DREAMING OF PROVENCE

JENNIFER SKULLY

Redwood
Valley
Publishing

Dreaming of Provence
A Once Again Novel
Book 1

A deathbed promise could open the door to a promise of love.

When Julia Bellerman loses her husband to cancer, she's cast adrift. For ten years, her whole life has been about caring for him. Now, before she can move on with her life, she must fulfill her husband's deathbed wish to scatter his ashes in Provence. And to let Ryder Wilding go with her.

Ryder, her husband's best friend. And the man she fell in love with a lifetime ago.

Ryder's first mistake was walking away from Julia. His second mistake was marrying the wrong woman—a marriage that ended in a nasty divorce. He's spent all the years since wrestling with the guilt of loving his best friend's wife. Now Ryder must take Julia to Provence to scatter her husband's ashes. He thought losing his best friend was painful, but keeping his hands off Julia will be the hardest thing he's ever done.

Can love overcome grief and guilt to give them a second chance?

ACKNOWLEDGMENTS

A special thanks to Bella Andre for this fabulous idea and to both Bella and Nancy Warren for all the brainstorming on our 10-mile walks. Nancy, thanks so much for being my beta reader and helping to make this story the best it can be. Thanks to my special network of friends who support and encourage me: Shelley Adina, Jenny Andersen, Linda McGinnis, Jackie Yau, Kathy Coatney, and Laurel Jacobson. As always, a huge hug of appreciation for my husband who helps my writing career flourish. And let's not forget our adorable cat, Wrigley, who keeps thinking the philodendron is an appetizer before dinner! Darling Wrigley, I'm trying to write, so please stop eating the plant!

DEDICATION

To Doris Beach
December 15, 1925 - March 18, 2021

My mother taught me what it means to grow old gracefully, lovingly. She always had a smile, she always knew who I was the moment I said, "Hello, Mummy," on the phone, even when she began to forget so many other things. She always laughed, and she taught me how to laugh. She loved her ice cream, and I will never eat another bowl of ice cream without thinking of her. Don't forget the wee bit of chocolate sauce, too. She loved to play Skipbo even when we had to start helping her just a little bit. She loved to sing, especially "The White Cliffs of Dover." She loved all the flowers on her patio. She called herself a silly sausage, and we were all part of the Silly Sausage Club. She was the kindest, sweetest person. And she will live in our hearts forever.

The house was as silent as a tomb. Will's tomb. Where they'd lived, where they'd loved. And where yesterday he'd died.

The doorbell pealed through the house like thunder. Julia's heart pounded as if all the walls had rattled around her. It took three seconds to gather her wits. She hoped to God it wasn't another sympathetic friend, or a flower delivery. She might just break down if it was. Why did people send sympathy flowers anyway? Were they supposed to cheer her up? Or maybe they were something she was supposed to cling to while she wept. Then again, she'd always sent flowers, mostly because it was the easiest thing to do.

But she would never do it again.

When the bell rang once more, she expected it this time and didn't jump. But she still hadn't decided whether to answer or not. The delivery company could keep the flowers. The sympathetic friends could come back for the memorial. She didn't want platitudes. She didn't want a hug. She didn't want someone to ask how she was holding up. She didn't want to cry in front of anyone. She didn't want to *not* cry. There was too much guilt, too much pain.

Worst of all, there was too much relief. How could she ever explain that?

As the doorbell chimed a third time, she wondered who on earth would be so persistent. Taking the last few steps into the foyer, she opened the door just to shut them up.

The man was short but muscular. His head was bald, and his teeth were shiny white. He tapped a clipboard he'd balanced against his flat stomach. "Mrs. Bellerman? I'm so sorry for your loss." His smile was perfect, with just the right touch of empathy, as if this were something he did all the time and knew exactly what the grief-stricken needed. "Hospice sent me to take everything off your hands."

Ah yes, he did do this all the time.

Will had in-home hospice care, including the hospital bed, the commode, the medical equipment, all the necessities to help a forty-five-year-old cancer patient pass out of this world as comfortably as possible.

And this man was here to take it all away now that Will had no further need.

He held out his hand. "My name is Isaac. I'm here to help with whatever you need."

Julia shook, his grip firm, his skin warm, his smile sympathetic. And the genuineness of that smile blurred her eyes.

"Is there anyone here with you, Mrs. Bellerman? I can call someone for you."

His job was dealing with grief, grieving husbands and wives, grieving sisters and brothers, grieving children, grieving friends.

"No, thank you." She blinked rapidly to clear her eyes. "Honestly, I'm fine."

"Sometimes it's good to have family with you. Or a friend. I can call anyone you'd like."

The family had been here yesterday when Will passed. His parents and Ryder and Julia's sister Felicity. They'd stood beside her when the hearse arrived at the house to take Will away. They'd fed her, rallied round her. She'd talked to her parents in Florida, and Will's parents had called his brothers, one in Atlanta, one in Chicago. Everyone was flying out tomorrow, though they'd all been here a week ago to celebrate Will's birthday.

He'd turned forty-five. Everyone knew he'd never see forty-six.

Of course, Felicity hadn't understood why Julia wanted Ryder Wilding, Will's friend and not even a family member, to be there for Will's final moments. Julia had called her sister, but only after Will was gone. She couldn't deal with any tension, and her sister was always tense about something.

Eventually last evening, she'd begged them all to go home, saying she was fine, she just needed to sleep.

But she could call Ryder now, ask him to sit with her while Isaac cleared out the bedroom. Ryder would be here like a shot. Will's best friend since junior high school and best man at their wedding, Ryder had been a lifeline from the moment Will got the diagnosis ten years ago. Will had survived for ten long years.

"Ma'am?" Isaac's deep voice rumbled over her, breaking her spiraling thoughts.

She'd stood there blocking the doorway, for how long she didn't know.

"I'm sorry. Come in. I don't need to call anyone." She waved him in. The truck sat on the driveway, the name of the medical supply company emblazoned across its side.

Seeing that name made everything real. At least hospice hadn't sent them out the same day to retrieve their equipment. Hospice had been good to them. A blessing, as much a blessing as Ryder had been.

"The bedroom's back here." She pointed toward the hall that headed down the bedroom wing of the T-shaped house. It had been their San Francisco Bay Area dream home when they'd moved to the suburbs after seven years of marriage. When they were searching for the perfect place to raise their children.

There'd been no children. There'd only been cancer.

They'd converted one of the four bedrooms into a den, another to a home office they both shared, where Julia did the household finances and Will had written up his patient notes.

She led Isaac past the guestroom to their master suite at the end of the hall. Bright and airy with a large bay window on the far end, it more than accommodated the hospital bed along with their king-size. Despite Will's illness, they'd slept in the same bed until they'd had to face that he needed hospice. Even when they brought in the hospital bed five months ago, setting it up in front of the window, she'd still stayed in the same room. She needed to hear him breathe while he slept. She'd looked after him every day and stayed with him every night.

Until last night, when Will was gone, body and soul, and she'd fled to the guestroom.

This room had ghosts, not Will's, but the ghosts of their lost dreams.

She wondered if *their* bedroom could ever become *her* bedroom, even once all the equipment was gone.

"It's all there," she said in a soft voice, giving Isaac permission with a flourish of her hand.

He passed her in the doorway with a politely murmured, "Thank you."

She stood for a few moments watching him break down the bed. Until she escaped to her office.

There were arrangements to make, the obituary to send

4

out. At Will's request, she and Ryder had written it weeks ago and submitted it to Will for his review. He'd made his tweaks and it was done, ready to go. Just waiting for Will to go, too.

There were trust details to look at, the lawyer to call, and authorities that had to be informed, social security, disability, insurance companies. And all Will's friends to contact, as well as his associates at the hospital where he'd once practiced medicine before it became too much for him. His parents were already making calls, and his brothers would also help with that when they arrived tomorrow. There were so many things to be done.

Yet she sat at her desk barely moving as the sun crept slowly across the rug. It seemed odd that the sun should still be shining the day after Will died, that this day in mid-March should be so cloudless and pretty. It usually rained in March in the Bay Area. It should have been raining.

Isaac wasn't loud, he was respectful. But she heard every clink and clank of metal. The dismantling of their life together.

There was no longer Will and Jules. Now there was just her. It seemed that she'd looked after Will forever. She couldn't remember what life had been like before he got sick, ten years ago, when they'd still had dreams of a future and a family.

Back then their lives had been filled with work and plans and house-hunting and friends and trying to have a baby.

Then her life had become filled with only Will.

Finally she turned on her computer, the facial recognition looking for her. Not finding her. As if she were a stranger.

She was aware of the slight puff of Isaac's breath as he carried disassembled pieces out to the truck.

The computer gave up and told her to sign in with her pin number.

Her desktop background popped up, a photo of her and

Will at the beach with the dog. God, she missed that dog. They hadn't gotten another pet after Star died. By then, Will had been diagnosed. There was no room for dogs. No room for children. No room for anything but his cancer and her fear.

Maybe now she would get a dog. Or a cat.

The realization hit her like a sharp stab right behind her eye. She was already planning her life without Will: She could do this and she could do that, get a dog, get a cat, when really, she had no idea what she'd do. For so long life had been only about Will. She had no clue how to adjust.

She'd scared herself yesterday with her thoughts when the hospice aides had come to bathe Will. When they'd told her his time was close.

She remembered the thump of the woman's words in her chest. If they turned Will, the aide said, he would pass, that's how close he was to the end. Then came the awful thud of Julia's thoughts inside her head. *Turn him. Just turn him.* And finally shame when she realized what she'd been thinking, what she'd been praying. As if she wanted him to die.

The truth was that Will had already checked out. He'd had a host of visitors a week ago. His brothers had flown out to see him, his parents had visited every day, so many of his friends had dropped by. No one had expected it to happen so fast, yet it was clear now that Will had been saying goodbye.

The moment they were all gone, when the house was quiet and empty, Will seemed to turn himself off. Within two days he was in a comatose state. And three days later, the hospice worker was telling her that Will's time had come. But her Will had already left.

She'd taken the time only to call Will's parents and Ryder. When they arrived, the aides had begun the ritual bathing as the family crowded round the foot of the bed. Just as the nurse had said, when they began to turn him, Will's body

6

finally gave up. Julia saw the moment his soul rose from him in that last puff of his breath. There had been something visible, tangible, a shimmering in the air above him.

She'd looked at Ryder then. There'd been so much written in his gaze. Pain, grief, loss.

She had felt only relief.

And now she felt only guilt.

She'd tried to tell herself the relief was for Will, that he was no longer suffering. But she was out of her misery, too. And that was where the shame and disloyalty surfaced.

She heard Isaac as he once again passed down the hall, but this time the footsteps stopped outside the office door. She forced herself to turn, making sure nothing showed on her face. But she knew that without the shame and guilt, there was no grief in her expression either. He probably thought she was a heartless bitch.

Yet his voice was gentle. "I'm all done, Mrs. Bellerman. Is there anything else I can do for you?" He waited a beat, like the flutter of butterfly wings in the air, then added, "I could make you a cup of tea, if you'd like."

It was the kindness that almost shattered her. The generosity of his smile. The understanding in his deep brown eyes. Maybe it was because he was a stranger, but she wanted to throw herself at him and cry out every second of the last ten years. All the heartache, all the lost dreams, all the pain.

But in the next brief second, the moment was washed away. She could never tell anyone. Because then she'd have to admit to the relief she felt, too.

"Thank you so much, Isaac." She used his name to acknowledge her appreciation for what he was trying to do for her. Even if she couldn't accept. "You're so kind. But I'll be okay. Thank you for the offer, though."

He nodded, his bald head shiny in the light that fell through the floor-to-ceiling windows along the hallway.

Rising, she walked him to the door, tried to tip him, but he refused. Then he shook her hand in both of his, holding on one second longer, letting a sense of healing warmth pass between them.

Julia stood framed in the open door, waved as he pulled away, as if he were a lifelong friend she was sending off on a long journey. She wondered how many souls he'd comforted with that sympathetic smile, soft voice, and gentle manner.

She knew he was an angel, that he did *this* job because it was a calling, because he could offer comfort in a way friends and family could not.

She only wished she could have taken it.

Once again the house was too empty, too silent. When she trailed back to the bedroom, it felt vacant, unlived in. Will was gone. And so was everything that had become a natural part of their lives—the hospital bed, the medical equipment, the shower chair, the portable commode.

In the bathroom, she found the evidence of what was left of Will, an array of pills and tubes. She billowed the sweatshirt she was wearing, piled the bottles into the pouch she'd made, carrying them all to the kitchen. Leaning over, she shook the sweatshirt, dumping everything onto the counter, then fished a plastic bag out of the drawer and began opening the child-protective tops, dumping the contents into the baggie for disposal. She ended up needing three bags before every pill was packaged.

She didn't know why she was doing it today, of all days. It was just that there was nothing else to do. Or maybe she just couldn't think of the best thing to do. She couldn't talk to anyone, but she couldn't do nothing either. She couldn't look at her computer with all the pop-up messages telling her so-and-so had emailed her or messengered her or tagged her on Facebook.

For so long, everything had been about Will. And now, without Will, she had no purpose.

When the bottles were empty, she tore off the labels and ripped them up, which was probably some OCD thing she'd developed. She'd become obsessive-compulsive about not having a list of their prescriptions just thrown in the trash. Like someone was actually going to paw through the garbage to find all Will's pill bottles... and do what with them? Sometimes she thought she was going crazy.

Haunting the hallway again, she passed her office. But she didn't want to fill out all the death certificate information. It was too much to think about right now. In the bedroom, she began opening the bureau drawers. They'd long since gotten rid of Will's suits and dress shirts and ties. At the hospital, before he'd stopped being able to practice medicine, he'd mostly worn casual clothes, and his drawers were filled with polo shirts and T-shirts and shorts and jeans.

She wondered if Ryder would want any of it. It was all fairly new. Will had lost so much weight, they'd had to buy him a new wardrobe.

What was she thinking? Of course none of it would be good for Ryder. He'd always been more muscular than Will. Taller and broader and healthier than Will. Even in college, when she'd first met them both, Ryder had liked the workout room and his rowing team, and Will had liked his junk food. He'd never been overweight, but after thirty, he'd started to show a little paunch. She'd teased him, telling him it was cute.

But Ryder never had a paunch. During the couples' vacations they'd taken together before Elaine and Ryder had children, Will had always joked that Ryder was the eye candy. Julia had never regretted that she ended up with Will and Elaine got Ryder. Not even on the worst days with Will. Sure she'd been jealous in the beginning; she'd dated Ryder first and maybe things would have been very different if Elaine hadn't walked into their scene.

But now Elaine and Ryder had divorced. And Will was dead. Their paths had turned out so very differently than they'd expected during their college days. In the last ten years, she'd needed Ryder so much more as a friend than anything else. He'd been her lifeline. He'd gone through everything with her. She couldn't have been as strong without him.

So many nights, they'd sat on the couch talking quietly, sharing a bottle of wine at the end of a long, long day after Will had finally fallen asleep, sometimes restful, sometimes fitful. She'd never wished that she'd married Ryder instead. She'd never wished Elaine hadn't broken them up. And if she'd had one or two erotic dreams about Ryder, they were only because she was lonely, only because Will couldn't manage the physical intimacy she craved. She and Will had become intimate in so many other ways, but she couldn't deny that sometimes she'd wanted a man's touch.

That's all those dreams of Ryder had been, a need for something physical. She never would have acted on them.

She stared down into the drawer. The colors hadn't faded with too many washings and the jeans were still crisp.

But Will's clothes would never fit Ryder.

In the quiet, quiet, quiet house, the front door opened.

Her heart leapt as Ryder's deep voice carried down the hall. "Hey Julia, where are you?"

She told herself the leap of her heart had nothing to do with Ryder. His voice in the quiet had simply startled her.

But in that secret room she kept locked deep inside her, she knew it was a lie. That she'd been lying to herself about a lot of things.

❧ 2 ❧

Ryder opened the front door without knocking and walked in out of habit. It was what he'd done since Will got sick. He hadn't wanted Julia to have to drop whatever she was doing to run for the door. Will had even suggested it.

But Will was gone. That book was closed. Now they had to write a new story. Everything must start over. Even if Will had been gone only one day.

"Hey Julia," he called out, "where are you?"

He found her in the bedroom, just as he had when Will was alive. She'd always been with Will. Yet now she stood motionless just inside the door, in front of the closet and the bureau right next to it, drawers open, a plastic garbage bag at her feet.

Will's hospital bed was gone. As if he'd never been there at all.

"What you doing?" He immediately regretted the censure in his voice when her body stiffened.

"I'm cleaning out drawers." She didn't look at him, just

continued riffling through the clothing, the only things that remained of Will.

"Jesus, Julia, you don't need to do that yet. It's only been one day." Again he regretted his tone, especially when she wouldn't meet his eye. But hell, they hadn't even buried Will yet. The rest of family hadn't arrived. They hadn't even mourned him.

Yet the bedroom was already empty of Will's hospital bed and all the evidence that Will had lived here.

And died here.

Maybe that was why Julia needed to clean out the rest of his things. Not because she was washing Will away. But because doing *something* was easier than facing that he was gone.

"I'm sorry, I didn't mean that the way it sounded." He stopped, because in the moment he *had* meant it.

But everyone dealt with grief in their own way.

"It's okay. I know it looks strange." She rolled her shoulders in, bunching her body in on itself.

"Honest, Julia, I didn't mean it like that."

She went on as if he hadn't spoken. "It's just that I didn't know what to do with myself once hospice picked up the bed along with everything else."

Which was pretty damn heartless of them, in his opinion, the fact that they'd rushed over to grab what remained, like jackals. Though there was probably somebody else who needed the bed now that Will didn't. Having all that stuff hanging around was a bad reminder anyway. "Why don't we sit in the kitchen? I'll make you a cup of tea."

She laughed softly, the faintest hint of mania in it. "I must look really bad, because the guy who picked up the hospital bed offered to make me a cup of tea, too."

Julia didn't look terrible. She never could. But her long chestnut brown hair lay limp and unkempt around her shoulders, as if she hadn't brushed it when she got up this morning. The deep blue of her eyes had faded with grief and pain. He'd never thought she looked her age, always tall, slender, and perfectly proportioned. But he realized now that her face was gaunt. The months of Will's dying and the years of caring for him had finally taken their toll. The life seemed to have been sucked out of her right along with Will's.

Moving closer, he put his arm around her shoulder, subtly pulling her away from the bureau. The plastic bag was empty, the drawers still full. Julia hadn't actually done anything at all, except maybe reliving her life with Will, reliving yesterday as the life passed out of him.

She let him lead her down the wide hall, the noontime sunlight falling through the windows.

As they passed the guestroom, he saw that the bed was rumpled and thanked God she hadn't slept in the same room in which Will had died. At least not during the same night. He'd always thought that was a bad idea, putting the hospital bed in their room, but she'd wanted to be close by in case Will needed her in the night.

Yesterday Will had stopped needing anything.

The loss still ached in Ryder's bones. He still felt the fear and the pain when Julia called him to say the end was near. Will's parents arrived soon after Ryder did, but even then, he didn't think Will was with them anymore despite the fact that his heart was beating, barely. Hands clasped, they'd stood in a circle at the foot of Will's bed.

As the hospice aides turned him, Ryder watched Julia, the relief that had washed over her face, the sudden furtive glance at Will's parents as if she'd been terrified they'd noticed. By the time her gaze had moved to him, Ryder was already looking away. She would never know he'd seen. When he finally looked at his friend's face again, Will was gone. But then Will had been gone for days; he just hadn't died yet.

Ryder understood the relief Julia felt, not just for Will but for all of them. Watching his best friend turn into a wasted shell who no longer resembled the man Ryder had known since the seventh grade, that had devastated Ryder as much as it had devastated his marriage and his family.

He couldn't think about yesterday, not now. Just as he couldn't think about the past or his marriage or the fact that his kids still saw him as the bad guy.

There was only the present. There was only Julia. There was only burying Will.

In the kitchen, he sat Julia in the breakfast nook, then put on the kettle to boil. She'd always loved tea more than coffee.

Three bags of pills sat on the countertop beneath the cupboard full of mugs. "You've been busy." He pointed.

"I had to do something," she said, her face turned away, her voice listless.

He ached for her. She'd lost so much. First, there'd been no children, and Julia had wanted them desperately. Then Will got sick, and Julia gave up her interior design career. Everything became about making sure Will would live. Until all hope had died, and they knew Will would not survive. Ryder could only imagine how bad it had been for Julia. Yes, he'd been there through all the ups and downs, the raised expectations, the good times, the new treatments, then the return of the cancer, the crushed hopes. He'd taken care of Will, sat at his bedside, talked with him for hours. They were best friends, and Will's loss was like cutting off a part of his own body.

But it was so much worse for Julia.

Her life would seem suddenly vacant, her future unknowable.

The kettle boiled, and he poured her tea, let it steep, then added milk and a spoon of sugar the way she liked it. There'd been so many times he'd made her cups of tea and slices of toast because he didn't think she was eating enough. Julia had done so much caretaking that she'd forgotten to take care of herself. Ryder had tried to do it for her.

He set the cup in front of her, pushing it close until it touched her fingers and she reached out to warm her hands around the mug.

Ryder sat. "You don't have to do all that stuff alone. I'll help. I just thought you might want a few days before you start."

Finally she looked at him, the color bleached from her face, from her eyes. "You must think I'm crazy."

He shook his head, reached out to touch her hand. Touching her had seemed so easy and simple when Will was here, when Will was sick, when she needed comfort, a hug, a shoulder to lean on, to cry on.

But Will was gone and suddenly it seemed wrong. It didn't even seem right to be alone in the house with her. So he didn't touch her now. Instead he clasped his hands and leaned his elbows on the table. "Your mom and dad will be here soon. Maybe you should think about going back to Florida with them for a while."

"There's too much to do." She shook her head at the same time, as if she needed the extra negation. "I have to plan the trip to Provence."

"You don't have to do that right now. Give yourself a little time." To grieve, to recover. Though he was afraid she would never recover. Will's death had been ten years in the making, and it would probably take ten more years to get over it. If she ever did.

Again, she shook her head, even more sharply. "It was our dream. We were supposed to go for our twentieth wedding anniversary this year."

They'd gotten guidebooks, made a general plan of their route, considering the different sites they wanted to see.

Ryder had even helped, so had his kids, all of them playing into the fantasy.

But they all knew Will was never going.

"Julia, you can't mean to go on your own."

"I mean to do what he asked me to do. If you want to come along, that's fine." She looked at him.

And he felt the weight of the promise he'd made to Will.

I want you to scatter my ashes in Provence, beside the bridge outside Saint Jean de l'Ange. You and Jules. You're the two most important people in my life, the two people who've done everything for me. Promise me you'll do this one last thing.

Ryder had promised.

Maps were spread out on the table. She must have already been planning. Maybe planning stopped her from thinking, from remembering.

She reached out, snagged a map with her finger and dragged it over. "I want to follow the route we all planned together. You don't have to go the whole way with me. I know you're busy at work. You could just meet me over there if that's easier."

He couldn't let her go alone. Will would never forgive him. If anything happened to her, Ryder would never forgive himself. "I can take off two weeks."

She sighed with what could only be relief. She didn't want to make the trip on her own. He knew that. She would do it, but it might be her breaking point.

Ryder had already started clearing his desk, knowing this would come. With his cell phone and the internet, he was never too far away to get things done. But even the CEO was allowed to grieve.

"When do you want to go?" he asked.

"I don't know how long it will take to get his ashes," she said, almost too softly for him to hear. "We always planned to go in the early summer. That's what I'd like to do it, when the weather is warm and the flowers are blooming, especially the lavender in Provence. It'll be the prettiest time to lay him to rest. He'd like that."

They'd talked about the end a lot in the last few weeks before Will died. Ryder and Julia had written Will's obituary with his input. Will had laughed and told them to punch it up, to make him look like a saint. In many ways, that's what Will had been, the way he'd handled the cancer, the treatments, never giving up, always trying one more experimental procedure, one more new drug trial. He was always first in line for the newest thing, even if it was unproven. For Julia's sake, Will refused to give up. Until finally his body had given up for him.

There would be a memorial, not a funeral. Will had wanted to be cremated, because, he'd always said with a laugh, he'd been scarred for life by a childhood rhyme about worms. *The worms crawl in, the worms crawl out, the worms play pinochle on your snout.* Will didn't want the worms crawling in and out of him.

Five months ago, after hospice brought the hospital bed into the house, Ryder and Julia had gone to the funeral home, read the brochures, the pricing, talked logistics. As a unit, the three of them had decided what to do when the time came. Julia had wanted a casket, but Will overruled her. "Couldn't we just rent a casket since I want to be burned up anyway?"

When Julia phoned to ask, she was told, quite snippily, that they didn't rent caskets because it was unsanitary.

Will had laughed. "If the next occupant is already dead, what difference does it make?" He'd always been practical about his own death. And he got his way, going out in a plain cardboard box. "If it's going to burn anyway, why waste the money?" he'd said.

The night of the casket, as he thought of the discussion,

Ryder had held Julia in his arms while she cried silent, water-less tears after Will had fallen asleep.

Then Will had made him promise they'd scatter his ashes in Provence.

"I'll take you, Julia," he said, keeping the strain out of his voice. "Just give me the dates you want, and I'll make the arrangements." Again, he thought about putting his hand over hers and again he rejected the idea.

"Let's see what we can book for mid-June, when the lavender will be beautiful."

"Sounds good to me." He would do anything she asked, just as he'd done anything Will had asked. Three months away, mid-June gave him plenty of time to book the flights and the hotels and make sure that his people at work were up to speed. "Shall we talk about the memorial now?" They'd already decided who would speak, where it would be. Will had all the input. Now they just needed to make the announcement and set a date, a time.

She looked at him again with those tearless eyes. "Thank you." Then, slowly, agonizingly, she reached out, laying her hand gently over his, the warmth of her spreading through him.

He'd never admit aloud that he'd made a mistake all those years ago when he let her go. He'd never even allowed himself to think it.

And he wouldn't let himself think it now.

"That's the most ridiculous thing I've ever heard, Julia." Felicity's nearly lipless mouth thinned even more.

"It was Will's last wish," Julia said firmly, determined not to be browbeaten. "He wanted his ashes scattered in Provence."

Julia had chosen her local coffeehouse for this conversation with her sister. That way she could leave whenever she wanted. The midmorning rush had ended and they hadn't rolled into the lunch crowd yet. Julia had found an empty table in the corner so she could see Felicity arrive through the window, giving her a couple of extra seconds to steel her nerves.

She'd held Will's memorial six weeks ago, once she had his ashes. People might think it was odd, but the funeral home had split Will's cremains between Julia and Will's parents. While Will had requested his last resting place be in Provence, his parents wanted a spot nearby that they could visit. A couple of days after the memorial, Julia had gone with Verna and Harold Bellerman, along with Will's brothers, to a grassy cliff overlooking the ocean where they'd had many family picnics when the boys were young. No one had asked permission to scatter Will's ashes there, they'd just done it.

The second urn—Julia had bought a decorative wooden box—was now sitting on the mantelpiece in the living room where Julia didn't have to walk by it day in and day out. Seeing the box was like facing all her failures. They'd bought the house for entertaining, but after only a few get-togethers and Will's diagnosis, the partying had ended. Now, Julia rarely used the living room. When she thought about cleaning in there, she always found a quarter-inch layer of dust on the furniture.

That's what her life felt like without Will, as if she had dust motes clouding her mind, weighing her down. She'd returned to the big bed in their bedroom but had woken up in the middle of the night fighting off dust bunnies. She didn't know what to do with her life without Will. For so long, he'd been the center of everything. How was she supposed to go on? Should she go back to work? So many questions. And the house was empty. So quiet. Sometimes she took her laptop to a coffeehouse just so she didn't have to sit alone in all that silence.

Today, however, she'd rather be anywhere than a coffeehouse with her sister.

When Felicity had finally showed, fifteen minutes late as usual, Julia actually considered running out the back door. Felicity, however, would eventually track her down. It was better to get this over with now.

"It's just weird you going abroad with some guy," Felicity said. "What will people think? Will only died two months ago."

Julia forced herself not to wince. "Ryder isn't just *some guy*. He's Will's best friend."

Felicity's hair was a deep chestnut like Julia's but she wore it short in a fashionable bob. She dyed away the gray, and despite having turned fifty this year, five years older than Julia, she didn't look like the older sister. Even in middle age, Felicity hadn't gained a pound. While Julia had lost weight through stifled grief and unshed tears over the last ten years, Felicity had maintained her perfect figure with a regimen of exercise and diet. Julia's beauty had faded long ago. She'd once been pretty, but she never would be again.

And now her sister was castigating her for doing her duty.

Why did she put herself through this? Because it was yet another duty. It made their mother happy to think that her daughters were good friends.

Duty, however, might not be enough anymore.

Felicity gave a purse-lipped head shake. "Whatever. You shouldn't be going on holiday with him."

Julia wanted to growl like Marge Simpson. "It's not a holiday. Will and I were planning this trip for years. It would have been our twentieth anniversary. And before he died, he said he wanted both of us, Ryder and me, to scatter his ashes in Provence. There's a special place, a bridge he saw in a travel book. It's out in the country, a beautiful spot. That's what he wanted, and that's where I'm taking him."

Felicity ignored the explanation. "That's why it's going to look so bad. Because Ryder was at your house all the time while Will was sick. People will think there was something going on between the two of you before Will even died."

Julia looked down at the design in her latte foam. It could have been an olive branch. Or it could have been a vampire in a coffin. She chose the olive branch, gritting her teeth and overlooking Felicity's tone. She didn't always like what her sister had to say, but sometimes she needed to hear it. It wasn't just Ryder's ex, Elaine. Julia knew other people might talk.

And she knew her own guilty heart.

But she still tried to rationalize. "Everyone knows that Ryder was Will's best friend, his best man at our wedding. No one's going to say anything." At least not in front of her. It was a whole different story behind her back.

God, she was tired. Tired of not knowing what to do now, tired of having to deal with other people, tired of all the tasks that had to be accomplished after a loved one died. Tired of walking through that empty house. Should she sell the place? Just the thought of that made her tired, too. That's why she'd gone back to the bed she and Will had shared. Because there was a certain sense of comfort in not making a change.

"I know he was Will's best friend." Felicity traced a line on the table with her stir stick, as if subconsciously drawing a line no one should cross. "Here's what I don't get. You called *him* to witness Will's last breath. Instead of calling *me*." She put her hand to her chest in affront. "I don't understand that. I'm your sister. Didn't you even need me?"

Julia had known this question was coming, and she'd already devised her answer. "I called Will's parents. And Ryder called me just to check on us. So I told him and he rushed over." She didn't care about the white lie; it would save her sister's feelings. And it saved Julia, too. "Then things moved so fast, and I didn't get a chance to call you. When I finally did, you didn't answer." She kept any censure out of her voice because truthfully she hadn't even thought about calling Felicity until after Will was gone.

"Right. But you didn't leave a message." Felicity's eyes, blue like her own, were misty.

Julia couldn't be sure how real her sister's tears were or if they were only meant to add more guilt to the weight already crushing her shoulders.

"By that time," she said softly, "I didn't think I could get another word out. Not without breaking down." She was playing on Felicity's sympathy, though she wasn't sure her sister had any.

There were only three things in Felicity's life, her boys, her house, and her standing in the community. Even before she got married, she'd decided to be a stay-at-home mom. Her two teenage boys would be graduating college soon, one a senior, the other a junior, eighteen months apart because Felicity hadn't wanted to go through the teenage years twice. Like Will, her husband was a doctor, her gravy train, though that might be unfair. All Felicity wanted was the best for her children, and she'd married a plastic surgeon to make sure those future babies got everything they wanted. Not that she hadn't loved Barry when she married him. Julia just wasn't sure Felicity loved him now.

"I told Mom and Dad about this trip," Julia said, attempting to distract Felicity. Or at least get a little buy-in. "And they were fine with it."

She'd informed her parents when they were here for Will's memorial, and they hadn't seemed horrified. But she didn't go to Florida with them as Ryder had suggested.

There was too much to do. The life insurance, the trust, the bills, making sure she had everything together for Will's final tax year. The medical costs might have been crippling, but being a doctor with his contacts in the medical community, Will seemed to know about every experimental treatment and drug. He gotten into things on the ground floor, receiving much of it gratis for his participation in the experiments and trials. His need to cure himself had been like a mania. Some treatments had worked for a while, others sent him into a tailspin. But they'd given him ten extra years, some of that time fairly decent, but other weeks and months absolutely miserable.

The other factor that saved them was the trust from Will's grandfather. He'd left equal portions of his wealth to his three grandsons. With that money, Julia had been able to leave her career as an interior designer and become Will's full-time caregiver once he could no longer practice medicine. They'd been able to pay every bill on time. They'd even had money for caregivers who came in for a few hours to help him bathe and dress. Julia had managed the rest of the time, along with Ryder's help when he could visit. Six months ago, they'd had to turn to in-home hospice care, and the majority of it had been paid for by insurance. She'd been able to spend all her time caring for Will, without worries about bills and how she would pay for it all once he was gone.

She also had enough money left for this trip to Provence and to live on until she decided what to do with the rest of her life, no matter how long that decision took.

That was the hardest part. She had no idea where to go from here. So much of her life had been about Will that she hadn't even thought about what she'd do when he was gone. Should she try to pick up her career where she left off? Was that even possible? All her contacts were long gone. They'd planned for everything else, but never for how Julia would go on alone.

"Mom and Dad understand completely," she told Felicity. The words understated the facts. Her parents had accepted, though she wasn't sure they approved wholeheartedly.

"What about all our friends?" Then Felicity modified it to, "All your friends?" But what she'd said first was really the issue. What would *Felicity's* friends think?

"My friends are fine. I've been getting lots of cards and letters from everyone."

Her friends wrote to say how much they missed her, how much they'd like to see her. Though many had attended Will's memorial, you couldn't talk at those things. *She* couldn't talk at all, other than politely accepting condolences. But the truth was she'd isolated herself over the last few months of

Will's life, and maybe even long before that. She just couldn't talk with friends about Will's illness, about her feelings. Funny, it had been easier to talk with the hospice volunteers. Even now she wasn't ready to see people, to answer their questions about how she was doing, to open up about her feelings.

She'd only agreed to meet Felicity today because they were sisters, family, and it was an obligation. Now she wished she hadn't even done that.

"It would look a lot better to everyone if I went with you instead of Ryder," Felicity said, as if she'd made up her mind and wasn't letting Julia get in her way.

But Julia wasn't about to give in. Will had wanted Ryder. That was his wish, and they'd made a deathbed promise.

Besides, if she went with Felicity, one of them would be charged with murder before the trip ended.

Felicity huffed. She had that sound down pat, designed to make the recipient of it feel guilty or obligated. Or terrified it was the prelude to a tantrum.

Julia didn't let her get in another word. "We planned this trip for our twentieth anniversary. And I'm going there to scatter his ashes in the exact spot he chose. That's all there is to say about it." It was the only thing she could do for Will now.

It was the only way she could make up for the terrible, horrible, gnawing relief she'd felt when he was gone. *If* she could ever make up for that.

Felicity couldn't resist the last word. "As if Will was ever going to make that trip."

Her sister didn't think about the hurt she caused. She'd always been attached to the unvarnished truth. As long as it wasn't about her.

"That was never the point," Julia said. "It was something to keep our minds off reality. And it worked."

"Taking off for Provence with Ryder Wilding is like airing your dirty laundry." Felicity's voice always got strident when she was being this insistent. The couple at the next table turned to look. "Everyone's going to think—"

Julia held up her hand, cutting Felicity off. She'd had more than enough. Since she was extremely good at giving herself her own guilt trips, she didn't need Felicity's as well. Pushing away from the table, she said, "You can only air dirty laundry if there's something dirty to air. And there isn't. People can think what they want." *Felicity* could think what she liked. "Will asked for this. I'm doing it." She put her hands on the table and shoved herself up as if she were an old woman. "I'll call you when I get back."

Fists bunched on her hips, her mouth pinched, Felicity gave a well-I-never look that should have had Julia bowing and scraping and offering apologies.

But Julia was already turning for the door.

She wished she'd taken her half-finished latte. It might have gotten the bad taste out of her mouth.

✣ 4 ✣

WILL

God, I'm tired. It's been forever. I never thought I'd say this, but I just want to die.

I guess there comes a time when you have to give up. I should have done it years ago. It would have been so much easier on Jules. I kept thinking that all the treatments, all the experiments, all the enhanced drugs, all the new technology, that it would help us both. I used to tell myself I was doing it for her, that I could never give up because of her.

I realize now that it was all about me. I was afraid.

I'm still afraid.

I can't say I never believed in God or that I'm an atheist. I just never thought about God. I never thought about heaven or hell. But I think about it a lot now. And yeah, it scares the crap out of me to consider that there's nothing after you die, absolutely nothing. When you're gone, you're gone, your heart, your mind, your soul, all gone. Then I start to wonder if there really is a heaven and what will happen when I get there. Will they let me in? What if there's a hell? What if that's where I'm going for all my sins? I wonder which is worse, hell or absolute nothingness.

Sometimes it just doesn't matter anymore what comes after because the life you're living right now is worse than anything you can imagine will happen to you once it's over.

I've reached that point. I'll never get better. I'm going to die in this bedroom, in this hospital bed. I'm never taking Jules to Provence. I'll never make love to her again. God, I can't even remember the last time we made love. Or even the last time I wanted to. Wait. I do remember the last time we tried. But I don't want to think about that. I'll never give her the child she wanted. And now it's too late for her.

There are so many things Jules is too late for. All because of me. We rarely traveled, usually just weekend trips to Tahoe or the wine country. We had huge plans but they were for *later*, like our big trip to Provence. Something always got in the way, medical school, residency, getting our careers going, buying the house, planning to have kids.

But in the end, there was only cancer.

It's time to move on. Time to give Jules her life back.

Last week was my forty-fifth birthday. Mom and Dad were here. My younger brother Andrew and my older brother Owen, their wives, their kids, Jules's parents, her sister Felicity and family, Ryder and his kids. Jules threw an amazing party. I even got out of this bed. We had steak I couldn't digest, champagne I couldn't drink, cake I couldn't eat. Jules fed me mashed carrots as if I were a baby, and mashed pears for dessert. I swear, they dribbled down my chin.

We all knew it was my last birthday.

After dinner and cake, I sat in the living room with Dad. He forgave me for wrecking the car when I was in high school. He tried to hide the tears in his eyes when I told him I loved him. He's always been a hard guy when it comes to the word *love*.

CHAPTER 4

And Mom, she just flat-out cried when I admitted I was the one who kicked the hole in Owen's bedroom door. She didn't even remember the door; after all, we were just kids. I told her I never meant it when I shouted how much I hated her. I was an angry teenager.

I finally admitted to Andrew that I stole Heather from him when he was in the ninth grade and I was a junior. What freshman girl didn't want to go out with a junior? I wanted her and I got her, even though I knew Andrew had the hots for her, and he'd seen her first. It was an asshole thing to do, especially since I dated her only a month before realizing just how big a difference those two years between our ages actually made. Even though Andrew and I never talked about it, Heather tainted our relationship for the rest of our lives. Andrew is like Dad, though. All he did was squeeze my hand, but I'm pretty sure that was forgiveness. Andrew's not a touchy-feely kind of guy, even when there's the scent of death in the air.

And Owen, what's there to say about Owen? He was first, I was second, only eleven months between us. Which meant Mom was cramping up with morning sickness when she already had a baby to take care of. I'm not sure if that made her love either one of us less. But somehow for Owen and me, it always felt like there was a huge competition between us. How do you apologize for years of one-upmanship? For dirty lies and sneaky tricks? But I love him and I told him that. It was probably the first time ever. And it'll be the last.

But now they're all gone, flying or driving back to their own lives, their own families, their own homes, their own beds.

Now I can go, too. Everything's ready. Jules knows what to do. Beautiful, loving, caring Jules. She's lost ten years of her life. She gave up her career for me. Interior design had been her passion. She found the perfect home for us, decorated it with loving care, planned for the babies that were supposed to come. Now everything is gone. The living room where we'd planned to have lavish parties now has an inch-thick layer of dust. All her dreams are gone. All because of me. I want her to find whatever happiness she can. My cancer, my rot, stole her chance to have children. But I won't steal the rest of her life.

She's the only one to whom I didn't confess. You don't confess to something just to make yourself feel better, not when you know the depths to which it will hurt the one you love most. There are some secrets which should always remain hidden because once they're out, the pain can never be taken back, the hurt can never be fixed. I will never confess what I did. I'll take that terrible secret to my grave.

The only remaining thing to do now is to extract one last promise from them. I want that trip to Provence. Even if I'm dead, even if I'm just ashes, I want that trip.

And I want Ryder and Jules to do the scattering.

It's the only thing I have left to give.

It had been two months since the last time they'd sat at Julia's kitchen table—the day after Will died. With the maps and guidebooks laid out before them, she tapped on her computer keys, checking out accommodations and making reservations. It was after seven o'clock, and the sun had set, the breakfast nook cocooning them from the dark outside. The heat had just come on as the evening cooled, and warm air puffed around their ankles. Mid-May in the San Francisco Bay Area could still be chilly at night. Julia had made a chicken salad for dinner, and the dressing was still tangy on Ryder's tongue.

Sometimes at night he dreamed about Julia's taste.

They had the route Will planned out, they just needed to book the hotels. "I'd like B-and-Bs or very small hotels," Julia said. "That will make us feel more like locals."

She'd lost even more weight since Will's death. Dark circles turned her eyes into hollows in her face, and her collarbones were prominently outlined beneath her skin. Ryder had asked how well she was sleeping, but she'd merely shrugged and changed the subject.

"B-and-Bs are fine with me," he agreed. "A lot of them include breakfast, so we'll probably get more local food."

This trip was all about her, whatever she wanted. Ryder had assigned Tyrone, his CFO, to be acting CEO while he was gone. He trusted Tyrone to hold the company's reins, and if Ryder were to leave the firm right now, Tyrone would be the person he'd suggest as his successor.

Julia would be his number one priority while they were away, with as little worktime as possible getting in the way. She needed to regain her health. He'd make sure she tried every French delicacy. She could sleep late, and they'd take long walks. They weren't going to rush this trip. He would make sure they saw everything and did everything. A vacation, not just a duty they had to perform.

"Okay," she said, setting her fingertips on the keyboard and typing. "Let's book the train tickets from De Gaulle airport first." They'd decided that taking the train down to Provence, rather than flying into Marseille, would give them time to tour Paris first. It would also allow them to see the countryside at leisure, and they could rent a car when they arrived in Provence.

For the next hour they shopped for train tickets and car rentals and the perfect bed-and-breakfasts or small pensions, bantering back and forth about how long to stay in each town, what sites they wanted to take in.

As they worked through the list, Julia was engaged, encouraged, energized, more so than she'd been in months. It was good sign. This trip was exactly what she needed. To get away, to step off the merry-go-round of death-related tasks she'd been on since Will died. Yes, they would be scattering Will's ashes, but Ryder wanted to make sure she savored every moment they were in Provence.

When his phone rang, he glanced down to see his ex-wife's name pop up, and he thanked God Julia has just excused herself to use the restroom. He'd called Elaine a few days ago to arrange for her to take Tonya and Dustin the two weeks he'd be away. She hadn't answered, and he'd left a message, sent a text, too. They had a one-week-on, one-week-off custodial agreement. The kids were in high school—Dustin a junior and Tonya a freshman—and both he and Elaine lived within ten minutes of the campus. Of course Elaine wanted to get her dirty little claws into his desire to change his week, trying to wrest extra child support out of him. She got alimony, too. But all that would end once the kids had finished high school. He expected Elaine to marry some rich fat cat the day Tonya graduated. And not a moment sooner.

He picked up the phone, swiped to talk to her, as much as he would have preferred to make all the arrangements in a text. "Hello, Elaine," he said politely.

"You are such an asshole," she started with. He couldn't remember a single civil phone call since their divorce was final four years ago. Hell, there hadn't been a civil phone call long before that either, not since the day he'd discovered she was cheating on him. Yet somehow *he* was the asshole.

"I assume you got my message," he said calmly. Not that calm actually worked with her. Just hearing his voice set her off.

"You're going to give up the first two weeks of summer vacation with your kids to go on a holiday with *her*?" She said *her* so sharply it might have been *bitch*.

He hadn't informed Elaine why he wanted her to take the kids during his regular week. But he had told Tonya and Dustin, not wanting that information to come from Elaine. He hadn't asked them not to mention it. The last thing he and the kids needed was for them to be caught in the middle of lies. It was his job to take whatever shit Elaine dumped on him rather than let it trickle down to them.

"It's not a vacation with Julia Bellerman." His voice was steady, none of his irritation shimmering through. "We're going to scatter Will's ashes. You know full well he asked me to do that."

"Well, I bet you just loved that, didn't you. A way to be alone with *her*." Again, that inflection, the word *bitch* unsaid, but definitely there.

"It was Will's dying wish." He heard the weariness creep into his voice.

So did she. "Don't make it sound like this is all about Will. You're fucking her, aren't you?" Her voice started to rise. "I'll bet you were fucking her the whole time Will lay on his deathbed."

He held the phone away from his ear as she screeched, her voice bursting against his eardrums. "No, Elaine. I did everything for Will, not for his wife." He didn't say Julia's name, pointing out instead exactly who she was. Not *his* wife, but Will's. And Ryder had always respected that.

"You're such a liar. I knew it all along. You were fucking her right from the start. Did you even care how Will felt about it? Did you even care about how *I* felt? Mr. Holier Than Thou, I'm taking care of my best friend," she mimicked, her voice as snide and ugly as her words. "And all the while you were also taking care of the poor, pathetic wife."

"Stop it, Elaine," he snapped between clenched teeth.

This wasn't new. She'd accused him while Will was still alive. She'd tried to use her allegations against him in the divorce. It began with her complaints about the amount of time he spent at Will's house. Then she started accusing him of going there just to see Julia. She'd even show up at odd hours, as if she thought she'd catch them doing something.

He'd never done more than hug Julia or kiss her forehead when she was at a low point. Maybe he'd wished for more, maybe he hadn't. But he'd figured out long ago the mistake he'd made in marrying Elaine. He'd stayed for the kids. Until Elaine had cheated. There were some things he couldn't get past.

"How could you do that to your best friend? Especially while he was dying. You make me sick. And the moment he's gone, you latch onto *her*." That *bitch*, the epithet clear in her tone once more.

"That's enough, Elaine." His blood was starting to boil over. If he wasn't careful, he'd find himself on her doorstep ready to... "Just tell me whether you'll take the kids."

But nothing was ever enough for Elaine. "Don't think I'm going to make it easy for you. You know I can still go back to the courts and tell them what an asshole you are, that you're palming your kids off on me so you can fuck your best friend's wife. They might even award me full custody."

When he'd first become infatuated with Elaine, he'd never realized what an angry, bitter person she was. Before they were married, she'd hidden it well. Sure, she had a few outbursts, but instead of seeing the red flags, he'd told himself everyone got mad once in a while. Or maybe he'd just been clueless and thoughtless, unable to see beyond his own youthful and selfish desires. By the time he'd figured out the kind of woman Elaine was on the inside, it was too late.

Still, he'd thought if he toed the line, he could live peacefully. When he understood that was a fantasy to help him sleep at night, he considered divorce. Until Elaine got pregnant with Dustin. And the easy way out was no longer an option.

Maybe that's why he'd always liked the weekends and vacations they spent with Will and Julia. Because Elaine was on her best behavior. She was the model wife, and after the kids came, she was the model mother.

Now, however, she was the ex from hell.

He countered her. "It's one week. The judge will laugh you out of court. And I'm not paying your attorney's fees if you try."

In the midst of the divorce proceedings, he'd thought about asking the kids to choose who they wanted to live with full time, hoping they'd pick him. But neither would ever hurt their mother's feelings. They were good kids. In the end, he couldn't force a choice on them.

"Asshole," Elaine hissed like a viper. She'd been the snake in the Garden of Eden who'd destroyed everything. "If you want me to accommodate you, you better give me an extra month on both the child support and the alimony." That's what she'd wanted all along; turn him into the bad guy, then make him pay for it.

She didn't hang up, there was just a crash across the airwaves. He held the phone away, his ear ringing. She'd probably slammed her cell down on the granite counter. He wondered if she'd broken the screen.

He'd known this trip to Provence would cost him something. And the kids would never see a dime of it. He always paid for the extras they wanted. The additional payment would go to Elaine's manicure or hair or spa treatments or that new bag she coveted.

His ex-wife was perfection on the outside and a bitter, evil crone on the inside.

If only he'd never...

JULIA SHOULDN'T HAVE LISTENED. SHE SHOULD HAVE walked away as soon as she heard Ryder on the phone. What was it her mother always said? *Eavesdroppers never hear good of themselves.*

Elaine's voice was strident, deeper than anger, closer to rage. Julia had never understood her fury after the divorce.

But now, finally, she was hearing the story as Elaine raged on the other end of the line, every word clear. Elaine hadn't resented the time Ryder spent with Will after the cancer came. She'd resented the time Ryder spent with Julia.

She should never have encouraged him to come around so often. But she needed so badly to lean on him. It had been selfish, even if she hadn't realized it was ruining his marriage.

Their relationship, all four of them, hadn't started out smoothly. She'd met Ryder first, before Will, in their sophomore year of college. And she'd fallen hard for him. Later she acknowledged that she'd been way too intense. He was her first serious boyfriend. She'd dated in high school, gone to proms and homecoming dances, but there'd been no one like Ryder. The problem was that for Ryder, there'd been no one like Elaine. Julia noticed her at one of Ryder and Will's fraternity parties. Then Elaine started showing up at all the frat parties. She was exotic, stunning, exquisite, sophisticated. All the things Julia wasn't.

And Elaine had dazzled Ryder.

Ryder hadn't cheated on her or dumped her for Elaine, because they'd already been on the rocks. It was Will who helped her put herself back together. It was Will who made her realize she was in love with love, not so much with Ryder. It took a year but she finally let Will talk her into a double date with Elaine and Ryder. They were a foursome after that. Elaine was flamboyant, but she was good with irreverent remarks, making you laugh so hard you almost wet your pants.

But while Will and Ryder were best friends, she and Elaine were never close. It wasn't envy. It wasn't that Julia still pined for Ryder. Elaine simply didn't have any need for female friends. She only needed men. Julia wasn't jealous when they announced their engagement. She wasn't hurt when Elaine didn't ask her to be in the wedding. Nor was it out of spite that she didn't ask Elaine to be in her wedding, even though Ryder was Will's best man.

Over the years, they took their vacations together, Hawaii, Mexico, the Caribbean, because Elaine liked the warmth. And Julia had enjoyed those trips, as well as the weekend barbecues.

Until Elaine had the babies. Honestly, that was the only thing that bothered Julia. Because she and Will had failed at having children. Of that she was envious. She wanted babies more than anything. She'd never been sure that Elaine actually wanted to be a mother.

After that, it was as if Elaine finally had something over her. She would make Julia touch her stomach, feel the baby kick, a glow in her eyes that had nothing to do with happy motherhood. But once those kids were born, Julia fell in love with both of them.

Then Will was diagnosed with cancer, and everything changed yet again.

Now here they were, planning a trip to scatter Will's ashes.

Ryder sighed heavily, shoved the cell phone in his pocket. He looked so weary, shoulders slumped, lines of strain at his mouth. Despite that, she couldn't deny he was a beautiful man, even at forty-five. Tall and muscled, he filled out a dress shirt to perfection. His short, dark hair was now dusted with silver and his deep brown eyes were sometimes sad, but he still turned a woman's head. The way he had when Julia was twenty years old. But now he was so much more, handsome, distinguished, but also caring and thoughtful, even selfless, and an amazing father.

He turned, and the look on her face obviously told him she'd heard too much. "I'm sorry," he said, when she was the one who should have apologized for eavesdropping. "Elaine can get a little hysterical."

She wanted to ask him if she'd been the reason for his divorce. But there were some things a woman should never ask. "It's all right. I know she never liked how much time you spent with Will."

He snorted a laugh. "That's putting it mildly. That still doesn't give her the right to say some of the shit she does." Which meant this wasn't the first time. "But at least she'll take the kids while I'm gone."

She was about to fuss, saying this was her job, not his, that he didn't need to take her, that she could do this on her own.

But Ryder was determined. He'd made up his mind and he wasn't going to change it, no matter what she said. No matter what objections Elaine brought up. He'd made a promise to Will, and he would keep it.

He pulled out her chair, beckoned her. "Let's finish planning the trip."

While she didn't want to create more strife in his life, she was truly glad he was going with her. Because she absolutely *didn't* want to do this on her own.

JULIA'S DOORBELL RANG IN THE LATE AFTERNOON. IT couldn't be Ryder again; they'd made all their travel plans last evening. She prayed it wasn't someone offering condolences, even after two months. Julia still had no desire to talk. There was too much guilt and too much she couldn't say, not to anyone.

On her doorstep, she found Tonya Wilding.

"Oh my God, how did you get here?" She felt a grin

brighten her whole face, the first honest-to-goodness smile she'd had since Will died. And probably long before that.

"I took the bus. Then I walked the rest of the way."

Julia put her arm around Ryder's daughter and hauled her inside. "I am so happy to see you." She felt almost giddy with delight.

"Can we make a pot of your special hot tea with milk and honey?"

"Of course, sweetie. Come on in the kitchen." She walked Tonya back, her arm still around the girl's shoulder until she grabbed the kettle to fill it.

Tonya and Dustin had become her de facto children, and Will's illness had strengthened the bond. On weekends, Ryder brought the kids to visit. Will loved playing games with them. As they got older, he taught them games like chess and Stratego, games that really made them think. Elaine sometimes popped in for a few minutes, just for appearances' sake, but left quickly. At least until she'd overheard Ryder's conversation last night, Julia always thought that was due to Elaine's innate fear of illness, as if cancer were contagious. But Dustin and Tonya had never felt that way.

She put the kettle on to boil. "How have you been? How's school?" She smiled gently. "And how's that boy Nicholas?"

Tonya grimaced. "Turns out he's a total creep."

"What did he do?" Julia put her hand to her mouth in commiseration.

"He took this girl to a party and tried to get her drunk but she wouldn't do it." Tonya rushed her words, her face flushed. "I bet that if she'd gotten drunk, he would have tried to have sex with her. I think that's date rape, don't you?"

"A boy should never get a girl drunk." Julia shook her head sadly. "And if she is drunk, he should take her home right away. You're very smart to recognize all that."

Tonya's eyes brightened with appreciation. "Mother said I

was being melodramatic." She always said *Mother* in that special tone, a hint of sarcasm, a hint of love, but not a whole lot of respect.

"Well, I always say it's better safe than sorry." Awful things could happen to young girls at parties, and she was glad Tonya was smart enough to steer clear of a boy like that.

Tonya was a pretty girl at fifteen years old, her smile gleaming white, her eyes fiery dark. The brunette hair falling in silky waves down her back came from Elaine, as did the fire in her eyes. But Tonya had never lashed out. Her fire showed in her enthusiasm, whether it was for cheerleading or soccer or an English assignment or playing Stratego with Will.

The kettle boiled, Julia poured the tea, letting the bags steep before she added milk and honey, then carried the cups to the breakfast nook she'd sat in with Ryder just last night.

She could still smell his cologne. Or maybe that was her imagination.

Tonya drew circles on the table, then sipped her tea and added another squeeze of honey. "Okay, here's the thing," she finally said. "It's about this trip you and Dad are taking to Provence to scatter Uncle Will's ashes."

Julia could smell the leaves of Elaine's discontent stewing, and thought a long moment about how to answer. "Do you remember how Uncle Will and I used to plan this trip?"

"Of course. We all used to sit right here at this table and look at the maps." She pointed dramatically with her fingertip. "We picked out all the places you should see." She tapped her chest. "I chose Arles where they have all those Roman ruins, like a mini Rome."

"You certainly did." Julia wrapped her fingers around her mug, suddenly needing extra warmth. "Well, Uncle Will asked us to scatter his ashes over there in Provence."

Tonya shrugged. "Dad explained that. But Mother—" She added an eye roll. "—is on the warpath."

"I know," Julia said softly, keeping what she really thought of Elaine to herself.

Tonya raced on. "But I think she's being silly. You have to do what a dying man asks. Isn't there some sort of law about that?" She didn't wait for Julia to answer. "I mean, he said he wanted you and Dad to take his ashes over there and scatter them." She lowered her voice. "He even told me that, you know, when I used to sit with him at the end. He said his soul couldn't rest, that he needed you and Dad to do this for him. It was like the most important thing to him. And I told Mother all that, but she just went all squinty-eyed." Tonya curled her lip, saying, "She didn't like that at all."

"But are you okay with it?" The question had to be asked for Ryder's sake.

"Of course. Like you have to do it." Tonya's eyes went wide. "It's a sacred oath."

She wanted to hug the girl. Instead she reached out and tucked a lock of dark hair behind her ear. "Thank you for understanding."

Tonya hiccupped a sigh. "Dustin's not so easy, though. But I'm working on him. You can count on me, Aunt Julia."

Her heart melted with love for this beautiful, smart, caring young lady. "Thank you." She squeezed Tonya's hand. "You know you can come by anytime you like. You can text me. You can call me. Anytime you need me, sweetheart."

Tonya dipped her head, her hair falling over her face. "I'm sorry I haven't been to see you since Uncle Will's memorial. It's just Mother."

After what Julia overheard last night, it went without saying that she would never be allowed over to their house. "I understand. But you shouldn't sneak over here either."

"I didn't sneak." Tonya smiled. "She was at Pilates or

whatever it is she actually does. And I left her a note. It's just that I really really really had to talk to you. Because Mother makes it sound like we all hate you and Dad. But we don't. At least not *all* of us." She shrugged dramatically. "Dustin, I don't know about, though."

She patted the girl's hand. "It's okay. He has to come to terms with things on his own."

Tonya nodded energetically. "I'm working on him. I'm telling him that Uncle Will begged you and Dad to do it."

"And I love you for doing our work for us. But I think your dad really needs to work that out with Dustin himself."

"Yeah, I guess so." Tonya breathed in deeply, twisted her lips slightly, and let her breath out in a long sigh. "I really miss Uncle Will, you know." Though she was looking at the table, Julia could see that her eyes had misted. "Like you'd think someone who was as sick as he was wouldn't want us around, like we'd be a bother and all. But he was never like that. He was totally awesome to be around."

"He loved having you here. You two were so special to him." She wrapped both hands around Tonya's fingers. "You and Dustin were and are special to both of us. I can't express how much it meant to your Uncle Will that you wanted to come see him after he got sick."

"Course we did." Tonya blinked back her tears. "He was like my second dad, you know." She looked up at Julia. "And you're like my other mom." She blinked again, as if she thought another tear might sneak through. "That's why I'm sorry I haven't been by to see you. That was really bad of me."

Julia squeezed her fingers tight around Tonya's hand. "Don't be silly. You're not bad at all. You're busy. So am I. But I'm so happy you came by. And I can't tell you how you've perked up my whole day." She laughed. "My whole week, in fact."

Tonya brightened, as if having gotten out everything she

came to say, she could talk now about whatever she wanted. "Good. Because I have to tell you about this other boy. He's not even Nicholas's friend. Because I wouldn't go out with any of Nicholas's friends."

"What's this boy's name?"

Warming Julia's heart, Tonya told her everything.

❦ 6 ❧

F inally. They were on the plane. Provence and two whole weeks with Julia were just eleven hours away.

There were times during the last month when Ryder hadn't believed he'd pull it off. A crisis at work, a crisis with the kids, the never-ending crises with Elaine.

Julia had told him Tonya was worried about her brother's reaction to this trip—mostly because of Elaine—and Ryder had tried talking to Dustin about it. But his seventeen-year-old son didn't want to communicate. He'd said nothing was wrong. Ryder wasn't sure how to get him to talk about it.

He also had the feeling that Julia was getting strong push-back about the trip on her end as well. She'd never said anything, but he saw the commas of strain at her mouth. It was her sister, maybe her parents, all of them wanting her to take anyone but Ryder.

But she'd remained resolute, insisting to Ryder that he was the one her husband wanted.

So here they were on their way, finally. He intended to put the problems behind him for now and concentrate on Julia.

"I can't believe you booked us in first class," she said on a wisp of air. "It must have cost a fortune."

"I have miles, lots of miles." He was able to use miles for some but not all, though that hadn't mattered. He would have paid full price to make sure she had the best.

Elaine had always pushed him to climb the corporate ladder, to make more, to keep them in style. But he'd stalled out at CFO. Elaine had blamed Will and Julia Bellerman and all their needs. On the other hand, she'd complained that he spent too much time at work, that he didn't have enough time for her, didn't have enough time for the kids. But she was the one who refused to go to Will's, even when Ryder took the kids. They loved their Uncle Will, and they'd done everything they could to cheer him up, planning the anniversary trip he'd never go on, playing all the games he taught them, making him laugh right up until the end.

Four and a half years ago, after Elaine left—or rather when she'd cheated on him and he found out—he had fewer constraints on his time. The kids were growing up, usually at games or meets or over at friends. Now he spent time with them according to their schedule, not his. His stalled career took off again. Now he was CEO. He had all the money Elaine wanted. And very little to spend it on besides child support and alimony and the myriad of things that kids absolutely couldn't live without. Teenagers could also eat you out of house and home, especially boys, but Ryder had his kids only two weeks out of four. He scheduled his business trips around their needs, and despite what Elaine claimed, it was rare that he asked her to change weeks.

Now he could well afford first class for Julia.

"I want us rested when we get there. We'll acclimate to the time change faster."

Julia settled deeper into her seat. They shared a first class pod and after dinner he would encourage her to sleep, especially after a couple of glasses of champagne and a good meal. He'd booked an afternoon nonstop flight, which would get into Paris midday tomorrow.

With a good night's sleep, it would feel as if they'd never crossed time zones.

"This is the best champagne I've ever tasted." She smiled. "I'm not sure if that's because it's really good or because I'm so excited about our trip."

His heart gave a bit. He'd been afraid the purpose of this trip would make her maudlin, but once everything was arranged, Julia seemed to blossom, calling him late at night with tidbits about Provence that she'd found on the internet.

"You want steak or lobster for dinner?" They prepared damn good meals for the money he'd paid.

"We have to choose?" Her pretty blue eyes twinkled. Christ, he'd missed that twinkle. He hadn't seen it for... Hell, probably not for ten years. Will would have been ecstatic to see it.

"I'll get steak, you get lobster, and we can share," he offered magnanimously.

"Deal." Though they hadn't even taken off yet, the flight attendant came through to refill their champagne glasses. He caught a glimpse of the label, and it was indeed very good champagne.

Which gave him an excellent idea. Once they were in France, he would call ahead to each hotel before they checked in and order a bottle of champagne to be ready in Julia's room.

He didn't think about the fact that they weren't celebrating. He couldn't. All he could allow himself to acknowledge was that Will had planned this trip for Julia. And Ryder needed to make it the best it could be.

Announcements over the PA instructed them to buckle in, that the doors would be closing, and they'd soon be leaving. He'd worn jeans, a polo shirt, and he'd already taken off his shoes. He'd left his suit and tie behind in Silicon Valley. He'd left all the arguments with Elaine behind, too. He could only hope that when he returned from this trip, Dustin would understand its necessity.

The plane lurched as they rolled away from the gate, and he raised his glass. "Here's to Provence."

"Here's to giving Will everything he wanted." She clinked his glass.

They were traveling with Will's ashes in Julia's luggage. The funeral home had taken care of all the documents, but no one from the airline had even asked to see anything.

"To Provence." They tapped again, drank.

Long minutes later they were in the air, sharing a bowl of gourmet nuts. Julia had slipped off her shoes, too, and curled her feet beneath her once the seatbelt sign was off. The scent of meat and seafood drifted through the first-class cabin.

He reached for the letter he'd slipped in the front pocket of his computer bag and slid it onto the console between them.

"What's that?" Strain shot her voice higher the moment she saw Will's writing on the envelope.

"Will gave it to me. He made me promise to open it only once we were on the flight together."

"You didn't tell me." Her tone was suddenly razor sharp.

He'd been committed from the night Will extracted the promise from him. The letter was another push he couldn't ignore. "He asked me not to mention it, just to let you read it once we were in the air. I have no idea what it says. You can check the envelope. I swear I didn't steam it open."

But he'd wanted to. Because God help him, he wanted Will to give his blessing. He needed Will to write that he wanted his widowed wife and his best friend to find happiness for the rest of their lives. Together.

She gave him a soft, poignant smile, so typical of the months before Will died. "I wonder why he gave it to you and not me."

And that's why Ryder thought he knew what the letter said, because Will had given it to him. As if it were a present. "Open it," he said. "And we'll both find out."

She picked it up gingerly as if she were holding the box containing Will's ashes. She tore the top carefully, unsticking the glue without tearing the paper. And he wanted to say *faster faster*. Then she pulled the note out.

It was written on one of Will's personal note cards. For weeks before he died, he'd been sending out letters, to old friends, family, acquaintances, health care professionals, nurses he'd appreciated, doctors he'd worked with, even those who had worked on him. Sometimes Julia mailed them, sometimes Ryder did.

Julia opened the card, addressed to them both, and began to read aloud.

"This is for the two people I love most in the world. I'm not writing to make you sad. It might be hard to believe, but I had a good life. I had good friends, a good family, a perfect wife. I just wish it could have been longer. I gave this letter to you, Ryder, because I have one last favor to ask. You've already promised to take Jules to Provence for me. But I need something more from you, buddy.

Ryder's heart was pounding so hard as she read that he leaned closer to make sure he didn't miss a word.

"I need you to make this the trip of a lifetime for her. She's a good woman, and she deserves happiness. My illness took ten years of her life. I know that Jules is crying now." Her voice had thickened and her eyes were misty. Ryder felt misty himself. "And that's why I need you, my best friend, to be my stand-in. Because I can't do it. I want you to take her to every place we talked about, to see every sight, to live it all

49

with her because I can't. I want you to help create the memories that she and I can't create. I want her to have what I couldn't give her. I'm counting on you, buddy, my best friend, my best man. Jules needs you. You both did so much for me. And now I'm in a place where I don't need anything anymore. Except for you to be happy. I want to be able to look down on you both from wherever I am and know that you're finding good moments to make up for all the bad ones. I love you both. Please do this one last thing for me."

Ryder's chest ached and his eyes felt raw. Will didn't need to ask him to take care of Julia. But he needed Will to go one step further. Just one more step.

Julia read the last few lines, her voice heavy with unshed tears. "This letter isn't supposed to make either of you sad. It's not supposed to make you miss me. It's supposed to give you the freedom to enjoy every moment of life. You both deserve everything good that life has to offer. Eat, drink, and be merry, as they say. Do that for me and I can rest."

The note was unsigned, as if it needed not one extra word.

Yet for Ryder it did need more, so much more.

Julia focused on something in the far distance as she smoothed the letter on her lap, obviously blinking away tears she didn't want Ryder to see.

They were his tears, too, if she only knew.

Finally she swiveled her head to look at him. "We're going to do what Will wanted." She reached over the console between them and linked her fingers with his. "Eat, drink, and be merry. We're going to do it all. We're going to have fun. And we're going to laugh." Tears brimmed her eyes, but she didn't give in to them. "That's what Will always wanted for this trip, to have the best time of our lives." She squeezed his fingers. "He knew he wasn't going to be there. He always knew it would be you and me making this trip. And enjoying every moment is how we'll honor him." She gazed at him with her mesmerizing blue eyes, and he felt himself falling into her gaze. "We'll do it for Will," she said.

Eat, drink, and be merry? Be Will's stand-in? His stand-in for exactly what? As a tour guide?

Or in Julia's bed?

The letter needed to spell it out. Because Julia would never believe unless it was written there in Will's words. Yet Will hadn't gone that far.

And the chance was lost.

As much as it might kill him on the inside, he'd eat, drink, and be merry for Julia. Everything he'd done in the last three months, from the moment Will died, had been for her. He would pretend they were just friends on a vacation, show her the sights, make her smile, lighten her burden.

But he could never pretend he hadn't wanted Will's letter to give him the permission he craved.

And he could never pretend he didn't want Julia with everything in him.

JULIA RELISHED SHARING THEIR STEAK AND LOBSTER, surprisingly gourmet dining for an airline. But she'd never flown first class before. Not that she'd flown anywhere since Will got sick.

She was done crying. Will wanted her to enjoy this holiday, and she would, even though it meant saying her final goodbye to Will as she scattered his ashes. She could do this. She would do it for him.

After dinner, she watched a movie while Ryder read. Then she spread out the seat into a bed and slept like she hadn't a care in the world. She didn't wake until breakfast was being served and shortly after that, the flight attendant collected their trash and informed them they would soon be landing. Julia didn't feel any jet lag, just the way Ryder promised.

"I don't think I can ever go back to flying coach," she told him, laughter in her voice. She wouldn't stop laughing because Will was gone. He wouldn't want her to.

They arrived in Paris just before noon, made it through customs, collected their bags, and took an Uber to the hotel they'd found near the Arc de Triomphe. It was a large, old four-story building that might once have been a duke's townhouse. Wrought iron balustrades ringed the façade, and the huge double doors opened to a lobby that resembled the foyer of a palace, with marble floors and a wide carpeted staircase.

It was early and their rooms weren't ready, but the concierge stowed their bags, allowing them to head out for an afternoon of sightseeing.

Armed with the good walking shoes they'd both worn on the plane and Ryder's small backpack stuffed with water bottles and a guide book, they set out to see what they could of Paris in one afternoon.

"Shall we order an Uber? Or take the metro?" Ryder asked as they emerged onto the busy sidewalk.

"How far is the Louvre? Or the Eiffel Tower?" They were the two sights she wanted to visit. "If we can walk there, we'd see more of the city. And it's beautiful out." She held her hands up to the sun, not too hot, perfect walking weather, the sky a bright blue without a single cloud.

Foot traffic flowed around them, fashionably dressed women, tall Frenchmen, elderly ladies with rolling grocery baskets, and tourists. It was a gorgeous mid-June day in Paris, and the tourists were out in droves, dressed in shorts and snapping pictures. Julia wore leggings, jeans for Ryder, and their phones would serve as their cameras. She was sure they still looked like tourists.

Ryder consulted his GPS. "Round trip," he said, leaning close to show her the map on his phone. "It'll probably be three hours or more if we take our time and look at everything. Ten kilometers or so, about six miles. Are you up for it?"

She was weirdly energized despite the time change, and since they were taking the train to Provence tomorrow morning, she didn't want to miss a moment exploring Paris. "Let's be wild and crazy and hoof it." Without even thinking, she put her hand in his, and they navigated the teeming street together.

Paris was bustling and crowded and wonderful, its streets lined with shops and outdoor cafés surrounded by potted plants. They snapped pictures of the Arc de Triomphe, took the underground passage, and walked beneath the magnificent arch.

"Let's climb to the top." Ryder squeezed her hand, pulling her to the entrance.

"I didn't even know you could get up there." But she followed him. The queue moved quickly, and the view of new and old Paris, despite the protection bars, was breathtaking. The Eiffel Tower dominated the skyline, and with the clear day, even Notre Dame was visible far off in the distance.

Below, the traffic whirled around the circle like bumper cars. "How do they manage not to crash into each other?"

Ryder shrugged a non-answer, shaking his head.

There were no lines on the pavement and yet there was a strange order to it even with all the vehicles jamming the roundabout.

They wandered along the Champs-Élysées, peeked in luxury shop windows, picked out French macarons, eating them as they strolled. It was amazing and thrilling. Pigeons flocked at their feet, and young people on electric scooters whizzed through every break in the crowd. Will would have loved it, the energy, the excitement, the extravagant view, but she refused to let thoughts of Will sadden her. He would have hated that.

Ryder was the keeper of the guidebook, pointing out all the sights, leading them on a short detour to the Place Vendôme, then back through the Tuileries Garden, the air redolent with an ocean of flowers.

Approaching the Louvre, Julia hung back from the entrance on the Rue de Rivoli, holding Ryder's hand. "I really don't need to go inside."

He stared at her aghast. "Don't you want to see the Mona Lisa?"

She shook her head. "Too many people in line. What I really want to see is the glass pyramid. You know, they have a small replica of it at the Legion of Honor up in San Francisco."

"I didn't know. You'll have to take me there sometime."

Her heart gave a little kick. She hadn't thought past this trip. "I'd love that." There were so many favorite things in the museum she would love to show him. She couldn't imagine why she and Will had never taken Ryder and the kids there.

But though she loved the Legion of Honor, the Louvre Pyramid was spectacular, with the contrast between the old architecture and the new engineering. "It's awesome, powerful." She took picture after picture. "You're not bored, are you?" When he shook his head, she held out her phone. "Selfie time. Your arms are longer."

He put his arm around her, pulling her close, his body heating her through as he snapped their picture. It felt almost too good.

Then he said, "Say cheese," and she laughed as he took another photo.

The picture was perfect. They didn't look like two people

taking the train tomorrow to scatter her husband's ashes in Provence.

After the Louvre, they crossed the Seine, strolling along the water. They'd walked hand-in-hand most of the afternoon, stopping often to take pictures. Julia told herself it was a safety issue, so they didn't lose each other on the crowded walkways.

But she liked the feel of her hand in his. A lot. Too much. Just the way she'd liked the feel of his body snug up against hers as he'd taken that perfect photo.

A photo in which they looked like lovers on a holiday.

7

She and Ryder followed the view of the tall spire to the Eiffel Tower, then stood silently, almost reverently, at the end of the concourse to view the iconic structure.

Julia sank onto a bench, pulling Ryder down beside her. She had to simply look at it, breathe in deeply as if the air around it were different, special. She'd never been to the Empire State Building, but she imagined it must instill this same feeling of wonder and amazement at man's ingenuity and drive, a vast structure, so immense it made you feel like a small and insignificant ant.

"It's so much bigger than I imagined." Julia breathed in its majesty. "Did you ever read that book *Paris* by Edward Rutherford?" She tipped her head to glance at him. And realized he was looking at her instead of the tower. His gaze on her made her belly flutter.

"No, I never read it."

He probably didn't have much time for reading. He was a busy CEO, the father of two teenagers. When would he ever have time to read? Except on the plane last night. She'd actually found it amazing that he was reading an e-book instead of analyzing profit and loss statements or proofing proxy pamphlets.

"I have it at home," she said. "It's a huge book, but a good part of it deals with the building of the Eiffel Tower. As well as the long history of Paris. It's a fabulous story. I love all his books."

"I'll buy it for my e-reader, if you're recommending it."

She laughed at him. "Like when would you ever have time to read a thousand-page book?"

Her hand still in his, endlessly in his, he tugged her closer and leaned down to say, "I like to read at night, before I go to bed. It relaxes me."

The words felt erotic, like sweet nothings whispered in her ear, as if she were lying beside him in bed.

They were only just starting this trip, and she had to stop thinking like this. They'd had their chance twenty-five years ago, and they'd both made mistakes. There'd been too much living and dying and divorcing and child-rearing in all that time since. They could never overcome those years. They weren't the same people anymore. Ryder had grown into a caring, empathetic friend, and a truly wonderful father. While she had lost huge pieces of herself in the cancer years. Now, she couldn't bear to imagine what Will would have thought if he knew she was having fantasies about his best friend before they'd even scattered his ashes.

"Shall we climb to the top?" he asked.

She shook her head, not wanting to brave the queue snaking its way across the concourse. "We'd be in that line for the rest of the afternoon. I only wanted to look at it. To know I've seen it."

"But the view from the top?" It was either a question or a statement.

She tried to explain how she felt. "We could have spent more time here, but I didn't book another day on purpose. I wanted to see the main attractions, but I don't really want to be a tourist in Paris. I just want to get to Provence." She wanted the trip that she and Will had planned, with Ryder and his children's help.

"We can always tack on a few days at the end, if you like."

She looked at him. He had two weeks, all he could spare, yet here he was offering up more. If she wanted it. She didn't know if the invitation meant anything. Maybe it was like the handholding, something to make sure they didn't lose each other in the crowds around them. Maybe he was thinking about all the money they'd spent on the flights—or rather all the money *he'd* spent on first class tickets—and wanting to make the most of it since they were here.

For now, however, they bore the burden of Will's ashes.

They strolled to the tower itself and waited in the relatively short security line so they could at least walk underneath it even if they didn't go to the top. Julia was dizzy staring up, marveling at its engineering. The tower had never been meant to stand forever, just like the Palace of Fine Arts in San Francisco. They were both part of international expositions, but the French hadn't been able to let go of the Eiffel Tower any more than San Franciscans could let the palace go to rack and ruin.

It was late in the day when they headed back over the Seine and through the Jardins du Trocadéro, also part of the same 1889 exposition, then on to the Arc de Triomphe and their hotel. She should have been exhausted with the time change, the jet lag, and all the walking. Instead, she was famished. All they'd had since breakfast on the plane were macarons and coffee.

"I don't want to go to the hotel yet." She stopped Ryder a block away. "Let's find a place to eat."

"How about down there?" He pointed to a bistro with sidewalk tables beneath a green and white awning. It looked very French, just what you'd expect if you were a tourist, maybe even overly touristy, but Julia didn't care.

The menu was in both French and English. She'd read and heard so much about how haughty the French were, but so far they'd only been treated with politeness. And there'd been no dog poop in the streets, another thing tourists warned about.

It was warm and the host shepherded them to an outdoor table. He spoke English in a pleasing accent, regaling them with the highlights of the menu. She ordered mussels and Ryder chose the veal.

"Shall we share again?" he asked when the waiter had gone.

"I'd love to." Sharing the steak and lobster on the plane had been oddly intimate, something reserved for couples who'd been together for years. Or old people who couldn't manage an entire meal.

They weren't old, though in the last ten years, she felt as if she'd aged twice that. But here in Paris, with Ryder, she wanted to feel young again. If she concentrated hard enough, she could pretend. Her parents were in their late seventies and still vital, enjoying their retirement. Her grandparents had lived into their mid-nineties. On that scale, she had half her life left.

She just didn't know what she was going to do with all those years.

Or with whom she would spend them.

THEY BOARDED THE TRAIN AT TEN THE NEXT MORNING.

Ryder could only call yesterday glorious. He'd rarely thought about death and the reason they were in France. He was pretty damn sure Will wouldn't have wanted them to dwell on it.

After the long day, Julia had started to fade around eight o'clock. He'd escorted her to their rooms, opened her door, made sure all the bags inside were hers, knowing the rest would be in his room.

Just as he'd ordered, champagne sat chilling in its bucket with a plate of chocolate-covered strawberries on the side.

"Oh my God. Did you do this?" She turned to him with beautiful shining eyes, and the look on her face was worth everything.

"I know you need your bath about this time." There were many nights that he'd stayed later with Will so Julia could unwind, enjoying the luxury of a bath, accompanied by champagne and chocolate.

Hands on the doorjamb, she leaned into the bathroom. "Look at that soaking tub. It's absolutely perfect." She turned and for a moment he thought she might throw her arms around him.

Or invite him to stay.

God help him, as much as he wanted it, he would never do it. Will hadn't expected his stand-in to take his place in his wife's bath and bed as well.

Julia stepped back just as quickly, as if she'd had the same thought.

He backed out, leaving her to her bath.

And yet he'd lain on his bed in his own room imagining her in the scented water.

He'd called his kids, too, though only Tonya answered.

But even after the brief call—Tonya was out having fun with friends—his mind wandered back to Julia.

This morning they'd risen early, had a French breakfast in the hotel dining room—juice, coffee, and a baguette slathered in jam—and headed out to catch the train.

The trip to Provence would take approximately five hours, and they sat across from each other in comfortable seats, a collapsible table between them and the countryside flashing by outside the window.

At noon, they moved to the dining car for a gourmet lunch. On white tablecloths with matching napkins, patrons dined on real china and drank from crystal goblets. They were traveling first class again, and it was luxurious. Nothing but the best for Julia.

"This is what we need in America, a fabulous system of high-speed trains," Julia said.

He sipped their after-lunch coffee. "California already tried the high-speed rail. It's cost billions so far and if we're lucky, we'll be able take it from Bakersfield to Merced."

She wagged her finger, a gleam in her eye. "No politics," she singsonged at him.

He laughed softly. "You're right. No politics. So what would you like to talk about? Anything. It's up to you."

If she needed to talk about Will, he would listen.

"Well," she said, drawing a pattern in the tablecloth with the tip of a spoon. "You know that night we were planning our route and booking hotels and I heard you talking to Elaine?" She ended on a question, as if he could put a stop to the conversation if he wanted to.

"I remember." She'd heard everything because Elaine had shouted loudly enough to break his eardrums if he'd had the phone right against his ear.

This, too, he would discuss if Julia needed to.

"We didn't really talk about it that night, but I have to apologize for both of us, Will and me."

What the hell? But he didn't say it. "There's nothing to apologize for."

"Yes, there is. What Elaine said about..." She shrugged, letting the sentence trail off.

Neither of them could say the words out loud. Not the ones Elaine had used.

Julia drew a deep breath. As if she were steeling herself. "About us, what she thought was happening. Which of course it wasn't," she rushed on to add, as if she needed to explain to him, too. "But I'm sorry Elaine's fears about it broke up your marriage. We never would have let you come over so much if we'd realized the harm it was doing."

Damn Elaine. "It wasn't your fault. It wasn't Will's." He chose half the truth. "We were in trouble long before that. I was staying in the marriage for the kids. She just wanted to pick on whatever she could and blame me for all our problems. But it was never your fault, or Will's. Elaine was unhappy with *me*," he stressed, his hand on his chest. "I never measured up. If I was controller, then I needed to be CFO. And when I was CFO, I should have been CEO. I thought spending time with the family was more important than climbing the corporate ladder. But Elaine wanted the money." And still complained about him not spending enough time with the kids as well. He couldn't win.

"I'm sorry." She reached out, but pulled back almost immediately, despite the fact that her hand had rested in his most of yesterday, as if his touch was now different because they were talking about Elaine.

"Don't be sorry," he said. "Not all marriages work out. A lot of us end up wanting different things. We grow apart instead of growing together."

There was only so much truth he could reveal, and Elaine's affair was a truth he'd keep to himself. He didn't want to say everything was his ex-wife's fault. He didn't want to be the kind of man who couldn't take responsibility for his mistakes and blamed everything on his partner.

He'd certainly made his share of mistakes. Though he'd never had affair, he'd thought way too much about Julia. And he'd regretted the choice he'd made all those years ago.

The absolute truth was that as he'd spent more time at

the Bellermans' house, he'd started lusting after his best friend's wife. Elaine had obviously picked up on that. But even so, he'd grown tired of the fights and the bickering, not just about Will and Julia, but about everything in their marriage from the way he washed dishes to the amount of time he supposedly *didn't* spend with the kids and the money he *should* have earned but hadn't.

Elaine wasn't the only one at fault. He'd stopped trying, stopped caring. "She wanted to go to marriage counseling," he said. "I refused." He'd checked out of the marriage long before Elaine cheated on him.

"I know you said not to say sorry again. But I am." She smiled sadly at him. "I mean, I should have known things weren't good, especially when she stopped coming around the house. It was just you and the kids. But quite honestly." She shrugged. "I thought it was because Elaine couldn't handle being around sickness, that she didn't know how to deal with it. A lot of people don't. And she'd always seemed so uncomfortable."

It would be nasty to say that Elaine stopped coming around because it wasn't fun anymore. She liked the parties and the beach vacations and the night-clubbing and the dancing. She wanted fun. Will's illness had put a stop to all the fun times.

But telling Julia that would only hurt her.

Instead he agreed with her assessment. "She was never good even when the kids were sick," he said with a touch of humor. "But I don't want to do a lot of Elaine-bashing. She loves the kids, and she's a good mom, for the most part. We just weren't meant to be together forever." He put his hand on Julia's, telling himself it was for reassurance. "It had nothing to do with you and Will. What you overheard Elaine say that night on the phone, she was just feeling mean. She never truly believed that."

But she had. It wasn't the first time she'd tried to beat him down with that accusation. She was just more vocal now that Will was gone.

In fact, she'd turned downright vicious.

They'd finished their coffee. "Shall we return to our seats?" He was ready to put an end to the conversation.

Julia agreed by smiling.

But they were almost at their seats when she turned back to him. "What bothers me is that I never paid attention. I never asked if you needed to talk about it. Or how you were doing. Or what you were thinking."

He put his hand over her mouth. "You need to stop with the guilt trip."

It was only after he'd done it, when he felt the warmth of her lips and her breath on his palm, it was only then that his knees felt suddenly weak with the need to touch her, hold her. And so much more.

This was the real reason he was a divorced man. Because he had feelings he'd never been able to control. Because he had regrets he couldn't stop. Because he had a guilt so much bigger than Julia's.

He dropped his hand back to his side, masked his emotions with a smile he hoped wasn't obviously false. "Stop feeling guilty about everything, Julia. You were dealing with so much. And I wasn't ready to talk about Elaine and me." He shook his finger in her face, making sure he still had that phony smile plastered on his lips. "Promise me you won't say one more thing about guilt during this entire trip. This is a guilt-free zone."

She answered with a rueful smile. "All right, I promise, guilt free."

He'd made her promise, but he wasn't sure he could hold up his end of the bargain. Because he was totally guilty for lusting after his dead friend's wife.

❧ 8 ❧

Julia knew they were in Provence when the first lavender field spread out across the countryside. The flowers were gorgeous, stretching for miles and miles, some blue, some light purple, some dark lavender, the color depending on the clouds above and how the light played across the fields. It was the beginning of the season, and the sight would only get better. She took pictures, but they were moving too fast and all she got was a smear of color.

"You'll have plenty of photo ops," Ryder assured her.

Her lips still tingled with the feel of his hand on her mouth. She shouldn't have liked it so much. She wondered if he'd felt the effects, too, especially with the way he'd withdrawn, fast and sharp, as if he'd experienced the same jolt she did. Or maybe he'd simply realized that he'd stepped over some invisible boundary.

He talked as if nothing had happened, as if there hadn't been that flash of heat between them. She wanted to ask but she'd already pushed too hard, crossing *his* boundaries when she'd asked about Elaine and the divorce. Yet she'd had to say all that, mostly to ease her guilt.

She kept thinking about Will's note, too. Ryder was his stand-in. If Will had been healthy and this was their anniversary trip, they would have spent more time in bed than walking around the town. Wouldn't they? Then again, they'd been married for twenty years. And sex had never been, well... Maybe people after twenty years of marriage were all about the sightseeing, not the lovemaking. She had no way of knowing because they hadn't been a typical married couple for the last ten years. Will had been sick for so long.

But Ryder was healthy, robust, tall, handsome, fit. And sexy.

She had to stop thinking this way. Will hadn't meant that Ryder should be his stand-in in every way. Of course not. Ryder was just supposed to take care of her. As if she needed taking care of. She could have made this trip on her own.

But would it had been maudlin instead of enjoyable?

Ryder was an excellent tour guide.

He'd spent the train ride pointing out huge châteaux and castles and cathedrals dotting the landscape. Some were downtrodden with years of neglect, but many had been restored and flourished, rising up magnificently from the landscape, their gardens manicured, their spires gleaming. She'd read somewhere that the old houses were white elephants, money pits, and maybe they were, but someone had found the money to refurbish a few of these national treasures.

"Wouldn't it be absolutely amazing to stay in that gorgeous château?" She pointed across a field of lavender to a château on a smaller scale, dormer windows in its peaked roof, its façade a pale shade of coral in the sunlight.

Ryder leaned forward to gaze out the window. "Didn't you book us into a château that operates as a bed-and-breakfast?"

She nodded. "Yes. It's just outside Saint Jean de l'Ange."

He turned to her. "That's where the broken bridge is, right?"

She stared into the distance, through the fields of lavenders, the old mansions, the monasteries, and into the past. "Right. And that bridge isn't even on any map. I mean, when you look up 'broken bridge in France' on the internet, the only one that comes up is Saint Benezet's Bridge near Avignon. But this one was just a picture in a travel book Will came across in a secondhand store. Off the beaten track. Unknown to tourists. And that's where he wanted me to leave him." The travel guide had given pretty specific directions on how to get to the out-of-the-way place. She prayed she could follow them.

They'd have to carry Will's box out there. She'd gotten used to the weight, but if she gave it too much thought, she felt the wretched absurdity of carrying her husband's cremains around in her luggage.

"We should be there on Saturday," Ryder said.

Only three days away. She didn't want to feel the ache around her heart. Instead, she allowed herself to be buoyed by the excitement Will had felt about the trip. "He said that bridge was the most beautiful place on earth, especially when the flowers are blooming all around."

"It'll be perfect." Ryder agreed with a smile, as if he, too, refused to let the grief overwhelm him.

Julia had cried little since Will's passing. She'd shed her tears in all the years before. Now all that was left was the relief she felt, the knowledge that not only was Will's ordeal over, but hers as well. And of course, there was the guilt over those very feelings.

Finally arriving in Aix-en-Provence, the first town on their itinerary, they departed the train and rented a car. They checked in at the pension, a quaint little place on a cobblestoned side street, with white window frames and green shutters, its walls covered in ivy.

Then they set out for a walk down the Cours Mirabeau, a lushly tree-lined boulevard famous in the town for its fountains, its historic mansions, and its restaurants. She'd expected there to be fewer tourists than in Paris, but the crowds had found Provence as well, dressed in shorts, laden with bags as they strolled through the markets filled with fragrant foods and brightly colored goods.

She'd forgotten what it was like to be a tourist, to just stroll, to stop where you wanted, never to make it to a particular destination because you found something else that piqued your interest. She'd spent so much time hurrying, always needing to get somewhere, to the pharmacy or the doctor's office or the hospital, or back home because Will was waiting for her.

Just as with their sightseeing yesterday, this felt like freedom.

Once again, Ryder held her hand as they walked. Once again, she felt the warmth of his touch. Once again, she told herself it didn't mean anything. That it *couldn't* mean anything.

And yet, when she stopped at a shop window, the touch of his hand at the small of her back was warm, almost sensual. When they studied the restaurant menus—which were all in French, unlike the bistro in Paris—Ryder leaned close so he could read as well. She was aware only of his heat and his cologne, something that smelled like the outdoors at home, like the forest and redwood trees. Like Ryder and no one else.

"I know a few words." He pointed at the menu. "Like beef and chicken and fish. And I'm pretty sure that's duck."

"That sounds mouthwatering." The problem was that with Ryder, everything was mouthwatering.

He held up his phone. "When we actually order, I've got a translation app we can use to figure it all out."

She smiled. "Maybe we should just surprise ourselves."

His answering smile made her tingle.

They took pictures by each magnificent fountain. In California, they had the missions and the painted ladies of San Francisco, but there was nothing like this, buildings erected centuries before the French Revolution.

"Shall we save the cathedral and Cézanne's studio for tomorrow?" Ryder asked. "You must be getting hungry."

She turned, laughing at him. "You mean *you're* hungry. I heard your stomach growl."

When Ryder laughed, he could stop a woman's heart or make it turn over in her chest.

"Food," she agreed. "And I want the duck."

The duck was scrumptious. Somehow, in the past ten years, she'd stopped enjoying food. Until this trip. Now everything seemed new and fresh. And the lobster ravioli Ryder had chosen was delicious, too.

She didn't want the day to end. Yet she couldn't stifle a yawn that struck over their coffee. It could have been the jet lag finally catching up.

"It's been a long day. Let's head back." Ryder stood, held out his hand, and she had no choice. She couldn't keep him here with her.

The pension she'd booked was delightful, the bed high off the floor with wooden steps to climb in, a small seating area by the windows with two comfy chairs, and a clawfoot tub that enticed her.

Ryder didn't come in, but he pulled her close for hug just as he had last night. Only somehow it seemed to last longer, as if she were clinging to him.

She wanted to beg him to come in, to stay with her just a little while longer, but he let her go, stepping back. "I'll see you in the morning for breakfast. We can tour Cézanne's studio and the gothic church, Église Saint-Jean-de-Malte, then maybe drive out to one of the wineries. Or we can just walk around, whatever you'd like to do."

"You've certainly done your research." She wanted to relax and walk and see everything. "We can do whatever we feel like doing." It was her newfound sense of freedom. "Thank you for a lovely day."

He reached out to tuck a lock of hair behind her ear. "Don't let the jet lag get you."

She felt the thrill of his touch along her skin. "I'm only a little tired. But nothing like I was expecting. Thank you for first class." She smiled for him. Ryder had made everything about this trip absolutely perfect.

"It was my pleasure." He gave her a quick peck on the cheek, and her lips hummed for more.

She really had to stop her wayward thoughts.

In the room, her bags were sitting on the rug in the middle of the floor, waiting to be unpacked. Then she saw the champagne and chocolate truffles on the table between the two chairs by the windows. The curtains were open over a narrow balcony and light streamed in, a combination of moonlight and city light that sparkled through the crystal glasses on the table. Two of them.

He'd ordered champagne for her again, this time with two glasses. Or maybe that was the concierge making an assumption. Ryder had told her to enjoy her bath, but there was far too much here for one person.

Moving her bags out of the way, she opened her door, heading down the hall to knock on his door one room down. When he opened up, she saw the suitcase on the high bed behind him, but he was fully dressed, still wearing his shoes.

She put a hand on her cocked hip. "You ordered champagne and chocolate again."

"For your bath," he said with the small tilt of a smile on his lips.

"Well, I can't drink it all alone, and I don't want to waste it like last night. You have to join me."

He shook his head, his smile growing. "It's all for you."

She grabbed his hand, pulled him into the hall. "Don't make me bring it over here. Because I will. Have just one glass with me. And some chocolate truffles."

There was a certain thrill in dragging him back to her room. She thought of the nights they'd shared a glass of wine after Will had gone to sleep. When she could let her guard down, let her smile crack, her shoulders slump. It had never felt as if they were doing something illicit. It had been more like collapsing after a long hard day.

This was different. This could be called intimate.

Julia didn't care. It was champagne and chocolate for two. And she was going to make Ryder share it with her.

In her room, he opened the balcony doors, letting the night air wash over them. They had a view of city lights on the bigger road and the voice of a lounge singer at the bistro across the narrow street floated up to serenade them.

"It sounds like a French ballad they would have sung during the war. You know, like all those old movies about French resistance fighters."

"You're such a romantic." His voice was kind, not mocking.

She smiled. The champagne was good, the truffles melting in her mouth.

She had the irreverent thought that Ryder's kiss would be as melt-in-the-mouth as the chocolate.

W ITH J ULIA SITTING BESIDE HIM IN THE SEMIDARKNESS AND the champagne bubbles going to his head, Ryder felt the romance in the air, as if they were a couple in love doing the grand tour of Europe.

She'd worn a short, pretty sundress today, her shoulders bare to the warmth of the sun. Her hand in his, he'd wanted to kiss her sun-pinkened skin, taste her.

"There's just something about European chocolate." Julia said, her eyes closed as she savored the taste on her tongue.

That was something he'd been aware of since they'd arrived, that she'd savored her food, every morsel, every bite, the chocolate, the cappuccino, the macarons, the duck. Even the pommes frites which she'd claimed were so much better than French fries though he couldn't see or taste the difference. Watching her eat had almost become a religion.

She'd lost weight over the years, while most women gained as they got older. Whether it was stress or fear or worry or maybe all of the above, he couldn't say. She'd always cooked healthy meals for Will, but Ryder had only ever seen her pick at her food. Until the last three days.

He was glad. She deserved good things in her life even if it was just good food.

"Here's an idea," she said, her eyes aglow in the moonlight through the open doors. "In every town we visit, we have to hunt for the best chocolate."

"Aren't the best supposed to be Belgian chocolates?"

She shrugged, her smile engaging, a sight he could almost feel on the inside. "I'm not sure. I've had Norwegian choco-lates, and they were divine. But don't you think it's a fabulous idea? We can start right here in Aix. We have to visit all the chocolate shops. Like other people go on wine tours, we'll do a chocolate tour."

He adored the playfulness. This was exactly what Will

wanted for her, to see her come to life again, to laugh, to enjoy every moment.

"The best chocolate, the best pastries, the best coffee." He was all for it.

She sipped her champagne. "The best coffeehouse is definitely that one we used to go to in San Francisco, near the university. Remember?"

"I remember." He felt the caress of the memory across his nerve endings. "It was your favorite." As a couple, all those years ago, they'd gone to that same coffeehouse on Saturday mornings. She'd said it was too expensive for every day, but it was her Saturday morning treat.

"They had the absolute best white chocolate mochas. There was some extra spice. It wasn't just the white chocolate. It wasn't even the cinnamon." She closed her eyes, tapped her lower lip, trying to recall what it had been.

"Cardamom," he remembered for her. He'd only sipped her mocha, never got his own. He was on the rowing team, and there were way too many empty calories in those things. But he'd loved watching her enjoy them. She didn't allow herself a treat often, but when she did, she enjoyed it with gusto, taking small sips, savoring the flavors, like she did now with the champagne and chocolate.

"You remember that Chinese place on Geary?" he asked.

"Oh my God." She gasped, putting her hand to her chest. "They had that Hunan beef so hot it made my eyes water. They had to leave a whole pitcher of water. But God it was good."

That had been another treat night for her. Once a month. Julia had her rituals. Mochas on Saturday mornings, dinner out on Thursdays once a month. At the time, there had been something stifling about it, as if because it was Saturday, that was the *only* thing they could do, nothing else. Sometimes he just wanted something different. Only later, when he'd lost all those things, did he realize how badly he missed them. He remembered trying to start rituals with Elaine, breakfast at the corner diner near their apartment on Sundays, a movie on half-price Tuesday. She'd hated it.

Excitement shimmered in Julia's eyes. "What about that Spanish place? The roast potatoes all crispy because they were deep-fried. And those meatballs." She groaned, breathing in deeply as if she could smell all the scents again. "Remember how we ordered plates and plates and plates and we were so stuffed we had to practically roll back to school."

They'd always shared their food, especially when they couldn't decide. *You get this and I'll get that and then we'll share.* Just as they'd shared the steak and lobster, the mussels and veal last night in Paris, the duck and his lobster ravioli tonight.

His heart literally ached in his chest. He'd forgotten all that. In the wake of Elaine's disdain for the small rituals he'd tried to add to their life, he'd forgotten all the rituals he'd made with Julia.

God, he'd been so young and stupid and unappreciative. He hadn't lost Julia. He'd simply walked away. And for what?

The only good things he'd gotten out of his mistakes were his kids.

Julia shot him a sparkling smile. "We never got into curries. I love a good curry once in a while, don't you?"

"You're making me hungry all over again." He handed her another chocolate. "This should shut you up."

Julia made him hungry for so many things. Hungry for his youth, for the past, hungry for her smile, for her taste. The dimly lit room, the chocolate, the champagne, the music drifting up from below, it was all so intimate and romantic, the memories so poignant.

Why did he ever leave Julia? It couldn't have been just Elaine's allure. It had to have been more. Maybe it was his fear of a bigger commitment. Or maybe he'd just been a selfish asshole.

Julia hadn't been a virgin when he first made love to her. But neither was she experienced. Had that mattered? Maybe.

He'd been an asshole kid who wanted something exotic and seductive, and the girl next door just wasn't enough. And it seemed that Julia was asking for too much, had gotten too serious too fast. How life changed. Now he craved the girl next door. His best friend's wife. He'd hidden it so well for so long.

But Will was gone.

It was so much harder now to deny or hide the things he wanted.

"There." He put his glass on the table. "I've had two glasses of champagne. It's time for you to take your bath." God help him, he wanted to join her. Wanted to beg her to let him in. Instead, he stood. "Breakfast at eight? Sound good?"

She saluted him with her glass. "That'll be fine. Thank you for the champagne and chocolates."

He took one step closer. Too close. The sweetness of her lotion mesmerized him, the champagne on her lips tantalized him. "And tomorrow we'll start our search for the best pastry, the best chocolate, and the best coffee." He leaned down to kiss her forehead, lingered just a little too long as he drank in her scent, turning him as lightheaded as the champagne had.

Then he left before he did something unforgivable.

❦ 9 ❧

WILL

I saw Julia first. Weeks before Ryder found her. Ryder was the go-for-it kind of guy. I was more gaze from afar, work up to it slowly, take your time, make sure it's right. Make sure she's not going to reject you.

But I waited too long. And Ryder swooped in. Sort of like I'd swooped in on the girl my brother wanted in the ninth grade. What goes around comes around. Not that Ryder stole Jules out from under me like I'd done to Andrew. I don't think Ryder had any clue I had my eye on her. We'd been best friends since junior high school, had planned all through high school to be roommates at university even though I went for premed and he chose business and accounting.

Despite our friendship, I never found it easy to share my thoughts. Especially when I hadn't even found the courage to ask Jules out. Ryder would have laughed at me. "What's taking you so long, dude?" Not unkindly, just getting me to act.

But like they say, in the end, the turtle wins the race.

The first time I actually talked to her was the first time

Ryder brought her to the apartment for pizza. How pathetic is that?

Her voice, it was like music. She was pretty and soft-spoken, smart and funny. She didn't spend the night, not that first night, not the second either, not even the fourth time he brought her home. She had a roommate, as in they shared the same room, not just the same apartment. Ryder and I each had our own rooms. There was privacy here.

It hurt deep down in my guts the first time they went to his room. I could hear him, but I couldn't hear her. I told myself that was because he wasn't any good at it. That he was just a taker, not a giver. That she didn't enjoy it.

Even though I knew none of that was true. Ryder was a good guy. He just got the girl I wanted.

A normal person would have moved out. Or at least found a girl of his own. But not me. I was a masochist. And Julia always included me. She loved this special white chocolate mocha down at a certain coffee shop. She had to have it, every Saturday morning. More often than not, she invited me to tag along. I don't think Ryder even resented it. In his mind, I was never a threat. Or maybe it was just that he trusted me. They included me in a lot of stuff. He was on the rowing team, and Jules and I went to watch him race. She had special restaurants, too, that she liked to go to, but she was frugal, and she only allowed herself a meal out once or twice a month. She didn't want to graduate with big student loans the way so many did. So she worked and her parents helped her out and she pinched pennies wherever she could. Except for those extravagant Saturday mochas.

Then everything changed because of Elaine. I saw her first, too. I knew immediately she was out of my league. She was stunning, with mouthwatering curves and luscious auburn hair that smelled like exotic blooms. But there was something hard about Elaine. Or maybe a better word would be *intimidating*.

Then Elaine saw Ryder.

Ryder was what women would call a hunk. He was six two to my five nine. He was one hundred seventy pounds of pure muscle compared to my one hundred eighty pounds of unexercised flab.

Where I was intimidated, Ryder was nonchalant.

I figure that intrigued Elaine. Maybe it intrigued her, too, that he was already taken.

I wouldn't say that Ryder cheated on Jules. It was just that Elaine was relentless. She wanted him. She was everywhere he was. While Jules was the good girl, Elaine was the bombshell party girl who just wanted sex. Elaine was the devil on Ryder's shoulder, whispering all the things that could be his if he didn't have Jules.

I'm pretty damn sure there was some female rivalry going on with Elaine, too. Like, why should Ryder be with some frumpy girl next door? Not that Jules was frumpy. But Elaine considered herself so much more of the sexy ideal.

When it came right down to it, Jules wanted commitment, and Elaine just wanted fun. Ryder was twenty years old, he didn't want to be serious. And how could he resist *fun*?

There was no huge breakup. He just told Jules he thought they should date other people. She agreed, hiding her broken heart. But I read her pain like it was written all over her face and her body.

So Jules was out and Elaine was in. Elaine had her own place, and suddenly I found myself alone in the apartment a lot of the time. Which was fine by me. That way I could pick up the pieces for Jules. Had I planned it that way? I honestly don't know. I just wanted to be there for her. She was hurting.

Then things started to happen for us. I asked Ryder if he minded. I think he was actually relieved that Jules had me, because he knew he'd been an asshole. And if she and I were together, somehow it lessened his burden of guilt.

That's how Jules fell for me. On the rebound from Ryder. Everything Ryder had done wrong, I made sure to do right. When we finally made love, I made it all about her pleasure. I never asked her about how it had been with Ryder, if I was better. I didn't want to know.

I don't know if she chose me because I was all she could get. Or because being with me allowed her to stay close to Ryder. I'll never know. And I'll never ask.

The bigger question has always been why Elaine *married* Ryder. Maybe that was her plan all along, even if she did say she was about the fun and relationships cramped her style. Maybe she thought Ryder had potential. Right out of college, he went for one of the big accounting firms, positioning himself on the partner track where he could make a lot of money or where he could transition to an executive position in industry. He was smart; he'd do it faster than most guys. Maybe it was all about the money.

But she never got as much as she wanted.

It was funny, funny-strange really, but Ryder and I didn't talk about our wives or our marriages, almost like they were a taboo subject. And yeah, of course they were. Because Ryder had been there first, made love to Jules first, made her fall in love with him. *He* was her first love, not me. And after Jules, I don't think he ever felt comfortable revealing anything about Elaine, probably from guilt. We were friends, the best of friends, but even friends shouldn't talk about some things if they want a friendship to survive.

So we never talked about why they got married or why Elaine had kids. A mother figure she was not. And I figured out pretty damn quick that she had them because she was afraid of losing Ryder, pure and simple.

Although from my perspective, her motherhood was my

salvation. Jules and I were godparents. When we had such a hard time getting pregnant, there were Elaine and Ryder's kids, both amazing little beings. They were the kids Jules and I couldn't have.

Then I got cancer.

And the good times ended.

Life as I knew it ended.

And Jules was changed forever.

❧ 10 ❧

They started their search for the best pastry the next morning, walking the streets until they found a boulangerie in the old town centre, with a line that stretched half the block outside.

"Didn't I tell you the one with the longest line has to be the best?" Ryder said, buffing his nails on his polo shirt and making Julia laugh.

Making her laugh had become Ryder's new goal.

They waited fifteen minutes to reach the front to select their morning delicacy, and not a single person complained or dropped out of the queue. There were meringues and cream puffs and croissants and brioche and fruit tarts and macarons and petit fours and raisin bread shaped like snails and eclairs filled with cream and opera cakes with layers of coffee buttercream slathered with chocolate ganache and something called a *mille-feuille* which was vanilla cream sandwiched between leaves of pastry.

"There's so much to choose from." Julia stood before the glass case like a child in a toy store.

"How about an éclair?" Ryder suggested.

"I can get that at home." Which meant she wanted something new and delicious and mouthwatering.

Ryder found his mouth watering and it wasn't the dainty treats in the case. It was Julia in another pretty dress, her sun-kissed shoulders beckoning his lips. He didn't want her to wear anything else while they were here, just those tantalizing sundresses.

"Oh my God, I've really got to have that," she decided, pointing at the *mille-feuille*.

The shop girl placed it carefully in a pink box.

"What are you getting?" Julia asked him, her eyes alight with excitement.

"I'm sharing yours."

She laughed, haughty, and loud enough to attract attention. "Don't even think about it, buster." She held the pink box protectively against her chest.

People in the line behind them nodded or grumbled or harrumphed. "See, they all agree with me. And they want you to hurry up." She didn't even drop her voice when she said it.

This was how he wanted her to be, heedless of their mission in Provence, just enjoying, even a little flirty.

Ryder grumbled, too, unsuccessfully hiding a smile, and settled for a buttery, flaky croissant. "And don't think you're getting a bite of this either."

Three doors down, they stopped in a coffeehouse and ordered two cappuccinos, taking them to a café table in the middle of the square where they were surrounded by chattering tourists, bored locals, and lot of pigeons.

"Pastries and coffee, that's all I need." Julia devoured hers, stopping at the very last bite. "Here, you need to try this." She reached out, the last morsel in her sticky fingers.

"I thought it was unsharable."

"I'll let you have one small piece," she said snootily, her eyes sparkling in the morning sun.

Ryder leaned forward to eat from her hand, almost overwhelmed with the need to devour the rest of the cream from her skin.

Instead, she licked her fingers in another mouthwatering moment, and he stretched out his hand to wipe away a streak of cream at the side of her mouth. "Someone's got to clean you up."

He licked it off his thumb, savoring her essence, so much more potent than the cream.

"Isn't this perfection?" She smiled and raised her face to the sky, eyes closed. "The sun and this divine taste on my tongue."

The divine taste he craved was her. He was growing, expanding. He wondered how long he could contain these feelings.

Then she whispered, "But I'm not sure this is the very best cappuccino. We're going to have to keep searching."

"And don't forget about the chocolate, too."

He would fulfill her every desire.

God, if only he could fulfill all of his.

The morning's jaunt was to Cezanne's studio, which they found fascinating, especially his paint smock still hanging on a hook as if he might walk through the door and put it on. After that, they toured the Aix Cathedral and Église Saint-Jean-de-Malte, the gothic church built in the 1200s.

Then Julia saw the Musée des Tapisseries, a museum dedicated to tapestries. She grabbed his hand, pulling him toward the old building. The façade wasn't as impressive as the Louvre, but inside was a needleworker's dream. Julia had taken up needlepoint in the long hours caring for Will. At night, while Will slept, Ryder sometimes sat quietly, just watching her as she decompressed after a long day, her nimble fingers moving in stitch after stitch.

These tapestries, from the seventeenth and eighteenth centuries, were impressive.

"I love viewing the tapestries at the Legion of Honor. They don't display them all the time, because they rotate their stock." She clasped her hands together, tipping her head dreamily. "What I wouldn't give to get a peek at everything in the basement."

"You really have to take me there." It was the second time she'd mentioned the Legion.

"I can't believe you've never been there." She touched his arm. "We'll make a trip up there sometime when we get home."

It did something to his insides that she was making plans. He couldn't bear the thought of her cutting him out of her life now that Will was gone.

The museum had once been a palace lived in by archbishops and other dignitaries, and they wandered from room to room, examining each intricate tapestry.

By the time Julia was done, it was well after two in the afternoon. "Let's get some bread and cheese and eat in the park," she suggested.

He paid for one of the last baguettes left in a nearby shop. The French went out early to buy their daily bread, and once the loaves were sold, that was it.

"Wouldn't you love to go out every morning to buy your bread and vegetables and everything you planned to eat that day, everything fresh?" Julia whispered, clinging to his arm.

France seemed to have freed something in her. From the moment they landed in Paris, she'd gone at everything with gusto. It could have been ten years of pent-up emotion, holding back everything she felt, saving Will from her fear and anxiety.

In the cheese shop, the lady gestured, obviously asking if they wanted samples of the different cheeses. Everything was fresh and aromatic. They tried Roquefort and brie, camembert and Fourme d'Ambert and Pont L'Eveque.

"They're all so good. I don't know which one to choose." Julia looked at him for guidance.

"I like them all."

"Anything but the Pont L'Eveque." She obviously hadn't enjoyed the strong, pungent taste as much as the other cheeses.

The saleslady laughed, said something in French, pointing to another cheese, this one a reddish-orange. Offering a tiny sample, she served it to each of them on spoons.

"Oh my God." Julia held her hand over her mouth as she savored the exquisite morsel. "This is crazy good. It has to be this one."

She couldn't pronounce the name and the sales woman said it for her. "Époisses de Bourgogne." Then added, "Bon," which Ryder knew meant good.

Ryder bought a round of it packaged in a wooden box. The lady added two small spoons to the bag, gesturing to indicate that the cheese was soft enough to need a spoon rather than a knife.

He paid for everything, refusing to take Julia's money. As they were leaving the shop, the lady pointed next door and said something that sounded like "vin." Ryder saluted her with a smile and did as instructed, going next door for wine, entering into a lively discussion with the proprietor about which wine would go best with the cheese they'd purchased. They ended up with a Sauterne, when Ryder was thinking of red.

"You really don't have to pay for everything," Julia said as they left the wine shop.

He wrapped his fingers around hers. "I want you to have the best without worrying about whether this wine costs more than that wine, or this cheese is cheaper than that one."

"Are you saying I'm a penny pincher?" She gave a mock glare that might have been half real.

"No. I'm saying that I want what I want and I don't care if it costs more, but that you shouldn't have to be the one who pays for that." This trip was all about giving Julia the best, and he knew she was bound to make choices that were about the cost rather than the luxury.

"Ryder."

He was about to put his fingers to her lips to shut her up, but he remembered the shock he got the last time. "Please, Jules, let me do this for you," he said, calling her by the name he'd let Will take over. Then he added, "And for Will," because he knew it would make her agree.

She sighed, then just as quickly smiled. "When a man wants to pay for everything, I guess I'd be an idiot not to say yes."

Her smile was close to turning his knees weak. "You're definitely not an idiot."

"Then thank you. I accept."

He felt as he had when he'd won a regatta back in his rowing days.

They wandered through an open-air market and comple-mented the meal with grapes and cherry tomatoes. Ryder stopped at a stall filled with colorful scarves and travel blan-kets and picked out a blanket they could use for picnics.

"What a great idea." Julia clapped her hands in delight. "Let's get wine and cheese and meats and have picnics every day."

"Sounds perfect."

The central park was dotted with picnickers and sunbathers and dog walkers. Julia kicked off her shoes like the twenty-year-old girl he remembered. No, this Julia was differ-ent. Back then she'd been studious and serious, though she'd laughed often enough with him. Later she'd laughed with his kids, played all the games, like kick the can or hopscotch or even hide and seek, where a child thought that if he couldn't see you then you couldn't see him even though his feet were sticking out below the curtain.

That was the Julia he saw now, eyes bright, smile wide, laugh lines at her mouth.

He took pleasure in tearing off a hunk of bread, spooning the soft, smooth cheese over the piece, and feeding her.

She laughed and propped herself on her elbows, her hair swishing across the blanket. "I'll be like one of those harem girls from the old black and white movies, where you just feed me grapes and ply me with wine."

She opened her mouth and he plopped in a grape.

It was idyllic, the sun, the scent of flowers, the old trees, the classic architecture surrounding them, and Julia, happy and carefree for the first time in ten years. It might be a façade, a picture she was painting for him and because it was what Will had wanted. Ryder didn't care, the moment was perfection.

Then his phone rang.

He fished it out of his pocket. It could be Tonya or Dustin. Or it could be work, he'd had a couple of calls about minor issues.

But of course it was Elaine, as if she knew he was enjoying himself and had to bring him down.

"Sorry, I need to take this," he said, because it might be about one of the kids.

Julia continued to smile as he rose to do Elaine's bidding, crossing to the shade of a tree several yards away. He didn't want Julia to overhear the same kind of abuse she had that night all those weeks ago.

"Having a wonderful time with your paramour?" Elaine drawled, her voice dripping with sarcasm.

He closed his eyes and turned away from the sight of Julia

on the blanket. "Do you want something, Elaine? Because if you're only calling to hassle me, I'm hanging up."

"Do I have to want something?" she imitated, her voice rising to a high whine. "Can't I just call up to talk?"

The answer was no. Their talking days were long gone. "What do you need, Elaine?" It was his last warning.

She obviously heard the inflexibility in his voice. "Why haven't you called your daughter? She's up there crying in her room because her daddy doesn't love her anymore."

"I talked with her the night I arrived." As he'd tried to with Dustin, but his son hadn't answered his call. Last night, however, he'd stayed later drinking champagne in Julia's room, and when he called, Tonya hadn't answered.

"You're such an asshole," she snapped.

"I know, Elaine. You've told me many times." Then he thought of the time difference. "It's too early in the morning for you. What's wrong?" His heart rate crept up. It was just like Elaine to argue with him before telling him something crucial.

"Tonya wanted to make sure she got hold of you before she left."

School had been over for a week. There was no reason Tonya needed to go out this early. Elaine was just calling to yank his chain, push his guilt button. And yet he hadn't been diligent about making sure he got hold of his daughter. Or his son.

He tipped his head back, stared up into the trees. He should have thought more about the kids. Tonya was sensitive. And Will's death, despite the years of illness, had hit her hard. She knew how special this trip was, and she'd wanted him to tell her everything step-by-step. But he'd been too busy with his own feelings to do right by her.

"Then put her on."

"Tonya," Elaine shrieked, not bothering to move the phone from her mouth. "He's on the line right now."

He didn't ask why Tonya hadn't simply called him herself, without the intermediary. He knew the answer. Because Elaine wanted the chance to grind him down.

"Daddy?" His daughter's voice was like a balm to his heart.

"You okay, sweetheart?" He didn't say that her mother had claimed she was upset.

"I'm fine. I just didn't want to miss your call again."

"I'm sorry, sweetheart. Let's arrange a time to call every day. What works for you? Noon? While you're having lunch?"

"But that means it'll be nine o'clock in France."

He laughed. She'd been checking the time change. "Despite being an ancient old fogey, I have been known to stay up past nine o'clock at night."

Tonya laughed softly. "Sorry about that, Dad."

"No problem. So how is everything really? You okay?"

His daughter sighed, and he could actually hear the eye roll. "Mother made it sound like such a big deal that we hadn't been able to talk for a couple of days. But I just wanted to know how everything's going. Are you enjoying yourself?"

"Yeah." They hadn't talked much that first night since she was busy with her friends so he gave her a recap of their first day. "We visited the Eiffel Tower and the Louvre and the Arc de Triomphe. Heck, we walked all over Paris, even crossed the Seine. Paris is amazing. I took lots of pictures for you."

"That is just so cool, Dad. Where are you now?"

"A town called Aix-en-Provence." Then he laughed. "Your Aunt Julia dragged me into a tapestry museum, if you can believe that?"

"That's awesome. She always likes to do things that are so different, not like everybody else."

"She told me they sometimes have tapestries at the Legion of Honor."

"Where's that?"

He was looking at Julia as she tore off hunks of bread, slathering them with cheese, putting one in her mouth, leaving one on a napkin for him.

"It's in San Francisco. I'm a bad dad for never taking you to any of the museums up there."

"You took us to the planetarium and the Academy of Sciences," she said in his defense.

He had. But there were so much more he should have done. "I'll take you when I'm back home."

"Maybe Aunt Julia will want to go, too."

His daughter definitely didn't have the same feelings about Julia that her mother did. "I'm sure she'd love that."

"So when are you going to..." Her voice dropped in pitch and softness. "You know, do the thing?"

He understood what she couldn't say. When would they scatter Will's ashes? "In a couple of days or so. There's a special place, by a bridge. He wanted it there."

"And you'll read the letter we wrote for him, won't you?"

"Of course I will, sweetheart. Julia will love it, too."

"I wrote it because I can write better than Dustin. But he wanted to make sure you tell Aunt Julia it's from him, too."

"I'll tell her, I promise. Is Dustin there?"

"He's still asleep."

"All right. Well, I'll call you guys around noon your time."

"I don't know where Dustin will be. He's out half the time."

"Which he should be," Ryder said. "It's summertime. You should both be out enjoying yourselves. I'll try his phone anyway."

"Well, I'll have my phone with me wherever I am. And I'll

tell Dustin you'll call him at noon. Then you can call me right after you talk to him."

"That would be great. I love you, sweetheart. I miss you." He blew kisses into the phone.

She groaned, but he knew she loved them. "I'll talk to you later."

"Love you, Daddy."

"Love you, honey."

Then his daughter was gone and he ended the call before Elaine could jump back on. He'd already heard everything she had to say. He liked the idea of a scheduled time to talk to the kids so he didn't miss them.

Now he could return to Julia without a guilty conscience, at least about the kids.

He had two weeks with her. And he wanted to savor every moment.

❦ 11 ❦

They settled into a pattern over the next two days. He got a few work calls, but mostly they toured all day, walking miles, seeing as much as they could squeeze in. They searched for pastry and coffee, but hadn't found the best-ever yet. And, of course, they delighted in their daily picnic. They bought everything fresh, fresh bread, fresh cheese, fresh fruit, fresh meat sliced right in front of them. And, of course, a bottle of wine. They took their dinners late, like the French did, usually at an outdoor bistro so they could watch people on the street, listen to music, and enjoy French delicacies. Then she'd return to her room to enjoy the champagne and a variety of chocolates Ryder inevitably ordered for her. The confections got better and better, from dark to milk to white to ruby, from truffles to chocolate-covered nuts to petite fours that melted in her mouth.

And Julia made him share.

Then their goodnight hug. She told herself she shouldn't enjoy it so much. But she wanted to cling tight to him, pull him down and put her lips on his, until he opened his mouth and kissed her, a real kiss.

Over the years, she'd forgotten the taste of his kiss, but not the sweetness.

It was as if he found excuses to touch her, guiding her with his fingers wrapped around hers, a hand on her elbow or at the small of her back as they walked, whether they were in a crowd or not. He often brushed a lock of hair away from her lips or pushed it behind her ear. They'd had their chance twenty-five years ago, yet she got the sense that he was on the edge just the way she was, that his body trembled with the need to hold her and his heart raced with the desire to kiss her. Maybe it was the circumstances, together for hours on end, sleeping in rooms next to each other, perhaps sharing a Jack-and-Jill bathroom as they had last night.

What had Will meant when he said he wanted Ryder to be his stand in?

With Ryder just on the other side of the wall, the questions plagued her late at night.

She had never, ever, not even once, given any sign that Will had been her second choice. Yes, she'd dated Ryder first, she'd made love with him, and yes, she'd loved Ryder no matter what she'd told herself later. It shattered her heart into tiny pieces when Ryder said he wanted to see other people. It was an easy excuse to avoid saying that it was over between them, and once he was gone, she knew he was never coming back.

But there was Will, who'd always been so sweet. He'd healed her broken heart. If she'd never felt the same intense, all-consuming love, she told herself it was because her heart was guarded now. And she *had* loved Will. Whatever she'd felt for Ryder had only been the blush of new love. It would have faded eventually.

But what was it she felt for him now?

God help her, what was it she'd been feeling for Ryder while her husband lay dying?

Her thoughts, and her guilt, tormented her in the middle of the night. But during the day, she did exactly what Will had told her to do, she took pleasure in every moment.

The food was lush, the wine was heady, the chocolate, pastries, and treats were mouthwatering, and the sights and sounds of Provence were as beguiling and evocative as love itself.

There was so much to see that they'd planned two nights in Aix-en-Provence, then headed east to Salon-de-Provence, famous for a fortress called the Emperor's Castle, a gorgeous Romanesque church, and the region's fragrant artisan soaps. Along with gifts for Tonya, Ryder bought several scents for Julia's bath.

He seemed to love pampering her.

The next day, after a morning in Salon-de-Provence, they headed for Saint Jean de l'Ange where they would look for the broken bridge Will had seen in a book and eventually decided it had to be his final resting place.

There was probably some sort of permission they needed to scatter Will's ashes in the French countryside. But Julia hadn't searched for anything about it on the internet, and no one seemed to care about the ashes packed in her suitcase. This was Will's last wish, and she wouldn't let anything get in her way.

Along the way, Ryder promised her there would be more pictures of lavender fields, pictures without a train window to distort them.

"Let's stop here." He pointed to a turnout. They'd been traveling on side roads rather than highways, immersing themselves in the French countryside. "I want a picture of you in the lavender fields to send to the kids."

"Are we allowed to just get out and walk around out

there?" Not that she saw a no-trespassing sign. Besides, if she wasn't worried about permission to scatter Will's ashes, why worry about walking in a lavender field?

Ryder mirrored her thoughts. "Live a little, Jules." He gave her a grin that could melt chocolate.

Only Ryder and Will had ever called her Jules. Ryder had started it, then Will had taken it over, made the nickname his own, and Ryder had stopped using it. Until now.

He directed her on the poses he wanted her to take. "Lean down and smell the flowers."

She breathed in the scent, closing her eyes, letting the aroma envelop her very soul.

"Rub some on your hands," he told her, holding his phone and snapping pictures.

As she did, the lavender's perfume broke free into the air, turning her giddy.

"Now walk through the rows, your arms out, your hands brushing the lavender."

She turned her face to the sky, closed her eyes, relishing the lush feel of the lavender against her fingertips.

"Lie down so you're surrounded by the flowers."

The scent seduced her, the sky above her, ringed by a corona of lavender. Ryder's voice seduced her, too.

She had never felt so worshiped by the camera. So worshiped by a man. The French sun on her skin was smooth like a man's touch. Like Ryder's touch all those years ago.

"Gorgeous," he murmured, looking down at her.

They were silent a long, sweet moment, a moment when he didn't take a single photo, when he just looked at her as if he were memorizing her.

It could have been the sun on her, it could have been the scent of lavender surrounding her, it could have been the landscape of Provence caressing her. Or it could have been Ryder. All she wanted was to drag him down under the wide-open French sky, lay with him in that field of lavender, cover themselves in the opulent fragrance.

She wanted it so badly that she had to jump to her feet and take several steps back until she could breathe again. She brushed off her sundress and her hair, laughed. "I'm going to smell like lavender all day." Did her laughter sound a little hysterical?

When they stopped for lunch, he bought her a lavender sachet. "To remind you of your trip."

But something burning in his eyes and the intensity of his gaze made her think he wanted to remind her of the moment he'd stood over her in the field, to remind her of the sensual feel of the sun on her skin and how badly she'd wanted his touch.

In the early afternoon, they rolled into Saint Jean de l'Ange, where they'd booked rooms in a magnificent château just outside of town.

"What would you like to do?" Ryder asked. "We could go to the bridge now if you want."

Julia's heart pounded. This trip was all about scattering Will's ashes, but now, when they were right down to it, she felt queasy. "I think," she stopped, not really knowing what she thought. Then she heard a small voice inside, whispering to her. *You can do this.* Maybe it was Will inside her head. Or maybe it was her own inner voice telling her she needed to face this. "Let's see if we can find the bridge today."

"Good," Ryder said, as if he too felt the urgent need to do this final thing for Will.

Their rooms wouldn't be ready for a couple of hours, and they left the bags in the trunk. Julia would need to retrieve the box when the time came.

For now, she pulled out the travel book Will had read, turning to the page that described the location of the bridge.

"After this book was published, there'll probably be crowds there," she said, trying to sound airy.

"We'll beat them back," he assured her, with the same light tone that neither of them really felt.

Sitting beside Ryder in the car, she spread the book open on her lap. "Here's what it says. Take the main road out of town going north." She ran her finger under the line in the book as she read. "We'll come to a big red mailbox right after a dilapidated wall, about three kilometers once we get back into the countryside, and then we turn left."

"All right," Ryder said. "Main road out of town, three kilometers, dilapidated wall, red mailbox. Let's go for it."

They seemed to have gone so far, Julia thought they'd missed it. But then there was a broken wall on the right, and a few yards further on, a big red mailbox. She'd been expecting a box like in America, where you drop your letters inside to be mailed. But this was someone's letterbox painted red. And right after it was a road to the left. "That must be it." She pointed. "That left right there."

Ryder took the corner a little too fast, the tires squealing. "Sorry about that."

"You don't think it's someone's driveway, do you?"

He shrugged and kept going.

The lane was narrow, one car only, the foliage thick after the spring rains, rhododendron and azalea bushes, their blooms fading now as the summer grew hotter. "See that water tower on the left, there should be another lane opposite it to the right." She felt her excitement rising as she pointed. "There it is, up there. We just need to look for the right turn." As they approached, she saw the break in the foliage. The road was barely more than a dirt track. "You think we're trespassing out here?"

"I haven't seen any sign at all," Ryder said. This time he

took the right slowly, expecting it. They bumped along, the car rattling.

"Okay, we should come to a big boulder on the right. And after that, there should be a turnout where we can park and look for a path."

He laughed softly. "I seriously don't think we'll be bothered by any crowds here. No one's going to take the time to follow all those directions."

She smiled at him. "Good."

On the left were rows upon rows of lavender and on the right lay a meadow dotted with trees.

Julia felt as if her heart were beating in her throat. She was half afraid of being arrested or a farmer shooting at them for trespassing. The other half was all about this final step for Will. He would be gone forever, living only in their memories. But then he was already gone; his ashes had nothing to do with it.

They came upon the big boulder suddenly and just beyond that, the parking turnout. Sure enough, there was a small sign beside two posts that could have been a gate at one time.

Ryder parked, and Julia jumped out, heading to the posts. Though the sign was in French, it had the look one would expect from a national or state park, faded pictures of wildlife, a small map. She turned back just as Ryder climbed out of the car. "I'm pretty sure it's a trailhead. It has to be the right place."

"Great. Let's grab your bag." He popped the trunk lid and slid her suitcase to the outside. Julia unzipped it and retrieved the wooden box which was about the size of a child's lunchbox. Will's whole life, she thought, reduced to a lunchbox.

"I can carry it in my backpack," Ryder offered. He laid it carefully on top of the travel blanket he'd already stuffed down into the knapsack. "All right, let's go."

"The guidebook says it's maybe a mile and a half in."

"Is the bridge right on the trail?"

She nodded. "I think so," she said, putting on walking shoes that looked odd with her sundress.

Ryder held out a tube. "You'll need some suntan lotion, too." He watched as she put it on, something hot in his gaze that warmed her all over.

The trail was overgrown, obviously not well-traveled. Tall grasses had encroached on the path and old trees provided shade from the sun. Julia led the way, climbing over a fallen log. Birdsong sweetened the afternoon, joined by squirrels chattering in the branches. Through a break in the trees, a hawk circled overhead, then divebombed some poor creature in the field. Otherwise it was quiet, no car engines, no planes overhead, no tractors in the fields.

They tramped for twenty minutes, and long before they reached it, she heard the water's musical babble as it tripped over the rocks. Then they broke through the trees and there it was, the bridge, surrounded by a profusion of wildflowers, lavender, red geraniums, blue hydrangeas. She wasn't sure how they all grew in the same soil.

It was as if the place were magical.

"It's beautiful." All the awe she felt infused her voice.

This was the place for Will, exactly what he'd dreamed of.

❧ 12 ❧

Ryder stepped up beside her, his fingers sliding into hers. It was so natural, the two of them here together, ready to do whatever Will needed, just as they had for the past ten years.

The bridge was made of ancient stone covered in moss, its broken boulders smoothed by time. As if a giant had chopped it down the middle, half an arch sprouted out over the gully. In summer, it was just a stream, but she imagined the water rushed high up the banks during a storm. Vines climbed the trees and dangled over the bridge. Over a thousand years ago, there might have been a Roman road that led here but it had long ago given way to nature.

Now it would be Will's bridge, the perfect resting place.

Ryder pulled the travel blanket out of his backpack and laid it on the grass. "Let's sit a while."

"Will would like that. Part of the ceremony," she mused. "Enjoying nature before we put him to rest."

With the water nearby, she would have expected bugs, and though she heard the buzz of insects, the creatures didn't bother either of them in this special place.

Ryder tugged out a bottle of champagne and plastic glasses she hadn't seen him add to the knapsack. Somehow she'd thought the French would find plastic champagne glasses a sacrilege. He must have had the concierge at the B&B in Salon-de-Provence search high and low for him. The bottle had been opened, the rest of last night's champagne they hadn't finished.

Lastly, Ryder set Will's box at the edge of the rug. She'd purchased it at a jewelry store, loving that it was constructed of different woods pieced together, the top inlaid with mother-of-pearl.

Ryder raised his glass. "To Will Bellerman. You are greatly missed."

"To Will, you were the center of my life for so long." She sipped the champagne. "I don't know what life will be like without you, but I'm sure it will never be the same." She felt an ache behind her eyes.

Ryder added, "I love you, man." They drank in silence.

And somehow she felt the essence of Will right there with them.

"He was a good man," Julia whispered. Because Will had always been good to her. Even when he got ill, he still thought about her, managing their savings and his trust money to ensure there would be enough left for her to live on comfortably when he was gone.

"He was always my best friend," Ryder said in the same reverent tone she'd used. "Sometimes I thought he was a better dad to my kids than I was." Pain and weariness etched his face.

"That's not true." She couldn't help touching his arm. "You've always been a great dad. No matter what anybody says."

"You mean no matter how much Elaine complains." His

sigh said it all. "I know she says that stuff just get to me. But we all wish we'd done things differently."

"Yes, we do." Sometimes she wished that Will hadn't put himself through all the treatments that never worked for long. His suffering had been immense. Though he sometimes had a few good weeks—once the cancer even receded for months, making them believe it was gone—but he was never cured. The cancer always came back. She wished she could have saved him all that. But she could never say that aloud. It would sound as if she'd wanted Will to die, and that wasn't true either. She wanted more time with him, yes, but she couldn't bear his misery. She'd prayed for it to end. "I wish I could've taken away all his pain."

"We all wish that."

They both blamed themselves for so much that wasn't their fault. What a pair they made.

"Are you ready?" Ryder finally asked.

She closed her eyes. Would she ever be ready? She hadn't been ready for Will to die, even as much as she wanted relief for him. And for herself. "Yes, I'm ready."

"How do you want to do it?"

"By the flowers at the base of the bridge. That's where he'd want to be." Then she had to add, "It's not Will. It's just his ashes. But somehow he'll be looking down and he'd like to be with the flowers." She laughed, hearing the shakiness of her voice. "Not that he was particularly a flower kind of guy."

Ryder didn't mock her. "It's peaceful here. That's what Will needed in the end. Peace."

The setting was serene, the babbling brook, the chirping birds, the buzzing bees. Yes, this was a good place. She rose, brushed her dress down. Then picked up Will's box.

She concentrated on the deep green of the moss covering the bridge. On the bright blue of the hydrangeas. On the crisp whiteness of the clouds overhead and the dark pink, yellow, blue and purple wildflowers that sprouted everywhere as if the bridge had magical powers.

Then she held out the box to Ryder. "I really need you to do this for me. I know it's not Will. But I can't look. I just can't." She ended on question, begging him. "Please?"

Ryder took the box from her as if it were filled with precious jewels.

She watched, but she tried not to see. Just as she hadn't looked as she'd stood by Will's parents up on that grassy cliff back home. The cremains were in a plastic bag inside the box, and someone had said they were like coarse sand. Julia didn't want to know. She just wanted Will to be at rest at last.

Ryder hunkered down at the base of the bridge with the brilliant flowers and the bright green bushes. He opened the box and she knew even if she could exactly see that he was sifting out the contents. Will would fertilize these flowers forevermore. He would become part of the magic, and his kindness, his loyalty, his beauty of spirit would make the magic even more potent.

When it was done, Ryder rose, closing the box.

Will was gone now. But his essence would remain here in this place forever, exactly where he'd chosen to be.

"Thank you," she said, so softly she almost couldn't her own words. Emotion clogged her throat, filled her eyes.

"What do you want to do with the box?" He held it, not handing it back but keeping it close.

She didn't know right now, she couldn't think.

Ryder understood because he didn't push, just took her hand, led her to their blanket, and put the box back in his rucksack. But before they sat, he said, "Tonya gave me something she wanted me to read aloud. She and Dustin wrote it together. Is that okay?"

"Of course." She squeezed his hand, felt his warmth and

his strength and his love for his children. "They loved him. Please read it."

He pulled the paper from his back pocket, unfolded it, held it in hands that shook slightly.

Then Ryder read aloud. "Dear Uncle Will. We want you to know how very special you are. All those hours you spent with us, teaching us how to play Stratego and chess. There's not a lot of people who would spend that much time with a couple of little kids that weren't even his."

Tears pricked the backs of her eyes, but, pressing her fingers to her temples, she kept them at bay. She needed to listen, absorb, remember, for Ryder, for his kids, and for Will. They'd been such an important part of Will's life, of her life. Tonya and Dustin were the children they never had.

"We wish we could have been with you every day. We wish we could have taken the pain away." Ryder's voice quaked with the same emotion threatening to overwhelm Julia. But he was stronger, and he kept reading. "Watching what the cancer did to you broke our hearts. But all our memories of you are also how our hearts will heal. Every time we think of your smile, we will heal. Every time we remember how you taught us to swim, we will heal. Every time we watch one of the beach videos and hear you laugh, we will heal. Every time we think of you and know that you are no longer in pain, we will heal. We will heal because we know—" Ryder's voice broke, then he breathed in deeply and started again. "We will heal because we know that we are loved by you. And because somewhere up there, you know how much we loved you. We will always miss you. Love, Tonya and Dustin."

They stood for a long, long moment in the quiet. Even the birds had fallen into a deep hush. The sun broke through the trees, shining down on the flowers around which Ryder had scattered Will's ashes like a halo. As if Will had heard every word, and the sunshine was his answer.

"How beautiful," Julia whispered. "They are so amazing."
How they'd both loved Will. She felt tears rising, choking her.
"Oh my God," she whispered, having no other words.

"They wanted you to have it." Ryder refolded the page,
held it out to her.

Oh God. She didn't deserve it. "No." She warded him off.
"I can't."

"It's okay, Jules. It's what the kids want."

She shook her head, her hair flying in front of her face.
"No. You don't understand. I don't deserve to hold onto those
words. Will did, but not me."

"Of course you do." His voice was soft, almost wary, not
understanding at all.

"Don't you get it?" She wanted to scream at him. "He
worked so hard to beat it." Then she choked out the next
words, as terrible as they were. "But I just wanted it to be
over." She slapped her hand to her chest. "I just wanted it all
to end."

"We all wanted his suffering to be over, Jules." He reached
out to her.

She had to step back. Couldn't bear it if he touched her.
"That's not what I mean. I wanted it to be over for *me*." She
covered her mouth, trying to hold in the cries, the tears. "I
was so tired. I couldn't do anything for him, for the pain, for
anything. I just wanted—" She couldn't finish those words.
"And when he was gone." She gulped air. Then she said it, the
thing she'd never admitted to anyone. "I just felt relieved.
That was all. Not pain or grief or anguish." Her voice
dropped to a whisper. "Just relief."

That was when she broke, crumpling like a puppet who'd
had all its strings cut. Finally letting go of all the tears she'd
been holding inside forever.

❦

RYDER DIDN'T KNOW WHAT TO DO FOR JULIA EXCEPT gather her in his arms, lowering them both down to the blanket, letting her tears soak his shirt.

Maybe he shouldn't have read the letter aloud, not right now. Then again, this was what Julia had needed for months. A release.

Maybe it was what they both needed.

He shoved the letter back in his pocket. He'd give it to her later, when she'd calmed down. When she was ready.

"It's all right," he whispered into her hair. "It's all right." Over and over. God. Her misery. It was killing him. "It's normal. I felt it, too."

But she'd harbored this guilt for months, since Will died, probably even before that day.

He rocked her in his arms. Her whole body shook, her sobs loud, her tears messy. They were tears for her broken dreams, for the children she never had, for all the years she would grow old without Will. She'd been stoic for ten long years. She'd stood by Will, sat through every doctor's appointment, gone through every treatment, heard every excuse for why it hadn't worked this time. And she'd been strong throughout it all.

She deserved this moment of release, not only deserved it but needed it.

And she deserved the relief she'd felt. "It was a relief for both of you," he murmured to her. Even if she thought it was just for herself, he knew it was far more. "Don't you think I wanted to see an end to it, too? For Will. For you. For all of us."

Still she cried.

And he held her.

He soothed her with his hands on her back, on her arms, his lips on her forehead, in her hair. He held her tight through every tremble, every quiver and quake. Until finally she had no tears left. She lay against him, breathing choppy breaths, sniffling. He delved into the knapsack and pulled out a packet of tissues. He'd come prepared.

She blew her nose, then took another tissue to wipe her eyes. "I'm sorry."

"You don't need to be." He held her face in his hands, forced her to look at him. "What you felt was normal, Jules. It doesn't mean you didn't love Will. It doesn't make you selfish."

"I'm not so sure." She looked down, not meeting his gaze.

"Look at me." He waited until she did, her eyes still blurry with her tears. "You're not a bad person. You did more for Will that anyone could have expected of you. You gave up your career. You did everything for him. And all you wanted was an end to the pain, his and yours. There's nothing wrong with that." He kissed her forehead, then held her away from him, his hands falling to her shoulders. "You know I wanted the same thing. I wanted Will to go. I wanted it to be over for everyone. I didn't want to see him suffer anymore. I didn't want to see *you* suffer." He squeezed her shoulders. "And I don't feel guilty for that. Will wouldn't want us to feel guilty."

Her gaze traced his features, lighting on his forehead, his cheeks, his nose, his lips. Then meeting his eyes. "Thank you," she said, almost mouthing the words. "Sometimes it feels better just to say it out loud. To someone. Like saying it takes the power out of it."

She didn't say she believed what he'd confessed. It didn't matter; he saw the shift in her, her eyes a little less bleak.

"Don't let it have power over you anymore." He knew the power of guilt, of what it could do to your insides.

She laughed softly then, put a hand to her cheek. "I must look a mess."

Her eyes and nose were red, her skin blotchy, her makeup gone. Yet she had never looked more beautiful to him.

"You look fine." He tipped her chin. "It's okay. It's just me. And I needed the tears, too." He'd cried his own tears as he'd held her. Tears for Will, tears for the beauty of his children's thoughts and words. Tears for the guilt Julia shouldn't have to feel.

She reached out, held a finger to his wet eyelashes, the touch so light it was like hummingbird wings.

He leaned in to kiss her eyelid. She leaned in to kiss the corner of his eye. He reached a hand under the fall of her hair. She stroked her fingers through his. He kissed her hair, softly, soothingly, the way he had so many times, comfort, reassurance, friendship, a way to ease the anxiety and pain in the moments when they were alone after Will had finally fallen asleep in his sickbed.

He didn't know when it changed. Or even how. Yet his kisses became something more, took him away to a place he hadn't allowed himself to go in twenty-five years. She seemed to melt into him, into his kiss in a way she'd never allowed herself. It was as if all the years melted away, as if it were the first time again, when he was crazy for her, when she had wanted him just as badly.

He opened his mouth, and she met him kiss for kiss, stroke for stroke.

He laid her back on the blanket, living and dying with every taste of her. So familiar and yet so far from him. So sweet and yet so hot. He held her close, their bodies like one. He cupped her face, tangled his fingers in her hair, relished the feel of her, the textures of her, the taste of her. It had been so long and he wanted so much more.

A soft moan rose up from her throat and set him on fire. He trailed his hand down her neck. Her arm, her back, her soft, round bottom. Then he pulled her close, tight against him, letting her feel what she did to him.

She wound her arms around his neck, raised her leg up his

thigh as he trailed his hand along her flank, down until he reached the hem of her sundress, until his fingers touched her warm, smooth skin. He broke the kiss to trail his lips down her throat, to the swell of her breast, his fingers riding up, up, up her thigh. Until he found the soft cotton of her panties.

He'd been there so many times, but this was all new.

Then Julia slipped off the strap of her sundress, baring herself to him.

And he took her in his mouth.

SHE'D NEVER WANTED ANYTHING MORE THAN RYDER'S KISS, Ryder's touch, Ryder inside her.

Oh God, she wanted it so badly. Right there. His mouth on her, his fingers stripping the scrap of cotton away.

Touch me, touch me, touch me.

Her whole body cried out for it, arching on its own, pleasure shimmying along her nerve endings.

Please, please, please.

She opened her eyes because she had to see. Because it was Ryder. Because she'd wanted this for so long.

Then she saw the hydrangeas glowing in the sunlight.

The hydrangeas where Ryder had scattered her husband's ashes.

Ryder's hand was up her dress, his lips pressed to her breast.

And her husband was there, *right* there. Watching everything.

"Oh my God, no." She scrambled away, backing up like a crab, tugging the strap of her dress up over her shoulder again. The strap *she* had pulled down to entice Ryder. "I'm sorry, I'm sorry, I'm sorry. I can't do this."

She felt hysteria rising in her like bile in her throat. She'd just cried her eyes out because of her guilt over Will, her relief over the end. And not seconds later, she was quivering for another man's touch.

Ryder was talking, his voice soothing, his hands smoothing her dress down over her thighs. "It's okay, Jules. I'm sorry, Jules."

Jules. Just the way Will used to say it.

She couldn't breathe, she might start crying all over again. What would people think? What would his kids think? What would her parents think?

"They don't have to know."

It was only when he answered that she realized she'd said it all loud.

"It was just a moment, Jules. We didn't do anything wrong. We were both emotional. That's all it is. You don't need to feel bad."

She hiccupped as if she'd just finished crying. "I want to believe you."

"Believe me. It was just a moment. And it's over now. It was nothing to feel bad about. I got carried away." But his hand was on her leg, soothing her, stroking her. "You can't feel guilty about everything for the rest of your life."

But she did feel guilty. And her body knew it hadn't been *just* a moment.

It had been years in the making.

She had to fight that feeling with everything in her. "You know I can't."

"I know we can't," he answered softly, but his eyes were still hot.

They could never go back. They could never erase all the years. They could never wipe out the guilt. They could never erase Will.

"We need to go." She rolled away, fast, to the edge of the blanket, standing, grabbing the empty champagne bottle and the glasses, shoving them into his knapsack while he folded the blanket.

Thank God he'd already tucked Will's box inside so she didn't have to see it again, a reminder of what they'd done.

"We need to go now," she said. "It'll be easier to find our way back to the car before it's dark."

But she didn't think they could ever find their way out of the mess they'd just created with that kiss, that touch.

IT WASN'T HIS MISTAKE. IT WASN'T HER MISTAKE. IT WAS just something they'd done, a moment they'd succumbed to. It wasn't that guilt didn't sizzle through him like bacon frying in the pan. Because it did.

It might even have been worse, like acid boiling in his veins. It seared his flesh. It ate through his heart.

But that kiss had happened. He was man enough to admit he'd wanted it. He shouldn't have done it. He knew that. But it had been so long. And he wanted her so badly.

Yet she might never get over it. Because in that moment, she'd wanted it, too.

That was the moment she would feel guilty about.

That was the moment she wouldn't forget.

And it was the moment he would always remember.

❊ 13 ❊

WILL

Julia should have been a mother. She was so damn good with Ryder's kids.

I loved them, too. It didn't bother them that I was sick. A lot of kids would have hated having to go to some dying guy's house all the time. But not Ryder's kids. Tonya and Dustin wanted to play games. They wanted to make me laugh.

With them, I *could* laugh. With all my heart, I could love two people who weren't my flesh and blood.

But I robbed Julia of having her own children, the thing she'd wanted so badly.

I clearly remember all that frantic sex when we were trying to get pregnant. When you become a baby factory, all the joy goes out of it. Not that sex had ever been easy for me. But the baby thing made it excruciating.

And still, Julia didn't get pregnant.

I know it broke something inside her every day. Especially when she was with Ryder's kids, showering them with all the love she couldn't shower on a child of her own. If they needed a babysitter at a moment's notice, she said yes, no questions asked. It was always Elaine who called, never Ryder.

Jules loved having them over, yet it made everything harder on her, too.

And made it harder on me because I was the problem.

We went to the doctor.

Oh yes, the problem was me. It was something I'd always secretly known about myself. Low sperm count. Low libido. Low virility.

Unlike Ryder.

It was almost like the scarlet letter *A* sewn on my shirt like the adulterous Hester Prynne. But for the opposite reason.

We didn't tell anybody that our childless state was my fault. I wanted drugs to cure me, but the doctors didn't offer any. We talked about taking my sperm, artificial insemination. Then they did tests, endless tests.

Finally, instead of telling me I had a baby on the way, they told me I had cancer.

I don't know how long it would have taken to find the cancer if I hadn't had that pesky fertility problem. It's very true; doctors are the worst at taking care of themselves.

That's when Jules really broke. She was like a rag doll who'd lost all its stuffing.

Of course, being Julia, that didn't last long. Because she had to be strong for me. She was always the strong one.

She never said it was all my fault. She never blamed me. She was stoic. She was wonderful.

Sometimes it made me sick to my stomach.

I went on as if everything were normal for as long as I could. I went to the hospital every day, worked until I couldn't take it anymore. I volunteered for every new drug, every new treatment.

But nothing would ever change the fact that I had broken Jules.

Or that I would eventually do something that if she knew, her love and trust would wither and die.

❧ 14 ❧

They were silent on the drive back to the château. Dinner was mostly silent, too, so different from the other evenings when they'd enjoyed a good laugh and a good talk.

It wasn't scattering Will's ashes that stood between them now.

It was that unforgettable kiss.

He wanted to tell her they'd done nothing wrong. But he knew Julia couldn't hear that right now. His shrimp tasted like sawdust. They didn't share food off each other's plate, skipped dessert, and didn't bother with coffee.

He didn't hold her hand as they walked, didn't put a hand at her back to guide her. There was no shared glass of champagne, no goodnight hug, no kiss on the lips, not even on the forehead, nothing at all.

Ryder feared they would share nothing for the rest of the trip.

He'd totally screwed up.

Then again, what happened seemed inevitable. After all

they'd shared, all the pain, all the worry, all the fear for Will, with all the emotions roiling inside them, it was bound to happen. As guilty as he felt about it, he'd *wanted* it to happen.

He and Julia stayed that night in the stunning château, his room dominated by an enormous fourposter bed and a massive marble fireplace. Every accessory was sumptuous, from the bed's thick eiderdown to the plush rugs covering the hardwood floors. The walls and doors were thick, barely a sound in the night except the chirp of crickets through the open balcony door. They shared a bathroom, and there the door wasn't quite so thick, something he now realized was a huge mistake as he heard Julia running her bath.

He couldn't help imagining her naked in the tub.

But she had stuck to that ritual. He wondered if it meant that tomorrow they could somehow get back to normalcy. Back to the camaraderie.

But he doubted it.

He'd sent champagne and chocolate to her room like usual. Had she poured a glass and nibbled on the chocolate? Or had she ignored it? He wondered if she'd used the bath scents he bought for her.

He lay on the bed listening. The subtle sounds of her bathing drove him a little mad. With desire, with guilt, with the sense that what they'd done had changed things entirely, that they could never go back, that they were ruined. The thoughts were overly dramatic, but he half prayed, half expected, half feared she would knock on his door and want to talk.

But there was nothing except the gurgle of the draining tub. An unbreakable silence fell next door, until finally he grabbed his e-reader to occupy his mind and shut out the unbearable quiet. Not that it worked. He remembered too well the taste of Julia, the feel of her, the scent of her.

His watch beeped telling him it was time to call the kids. What the hell would he say when his mind was so preoccupied with thoughts of Julia?

He called Dustin first, but his son didn't answer. Ryder gave it another five minutes and tried again. Dustin never picked up.

He called Tonya. She was his daughter and he loved her with everything in him, just the way he loved Dustin. But Tonya was so much more easygoing and accepting. "Hi, sweetheart."

"Daddy. How did everything go?"

He loved that she still called him Daddy sometimes even though she was almost sixteen. He knew it would change, that he would lose that part of her, and already he mourned it.

"It went well. We toasted Will with champagne. It was a lovely place, a lot of flowers, a brook, really peaceful, not a bunch of tourists tramping through. And the broken bridge is picturesque. Will's going to love that spot."

"Did you read my letter?" Her voice brimmed with hope and caution and fear.

"Yes." When he'd unpacked his rucksack, he'd found the box that had contained Will's ashes. And he'd placed the kids' letter inside. It was fitting. He'd find the right time to return the mother-of-pearl box to Julia. She would want to keep it, he knew, as well as the letter. "It was the most beautiful thing I've ever heard, sweetheart. I thank you and your brother so much for that."

"Did Aunt Julia like it?" He could almost hear her held breath.

He didn't tell his daughter that Julia broke down after the reading. But her breakdown had been a good thing. He knew it deep in his gut.

It was the kiss that ruined everything.

"She cried because it was so beautiful. It was a good afternoon. Everything was perfect for Will's send off."

She sighed wistfully. "I wish I could've been there."

"Me, too, sweetheart." With all his heart. "How's your brother doing? I called but I must have missed him."

She sighed, and he sensed the accompanying shrug. "He's fine. He's just Dustin. You know." The teenage years. He'd expected it with Tonya, but she hadn't reached the difficult stage yet. Dustin, however, had been acting out since the divorce. "Is he home with you now?"

"No. He's..." Her sigh was long-suffering, an adult sound, like a parent who just couldn't understand their kid. "I don't know. He's wherever."

"Well, tell him again that I'll try to talk to him during lunch tomorrow."

"Not that it will do any good," she groused. "Okay, Dad, I have to tell you something. So promise you won't totally freak out on me."

His stomach dropped. "I won't freak out."

"Well, it's like Mother has gone hysterical since you left. She's been on this weird rampage. About you and Aunt Julia."

He gritted his teeth. Julia had warned him about this.

"I can hear you grinding your teeth, Dad, that's bad for you," she singsonged at him.

He laughed softly. His daughter knew him too well. "Don't you worry about your mom. I'll have a talk with her."

"It's not like she's been mean to us or anything. Just so you know."

"I know." He had to give Elaine that, she wasn't a terrible mother, even if she loved to dad-bash.

"She's just really upset you went away alone with Aunt Julia."

Yeah. Elaine had been badmouthing him again. She'd done that since the day he discovered her sexting phone, and her affair somehow became his fault, nothing to do with *her*, but something he'd driven her to. He'd never told his kids about Elaine's affair. It wasn't fair to them to air their parents' dirty laundry, to start throwing around blame, to put the kids in the middle.

That, however, didn't stop Elaine from talking shit about him.

He shouldn't have to justify or explain, but after what he'd done today, guilt made him do it. "Aunt Julia needed me after Uncle Will died."

"I know, I know. I understand. Really I do. But you know Mother."

Oh yeah, he knew.

"Okay, Dad, I gotta run. I'm meeting some of the girls at the mall." Again.

I love you, sweetheart."

"Love you, too, Daddy."

He let his daughter's love and the sweetness of her voice flow over him for a minute. Then he called Elaine.

She answered with, "What do you want?"

He really hated Caller ID. She could start in on him immediately, knowing exactly who was on the other end of the line.

"I have only one thing to say. Do not start that crap with the kids about me and Julia. Do you understand me?"

She gave him a prim, prissy little snort. "I don't know what you're talking about."

He wasn't about to say that Tonya had tattled on her. "I know you, Elaine. And I know you're pouring vitriol in their ears all the time. There is nothing going on here. It is all above board. And you need to stop."

"Or what?" Her voice dripped with challenge and sarcasm, setting his teeth to grinding again.

There was no real "or what" about it. The only thing he could use against her was her affair, at least the one he knew about, though he suspected there'd been more. But that was a card he'd never play with his kids. So he just said," At least try to be a good mother. Leave them out of our battles. They don't need you putting them in the middle."

He hung up. Maybe using the good-mother trope was petty. Maybe hanging up on her was, too.

But petty was all he had now.

THOUGH JULIA HAD CLIMBED INTO BED AFTER HER BATH, she hadn't slept. It was only nine o'clock, too early to sleep. Other nights, she and Ryder had shared champagne and chocolate and talk. Now, though the walls between them were thick and the silence agonizing, she thought she could hear the soft murmur of Ryder's voice as he talked to his kids.

Ryder had two wonderful children. She had nothing. The thought sounded so disgustingly self-pitying, but though she'd tried so hard over the years not to succumb, self-pity seemed to be all she had left. That and the memory of this afternoon. Not of Will, but Ryder.

Tasting him had been glorious. The feel of his hands on her, his mouth on her, it had been the stuff of fantasies.

Of course she could never make the fantasy real. It would be a betrayal of Will. It would almost be like admitting that Will had been second best, that if Ryder had stayed with her all those years ago, they would still be together. That she would never have loved Will.

Though she always would have loved him. It might have been a different love, like a sister or a friend, not the romantic kind of love. But romantic love never lasted anyway, right?

Except that when she relived those moments between her and Ryder today, she had to admit to herself that it never been like that with Will. She'd gone a little crazy, needing Ryder so badly, wanting him so purely. It had been like that all those years ago, intense, consuming, there'd been nothing else but Ryder.

But this afternoon was just the pent-up emotion of the moment, the beautiful letter from the kids, the way it had spotlighted her guilt, made her feel unworthy, then Ryder's confession to feeling the same sense of relief that she had. She'd reacted to that, to not feeling so alone in her thoughts.

But still that terrible, guilty voice inside her persisted, whispering to her, asking her that unanswerable question. *Did you love Will enough?*

She had loved him. But had she loved him *enough*?

She didn't blame herself for his cancer. It wasn't as if true love would have miraculously cured him. But maybe she'd robbed him of something special and elemental. She could only pray he never knew that sometimes she'd dreamed of Ryder.

And now she was in danger of ruining her relationship with Ryder. What if he couldn't be her friend after what happened between them today? His friendship was all she had.

They'd barely spoken on the way back to the château, even less during dinner. God, she'd missed the time they spent watching the sunset, drinking champagne, comparing tonight's chocolate to last night's and the night before, talking about the day, the sights they'd seen, the pastries they'd tasted, the coffee they'd shared. She missed the good-night hug, the soft kiss of friends.

She wanted it all back. She didn't want anything to change. Those moments were too precious.

She fell asleep rehearsing everything she'd say to him.

And yet, despite all the rehearsal, the next morning she'd forgotten all the right words, remaining tongue-tied and brusque as they toured Saint Jean de l'Ange.

Ryder didn't hold her hand. They didn't search out the best pastry or the best coffee. He didn't buy cheese and bread and fruit and wine for a picnic. They ate in near silence at a little café they found on a back street.

Her heart couldn't stand it. Yet she couldn't say the words.

They toured the town's cathedral, but in her mood, she thought all cathedrals looked alike. Or maybe this was just a church. She couldn't tell the difference anymore. Maybe she was just exhausted because she'd woken so many times in the night thinking about Ryder and what they hadn't done and what she couldn't say.

Her throat ached from not talking.

Several times she'd opened her mouth, the words on the tip of her tongue, then she couldn't remember the perfect way she was supposed to say them, so that he would understand everything she felt and they could be normal with each other again.

In the city's park, he didn't spread out the blanket. They sat on a bench beneath the leafy shade of a tree. And didn't talk.

If only Ryder would bring up what had happened by the broken bridge. If he started it, maybe she could say what needed to be said.

The silence was torture as they watched birds swoop in for the bread a gaggle of children had thrown to them.

This was Provence. They should be enjoying the beauty of it all, the market square that had been built hundreds of years ago and was still used three days a week, the musicians in the corner of the park playing something lovely and lyrical with sweet abandon. The boulangeries had closed for the day, their baked goods sold. The town had turned sleepy in the afternoon, few cars on the narrow roads, only the tourists still walking about.

Just say it. The longer this numbing silence went on, the harder it would be to ever end it. They needed to deal with this or they would lose the friendship they'd built.

She couldn't say she found the courage, but she at least opened her mouth, and a few words spilled out. "About yesterday," she started. "I just wanted to explain." Not the right words, but at least they were words.

"You don't need to explain, Julia."

For a moment, she thought he might put his hand on hers. But he backed off. That's how it was between them now. He couldn't touch her anymore, not even for comfort.

And she hated that.

"It was my fault." His voice was low, harsh.

"It wasn't your fault." She found more words, letting them flow. "We got carried away. But we need to talk about it, because now everything is awkward between us. And I don't want it that way. I want us to go back to the way we were."

Ryder looked at his hands.

"What I mean is, we'll never let it happen again. It was just a moment. We can forget—" She didn't finish. She didn't want to lie. Because she would never forget. "I just felt like I... Oh, I don't know. I don't know how to explain." She felt as if she were standing off in the distance watching herself flounder. "This isn't coming out the way I planned."

He leaned forward, elbows on his knees, hands clasped. Silent.

Talk to me, she wanted to shout. Yet she was the one who'd been silent since it happened.

Finally he spoke, his deep voice gentle in the quiet afternoon. "Why can't it happen again, Julia?"

His words smacked her, leaving her stunned. Maybe she hadn't heard him right. Maybe her ears were ringing. "Because." It was all she could say, the only word, just like a mother would say to her child who wouldn't stop asking the same question over and over, no matter how much she explained. *Because I said so.*

Yet her mind reeled with his words. Why couldn't they?

Ryder finally looked at her, a long, assessing look with those beautiful, soulful brown eyes. "Will was my best friend in all the world. I loved him. I miss him." He let the next words hang in the air. Even before they came, she felt them like a slap across her face. "But Will is gone. And we're still here." A gentle pause that beat against her eardrums. "So why not, Jules, tell me why not? Because I have to tell you, now that I've tasted you again, I can't stop thinking about you." His eyes were deep pools she wanted to fall into.

"We can't *because* of Will," she stressed.

He shook his head slowly. "I thought about Will. And I've felt a whole lot of guilt about what I feel for you. But I remember that letter you read on the plane. And I'm starting to think Will wouldn't care. He wanted you to be happy. He wanted us both to be happy."

She felt the horror of what he was saying in her chest, like it was a creature scratching and screaming to get out. "That doesn't mean he wanted us to be happy *together*." Yet she felt the need and the desire deep in her heart.

He stared her down. "I think that's exactly what he meant."

"That's crazy, Ryder."

He touched her then, for the first time in twenty-four hours, his hand cupping her cheek, warmth seeping into her again after she felt like she'd been wandering in the Arctic.

"I know what I felt yesterday," he murmured. "It was so damn good. I want to feel that again. With you." He was so close she could see the flecks of gold in his brown irises. "Tell me you don't want it, too, Jules."

She couldn't tell him. All she could say was, "Things are different here. Once we get back home..." She let the sentence hang. Because nobody back home would allow them to be happy together.

"Then let's be happy while we're here. While it's just the two of us."

"I can't," she whispered. "I really can't, Ryder."

He stroked his thumb across her lips. "There's a difference between *can't* and *won't*. We *can* do this. But not if *you* won't."

"Ryder." All she could say was his name. Because more than anything she wanted to lean into him, kiss him the way she had yesterday, touch him the way she had all those years ago. He couldn't possibly know how badly she wanted it.

"I want you, Jules."

"Please don't call me that. It's the name Will used."

"It was what I used to call you before Will ever did."

Ryder had always called her Jules. He'd loved the name. Will had taken it over after the romance ended. And Ryder began calling her Julia.

"Say you don't want me. Say that and I'll stop."

She swallowed hard, felt her chest tighten and her muscles tense. She *needed* to say she couldn't do this with him.

But God help her, she couldn't get the words out. Because she wanted it so badly she ached in all the private pieces of her body. She'd wanted this for so long.

He touched her with his gaze. "Take me, Jules. I'm all yours. For as long as you want. Even if it means just until we go home. I'll take whatever I can get."

He was so close she could breathe in the male scent of

him, feel the heat rising off his skin along with all the hormones and pheromones and masculinity.

She no longer possessed the ability to say no. She didn't *want* to say no.

She answered him by pressing her lips to his.

❦ 15 ❦

The kiss was long and lingering and tasted so sweet his heart ached. Ryder cupped Julia's face in his hands and took everything she offered.

Twenty-five years ago, it had been all rushing hormones and overpowering need, but now his desire and passion were tempered with age and wisdom. He didn't want to screw it up by assuming.

He backed off, looked into her blue, blue eyes. "I'd like nothing more than to go back to our room in the château and make love to you until the sun goes down." He watched her pupils widen. "But what do you want, Jules?"

She blinked slowly, as if she were dazed by the sweetness of that kiss. "I don't know, Ryder."

He wound her hair around his finger, rubbed the silky lock against his cheek, grinning at her. "Do you remember how I always used to beg you?"

She laughed softly. "Yeah," she said, her smile morphing into a smirk. "It was always, 'Come on, Jules, please, Jules, I want you so bad, Jules.'" She mimicked his needy, hormonal pleas.

God, how he'd wanted it then, with her. It ripped his guts out now to admit he'd wanted Elaine with the same intensity. But it had been all sex with Elaine. With Julia, there'd been terrifying emotions as well, how much he wanted *her*, not just the sex, how good she made him feel just being around her, yet how much she wanted from him, things he didn't think he could do, fear that he couldn't be the man she needed.

Those emotions didn't terrify him anymore. "Come on, Jules," he whispered. "Please, Jules, I want you so bad, Jules."

"You always did know how to say just the right words to get exactly what you wanted." Her tone teased his senses.

He chuckled. "Is it working?"

He loved the sparkle in her eyes. He loved the smile on her face. That was really all he wanted. To see her laugh, to see her smile, to see her happy. Even now, if she turned him down, his heart would be at peace because she was smiling.

"I don't know," she said. "You still haven't found me the absolute best chocolate yet. I'm not even sure about the best pastry and the best coffee either."

"Then let's go find that chocolate right now." He nuzzled her ear, dropped a warm kiss on her lobe, felt her shiver. "Maybe I can seduce you with chocolate."

The town was small and quaint, with some buildings at least two centuries old, flats above the shops, balconies with potted flowers and leaves growing through the railings. The roads were narrow and cobbled, barely wide enough for a car, let alone a delivery truck. Decorative awnings adorned the shop fronts, their windows filled with colorful wares.

They discovered a chocolatier that hadn't closed down for the day or sold all their goods. The array in the case was vast, tempting, mouthwatering, and with Julia's hand in his, he felt her tremble of anticipation.

He should have gotten out his guidebook and looked for

the word *sample*. But instead he said it in English, "Sample?" holding his thumb and forefinger close together.

With lines on her face and gray in her hair, the sales lady appeared to be in her midforties just as they were. Maybe she read their auras, fresh with something blossoming between them, because she smiled wide, saying "*Mais oui,*" and pointing into the case. "Plain," she said with a heavy French accent, "or light?" They appeared to be dark chocolate and milk chocolate.

He looked at Julia, who glanced at the lady, one eyebrow raised. "Which is best?" She gazed longingly from one section to the other.

The lady smiled. "Both." She kissed her fingers, then added, "Perfection." She reached into the case, indicating with her index finger. "This one, a hint of merlot, a touch of cabernet, like the finest wine." She picked out a couple of small pieces and laid them on a white tray with a pretty doily.

They each took a bite, Ryder slipping the delicacy on his tongue just as Julia did.

She closed her eyes, moaned, and he wanted her so badly in that moment that he could have dragged her right out of the shop. Then the flavors burst on his tongue, and he couldn't disguise the groan deep in his throat.

"I can taste the hint of wine." Julia opened her eyes. "That is so good."

He imagined her saying that when they lay naked in the middle of the bed. When he was doing delicious things to her.

"I think we have a winner." He stared her down, letting a smile curve the edges of his lips.

Her eyes flashed. She got his meaning. Seduced by chocolate. Then he turned to the sales lady, repeating her word, "Perfection."

She beamed as if she saw the passion exploding between

them as well as the flavors. Maybe that was what chocolate was all about, the perfect joining of taste and body.

He had the woman fill a small box, paid, smiling at her, letting her know she'd made the right choice. Then he waved and grabbed Julia's hand.

As they left, the shop suddenly filled up, as if the tourists on the street had seen the magic flaring inside and had to secure their own little piece of heaven.

On the sidewalk, her hand in his, the chocolate and passion still sizzling on his tongue, Ryder pulled her close, wrapped his hand around her nape and kissed her hard, her sweet chocolaty taste so good it almost brought him to his knees.

"Get a room," called an American voice.

Ryder eyed the man. "Buy your wife some chocolate and you'll need a room, too." Then he led Julia away down the narrow, cobbled street.

She laughed softly. "You're terrible."

"No, I'm in an autoerotic chocolate daze."

She laughed again, full-throated, out loud, the Julia she'd been before Will got sick.

He slung an arm around her shoulder, walked her down the street. "Do we need anything else?"

She lowered her eyelids, slow, sexy, seductive. "Did you order champagne?"

He nodded.

"Then we just need grapes." She gasped. "No. We need mango slices. They'll be perfect with that chocolate."

This was the Julia he needed, laughing, happy, playful, excited. He wanted it for her sake, for all the agony, for all the disappointment, for all the years of Will's illness she'd suffered through.

Now she was the one seducing him. And he might never get enough.

They'd missed market day, so instead they found a local grocery. "This is going to be so good," Julia said, as she selected a package of freshly cut mangoes.

She had no idea how good it was truly going to be.

"I'm surprised they actually have it already cut up."

"Maybe they do it for the tourists." Then he took her hand. "We need one more thing." He led her down another aisle with bandages and first aid kits, and there he found exactly what he wanted.

Julia put a hand over her mouth, stifling a gasp and a smile. "I cannot believe you're going up to the checkout stand with condoms and mangoes. What on earth will they think?"

But what she didn't do was turn in on herself again, or back away.

"I'm pretty sure our purchases will say it all." He pulled her close to kiss her forehead. "After all, the French are experts at making love."

Indeed, despite the fact that elderly women and mothers with children stood in line right along with them, no one gave them a single odd glance. He paid for his purchases, handing the money to a teenage girl, who looked as bored as any American teenager.

They collected the car and headed back, turning into the long gravel drive, the château lit up by the late afternoon sun. Its shutters were open, the light on the windows reflecting in prisms of color.

Inside they climbed the wide marble stairs, the sun shining through the stained glass window above the landing. Her hand in his, Julia said, "This seems a little weird, like we're planning this whole thing. Isn't it supposed to happen spontaneously, like in a romance novel?"

He stopped on the landing, the foyer empty below them, the reception desk unmanned for the moment. "There's nothing unplanned about this, Jules." He tipped her chin with his finger. "Don't you know I've dreamed about everything I want to do you? About every way I want to pleasure you?"

She blushed, but he recognized the flare of heat in her eyes. "I think the chocolate will work." The words could have meant anything, that she was hungry, that she had a sweet tooth, but to him it was seduction.

He led her to his room and unlocked the door, the French doors open to the small balcony outside. Fresh air and the scent of flowers swept into the room. The bed had been made, and the room cleaned.

"Let's make a picnic." He laid out their travel blanket on the floor by the open windows. "Sit," he invited her.

She took his hand, letting him ease her to the floor. "Chocolate." He set down the box of merlot chocolate. "Mangoes." He opened the plastic lid, putting the container next to the chocolate. The champagne he'd ordered sat to one side of the balcony door, the glasses chilling in the ice bucket right along with the bottle. Beside the bucket was a plate of chocolate-covered strawberries.

Once he was sitting cross-legged and facing her on the blanket, he popped the cork, letting it fly out the open French door, accompanied by Julia's laughter. She tilted first one glass then the other as he poured. Then she opened the chocolate box.

"Now," she began to instruct him. "Just a tiny bite of chocolate, add the mango, then sip the champagne." She issued directions as if it were another of her rituals.

The tastes exploded in his mouth.

"Good?" The word was erotic in her soft, seductive voice.

He nodded. "Succulent." The way she was. Then he fed her a piece of mango, her lips kissing his fingertips. He savored the touch as much as she savored the fruit.

She seduced him with a look and a whisper. "Let's put the mango in the champagne so it soaks up all the bubbles."

She dropped a chunk into her champagne, making it fizz to the edge of the glass until she slurped up the bubbles before they spilled.

"Maybe I should add it more slowly." He slid a bit of mango down the side of the glass and into the champagne. It foamed but didn't overflow.

"Now we let it sit there until the glass is empty. Then we eat the fruit and all the champagne it soaks up." Her features were so alive, her eyes so bright. Like the Jules of ten years ago.

He popped a piece of fruit in his mouth, sucked on chocolate, leaned close, and slipped his hand around the nape of her neck, pulling her in for a kiss, long and sweet, mango and chocolate and her taste mingling in an exquisite ambrosia.

"Now *that* was the best," he murmured against her mouth.

Pushing him away, she grabbed another chunk of mango and drew it across his lips, then leaned in to lick him clean.

It was sexy and tantalizing, erotic and mind-blowing.

They ate chocolate, sipped champagne, devoured the fruit, finished off the chocolate strawberries. Until he was so damn hungry for more.

"I've got an idea." He trailed a bit of fruit across her chest just above the line of her sundress, then took a long, long time licking off the juice.

She was breathing hard by the time he pulled away, and she flicked her finger at him. "Take off your shirt."

He liked this game, yanking his polo shirt over his head and throwing it across the room. She drizzled mango juice on his nipple, and when she sucked him into her mouth, it was crazy good. As she licked him clean, a wild surge of desire shot through him. He wanted to dive into her, take her, make her feel everything he felt.

"Unzip your dress." His voice came out harsh with desire.

She held his gaze as she reached behind, and slowly, slowly tugged the zipper down, a quiet rasp in the quiet room.

It was like playing strip poker. He would make sure they both won.

Then he reached out and slid the strap of her dress off one sun-bronzed shoulder.

❧

IT WAS DARING, IT WAS FUN, IT WAS SEXY.

Julia couldn't remember the last time she'd felt any of those things.

But as Ryder slipped the strap off her shoulder, he catapulted her into his seductive, sensual world. She'd made love with Ryder before, all those years ago, but somehow this was new and alluring and tantalizing.

She held his gaze, watched the colors change in his eyes from earthy to fiery.

She'd expected him to pull on the strap until her breast fell free, but he stopped, her dress caught on the upper swell. And she thanked God she wasn't wearing a bra.

"The other strap, you take it off." His voice was rough and raw, as if he needed her so badly he was afraid to touch, afraid he couldn't stop, afraid he'd take her before she was ready.

For one brief moment, she thought of Will and let the guilt wash over her, let the questions beat in her head.

But only for a moment.

Then she gave up all her fears and guilt and embarrassment, telling herself she'd think about it all tomorrow.

There was only now, there was only Ryder.

And God, she was ready.

❧ 16 ❧

Julia ached for everything Ryder promised.

Slipping one finger beneath the strap, she slowly pushed it down her arm. It caught on the swell of her breasts, clung there. Waiting for him to do something.

They both remained completely still for two heartbeats, their eyes locked. As if it were somehow a contest of wills. Who would dive in first?

Then he reached out, just as slowly as she had, and with only his index finger on her breastbone, he dragged the dress down, down, down.

Until her breasts were free.

She gasped as air wafted over her bare skin. And she hardened, both from the warm breeze and the intensity of Ryder's gaze.

"You are so gorgeous."

Julia loved the reverence in his voice, as if she were some awe-inspiring beauty, even though she was forty-five years old and too skinny with too many bones poking out.

Yet she denied nothing. She needed his pretty words

stroking her ego as much as she was dying for his hands to stroke her body.

"Lean back," he directed, his voice low, his tone unyielding.

Julia propped herself on her elbows, waiting desperately for his next move.

Ryder scooped another piece of mango out of the tub, held it over her until a drop fell on her breast. Then he rubbed the fruit all over her chest, the sweet citrus scent mingling with his heat and his pheromones.

He bent his head to her.

She couldn't help the moan that fell from her lips as a thrill shot through her. When he sucked her into his mouth, teasing her with his tongue, she cried out softly. Then she braced herself on one elbow, reached up to sift her fingers through his thick hair and hold him tightly to her.

He started on her other breast, taking so deliciously long to pleasure her that she thought she might come just from his mouth.

She was barely aware when he started to pull down the dress, all the way down, telling her, "Lift," as he slipped it over her hips and whisked it off her legs, the sensation almost sensual, as if it were his mouth on her. Then she lay before him clad only her pink cotton bikinis.

She squeaked when he drizzled champagne into her navel, followed by a piece of mango. "I'm going to eat you up." Then he dove on her stomach, sipping the sparkling wine, eating the mango.

And setting her skin on fire.

She thought about the open balcony doors. She thought about the birds and the bees and the squirrels and people who might be enjoying a stroll outside.

And she didn't care if anyone heard her cries.

He tantalized her with his tongue, licking, nibbling with

his teeth, sucking little rings into her skin with his mouth. It had been so long since she'd been touched this way.

So long that she'd ached for a romantic touch, a loving touch, a sexy touch.

Ryder's touch.

She wouldn't think about Will. Not now. She was going to give herself tonight. No fear. No guilt.

When Ryder tugged on her panties, the cotton slid sensuously over her thighs, down her calves, caressed her feet, setting every nerve on high alert.

"You're utter perfection, Jules." He kissed the quivering flesh of her belly.

He dripped champagne between her legs. This time she didn't squeal. This time it was hot, sizzling, and when he spread her legs, he stroked her with mango. Then he took the bite of fruit between his lips and dove on her, juice and champagne all over her. Ryder all over her. He ate the mango laced with her flavors. Then he licked and sucked, cleaning every last drop of juice before he hit her quaking center.

Her body shuddered and trembled, her legs fell wide, giving him all the access he wanted. All the access she craved.

He took his fill of her. Then he touched his tongue to the hidden bead, and when he licked her, she almost came off the floor. She scrabbled her fingers in the blanket, holding on tight, her eyes squeezed shut, the pleasure so much greater than she'd imagined. The image seared itself against her eyelids, burning forever into her mind. Ryder between her legs.

Her hands found their way to his hair, clutching, tangling her fingers in the thick strands.

It was his turn to moan. As if her touch in his hair was as sexual as his mouth on her.

Then he stopped playing and went at her with gusto.

She flew high up on a mountaintop almost immediately.

As pleasure streaked through her body, she didn't know how it could feel this good. Like nothing she'd ever felt before.

Until he slid his fingers inside her.

And Julia shot into the sky.

SHE SHOOK AND SHUDDERED AND ARCHED, TAKING HIS fingers deeper, soft mewls of pleasure and agony falling from her lips. Her body contracted around him, her legs tightened around his head, pulled him in deep, keeping him exactly where she needed him. He didn't let go, teasing every last cry and gasp from her with his tongue and his touch inside her.

Then she was pulling at his hair, muttering, "Oh my God, too much, too much, oh my God."

Only then did he ease back. Watching her. Her gorgeous breasts rose and fell, her heart fluttered, her skin quivered, and she was breathing hard, tugging his hair as if that intensified the last blasts of pleasure.

Then her bones melted, her legs falling wide, her arms outstretched. Ryder crawled up her body until he was on top of her. She opened her eyes as he blotted out the sun. Without giving her a moment to think, he swooped down on her mouth, going deep, twisting his tongue with hers, sharing her taste.

He was rock hard in his shorts, but he wasn't ready to give himself over to the throes of his own ecstasy. There was so much more he still had to give Julia. He was a forty-five-year-old man now, not a twenty-year-old kid, and he could last a very long time. She lay there for everlasting minutes, then wound her arms around his neck and dove deeper into his kiss. Their chests were sticky; she'd need more cleanup. A lot more.

He had such big plans for her.

Backing off, he straddled her. "It's bedtime."

Standing, he gazed down at the glorious sight of her, the late afternoon sun highlighting the flush of her naked body, glistening in the mango juice he'd missed licking away.

Her eyes were blue and wide, her lips red and parted. "Thank you," she whispered.

"Don't say thank you yet. I'm not done with you." Turning to the bed, he stripped back the comforter and sheet. He'd already laid the condom on the side table.

She watched him, still motionless on the floor, her legs gloriously, wantonly splayed. Skirting the blanket, he closed the balcony doors, then leaned down and hauled her high in his arms, turning to throw her on the bed, surprising a laugh out of her.

Then he shrugged out of his clothes.

Her gaze fell to his erection.

Crawling across the big bed, he straddled her. "I closed the doors," he told her, "because I want you to scream."

"Someone could still hear."

"The doors and walls are thick, no one will hear. Not a single sound. Except me and I want to hear everything."

He trailed a hand back and forth over her breasts, bringing the tips to diamond-hardness. "I can see now that I didn't clean you up properly. I have a lot more licking to do." He started with her lips, heading down her throat, then to each breast, reveling in her skin's salty taste and the mango's sweet juice.

He'd never been able to control his dreams. And his dreams were all of Julia.

Yes, even when he was married, when things had gotten so bad, when he and Elaine literally couldn't bear the sight of each other.

His solace had been his dreams of Julia. His guilt had been his dreams of Julia. His fear and pain had been his dreams of

Julia. And his ultimate pleasure had been all those dreams of Julia.

She smelled of sugar and spice and everything nice, the rhyme sounding off in his head. He licked her, he licked his fingers, then he trailed his hand down her abdomen, glided between her legs, and gloried in the gasps and moans that fell from her lips. He followed the moist trail, licking away the sticky mango juice everywhere he could find it. Until Julia trembled, her hands fisted in the sheet, her body arching to meet him.

This time he wanted to watch her, so he used only his fingers, slowly, over just the right spot inside, watching her tension build until she tossed her head on the pillow. Then he slid out to circle and swirl around the sweet, hard nub and sent her tumbling over the edge.

This time her cry was full-throated, as if she were releasing something from deep inside, something more than her climax. He kept the rhythm, feeling her contractions, one after another after another, until she collapsed on the bed, whispering, begging, "Stop, stop, stop."

But he didn't stop. He was on her again, tracing his moist fingers over her lips, then licking his fingers clean, and finally kissing her. The sharing was intimate and kinky, as if she'd had a hand in her own debauchery.

Straddling her chest, he leaned over her until she wrapped her hand around him and took him between her lips. He wouldn't finish this way. He had to finish inside her. But he needed her mouth on him. "Taste me, lick me, then I need to kiss you again."

He pumped slowly, keeping it shallow, but reveling in the feel of her, her tongue swirling around his tip, her lips drawing on him, her teeth grazing him. When he was close and hard, he pulled out, grabbed a condom and rolled it on.

Her fingers fluttered on his thighs, and he backed off to kiss her, tasting his salt and her sweet.

It was a communion. A connection. A sharing. It wasn't just sex. It was their minds and hearts and souls melding.

He crawled once more down between her legs and relished the taste of her on his tongue, playing her until she was on the edge again. Then he rose above her and plunged deep.

She cried out, her tight body flexing and contracting around him, until she grabbed his butt cheeks and pushed them to a hard, fast rhythm. She moaned, cried out, wailed even, her sounds a sensual symphony. Without a doubt, she was riding the wave of another climax, giving him permission to crash down into oblivion right along with her, her touch on him, her body around him, holding him in tight, turning his senses into a firestorm of pleasure.

Finally, Julia's lips were on his.

And ecstasy claimed them both.

THEY WERE BOTH STARVING FOR DINNER. "I SHOULDN'T BE hungry after all the champagne and chocolate and mangoes," she said. And sex, she thought.

Ryder just smiled, the tangible reminder of the workout he'd given her. No wonder she was starving.

A bistro in town had one last table outside. Which is exactly where Julia wanted to be. The evening was warm and sultry. Or maybe that was just her mood.

She was sated with good sex. *Great* sex. She was dying to talk about it, go over every single detail, how good it was. *Yes, again, please.*

But she kept that to herself and asked instead, "Do you want to share again?"

He gave her the sexiest lady-killer grin. "Oh, I'm dying to share with you again, all right, but not my dinner. I'm hungry enough to eat a whole side of beef." He leaned in, adding, "I have to keep up my strength for the rest of the night."

She felt like a woman on her honeymoon, the envy of the two middle-aged ladies at the next table, American by their dress and the midwestern twang. They'd obviously overheard Ryder, eying him like *he* was the side of beef they wanted to eat.

When the calamari appetizer came, he fed one to her. Nothing had ever tasted so delicious. She ordered the house specialty, coq au vin, and Ryder had the medallions of beef. There was more food on her plate than she could possibly manage, and Ryder stole a chunk of her chicken.

She slapped his hand. "Hey, you said no sharing."

He laughed. "I'll let you have a bite of mine if I get a bite of yours," he said, heavy on the innuendo.

"You are so bad." She mock glared at him, but he still laughed.

Ryder had always been a man full of humor, full of practical jokes, full of fun. Until Will got sick and everyone changed. Especially her, certainly Will, but even Ryder.

But this was the man she remembered, the man who chased his kids down the beach, the man who made them giggle, the man who could make anyone laugh. Even Elaine.

It wasn't until this moment that she realized how much she'd missed the Ryder of ten years ago, not just the Ryder from her university days.

The entire meal from start to finish was tantalizing, sexy, romantic. He stole off her plate, then fed her bites off his fork, whispering naughty sweet nothings about all the ways he wanted to pleasure her. Those were the things brand-new lovers did. And that's what they were, lovers. Even if it only lasted through the night. Or the rest of this trip. When they got home....

Julia refused to think about home.

"Caramel flan for dessert?" he asked. "We can share."

"No way. I'm not sharing my flan. I want it all."

He gave her a look so close to a touch that she trembled with desire. "I want it all, too, everything."

The two ladies at the next table were riveted.

The flan drizzled in caramel was delicious on her tongue, almost as good as Ryder. And despite the fact that they each had their own dessert, he insisted on feeding her tidbits from his bread pudding. "I need to fatten you up."

"That's not a nice thing to say to a lady." Mostly because it was true.

Her collarbones jutted out, so did her hipbones. Her only concern for the past ten years had been Will, and she'd stopped taking care of herself without meaning to.

She added, "I especially liked it when you fed me pieces of mango," as much to tease Ryder as to keep her mind from wandering places she didn't want to go.

"I liked it better when I ate it—"

She put her fingers over his lips. "Do *not* say it." She slid her eyes to the right. There were some things their American neighbors didn't need to know.

Ryder gave her that look again, the one that set her skin on fire and promised so many dirty, delicious, delectable things later tonight.

❧ 17 ❧

They enjoyed their dessert and coffee and sexual banter, all while serenaded by the music drifting to them from a bar across the street, a low, sweet song in lyrical French, probably a ballad about lost love.

When the dinner was done, Ryder threw down some bills and stood, holding out his hand. "A walk along the river?"

"I'd love it." Julia put her hand in his, feeling as if the night were just beginning.

A pretty cobblestone walking path edged the river that meandered through town. The parting sun still warm on her bare arms and Ryder's hand around hers felt sweet, safe, caring. Other walkers had the same idea, strolling hand in hand, exchanging quick kisses, enjoying the warm French night.

"I vote that this afternoon's chocolate was the best we've had yet," Ryder said.

She looked at him. "The best mangoes and the best champagne, too."

The afternoon had been more exquisite than any she

could remember, a day she would retrieve from her memory banks in long, lonely nights back home.

"Oh, yeah, way better than anything." He leaned in close, his breath warming her ear, his hand tight around hers. "And more to come. I am so not done feeding you the best chocolate you'll ever have." Then he whispered, "And more."

Her body felt light and warm and languid, enjoying the moment, yet longing for the promised pleasure.

"Let's sit for a while and enjoy the sunset." He led her to a bench overlooking the river where the trees along the path were thick and leafy. Above the branches, the sky turned glorious shades of pink and blue and purple, stretching their tongues of color across the clouds.

It was so serene, so beautiful. It made her forget every bad thing. There was only the present, sitting here with Ryder, the afternoon making love with him, dinner, laughing and talking and sharing and pretending they were a couple.

She wanted nothing more than to pretend. She didn't want to think about yesterday when they'd scattered Will's ashes. She didn't want to think about the day they would board the plane to return home, to reality, to their lives, to their families. And though this afternoon she'd told herself she wanted only one night, she knew she was going to steal every moment of this trip with him.

"Bellissima," he whispered.

She laughed softly. "Isn't that Italian?"

He lifted her hand to his lips, lingered there. "You're beautiful in any language."

She leaned her cheek against his shoulder, and they sat in comfortable silence, watching the sun as it dipped lower in the sky, the shifting colors of pink and red and purple, before finally disappearing behind the trees.

"I don't remember the last time I just sat and watched a sunset," she mused.

"I'm not sure I even remembered what a sunset looks like."

They were victims of their busy, complicated lives. "I'm going to make it a point to look at the sunset every day from now on. I'll go out to my garden and smell the flowers. I think I'll plant bulbs and watch them come up in the spring."

"I'm going to watch my children grow up. I'm going to be a part of their lives. I'm not going to be an absentee dad anymore."

She stroked his arm. "You never were an absentee dad." That had just been Elaine's bullshit.

"I was."

Sitting up straight, she tapped his chin to get him to look at her. "You spent so much time with the kids and with Will. He loved those last few years when he had Dustin and Tonya to dote on. It meant the world to him. And you were so generous to bring them around so often."

"The sad thing is, I did it for Will, not for them. I know they loved spending time with him. But it was Will, not them, that I did it for. And that's so wrong. Everything I did should have been for them. I should have made time to go to their games, to help with their homework, all the things I left to their mother."

"You're way too hard on yourself."

He shook his head. "I didn't do right by my kids." In the fading colors of the sunset, she felt the blueness of his mood.

"I can't decide what to do with my time now," she mused to herself, wanting to draw him out of his melancholy. "I suppose I could go back into interior design. I've been out of the game so long, though. I'd have to start over from scratch. Find new clients." She shrugged. "But I think I want to try something different."

"Like what?"

She patted his thigh. "You're supposed to tell me what to

do," she said, humor lacing her tone. "That's why I brought it up. You're my sounding board." She had so much thinking to do, but she also felt his mood rising, as if all he needed was someone else to think about, someone he could help.

"Seriously?" he said. "I think you should become a caregiver. You're so good at it. You give people hope. You make their last days easier. You know how badly they need family around them. And so many don't have any family, especially if they're older and in nursing homes. Nobody comes to see them. You could be their savior, Jules."

"I'm not sure I could handle it." She sat there for long moments thinking about watching people die. It had taken so long for Will. Could she go through that again?

"It's completely different when it isn't your loved one. You feel their pain, you try to ease it, but there's also just enough distance to be empathetic instead of overwhelmed. How do you think nurses do it? They have to distance themselves from so much emotion. They think only about the comfort they're giving. That could be you."

"I never thought of that." She remembered Isaac the day he'd collected Will's medical equipment. How badly she'd wanted to talk to him, pour out everything. If only she'd been able to let go. "I could be there for the families."

"That, too. You know what it's like. You could be the shoulder to cry on, the person they have a glass of wine with in the evening when their loved one is finally sleeping."

Ryder had sat with her in the evenings. But she'd also had hospice volunteers to stay with Will when she ran errands. They didn't dispense medication or do many of the normal caregiving tasks like bathing. There were trained hospice aids for that. The volunteers were there as company for Will when she had to go out, but sometimes when she returned home, they didn't leave. Sometimes they stayed just to listen to her.

"You know, I could be a hospice volunteer." The volunteers had been a godsend for her. It would be a way of giving back.

Ryder snaked his arm around her waist. "You'd be good at it, Jules. You know how it feels."

For the first time she felt excitement about what lay in front of her when she returned home.

"Do you have enough money to keep you going if you volunteer instead of getting paid?"

"You mean no new income? At the age of forty-five?" She didn't have to think. "There's still money left in the trust from Will's grandfather, which is mine now, no restrictions, plus our own investments. And the medical bills are all paid for, too. I could also sell the house if I really need to and move into something smaller. After all, it was meant for a family."

Ryder knew about all the experimental stuff that Will had done, most of which he'd never had to pay for as long as he was part of this or that study.

Money was the one thing she didn't have to worry about. "If I don't live extravagantly, I could do it."

"You can do anything you set your mind to."

"I really can do it." A thrill buzzed through her veins. "I'd love to help people, make them feel less isolated, help them cope." She sat up, looked at him, really looked. He was so beautiful. So perfect. So masculine. The years had only added to his good looks. And he was smart. "Thank you. I don't think I would ever have considered that on my own."

"Anything for you, Jules. I just want to help you move on. In the best way possible. And you know how proud Will would be."

"Yes, he would be proud. He was always asking me what I was going to do after he was gone. I just couldn't think past the moment, because it meant thinking about his death. So I never answered him. I never even thought about it."

"You already have an in with hospice since you know so many of the nurses and aids and the management and how the system works. They'll take you no questions asked."

"I want to do what all the volunteers did for me and Will. I can do that in people's homes as well as go to facilities, wherever I'm needed. I want to give back."

He stroked his fingers down her cheek. "You always give back. That's who you are. You just had to figure it out." He leaned in for a sweet kiss, and suddenly it wasn't enough.

She parted her lips. Begging for more.

Ryder gave it to her, leading her down the road to passion.

It wasn't long after dark when they arrived back at the château, climbing the stairs hand-in-hand. They nodded to the Spanish couple three doors down from them, passed a German family on their way out for a late dinner or a stroll. At the beginning of the tourist season, the château wasn't fully occupied. In a few weeks, as Europeans started taking vacation and the weather grew warmer, everything would get more crowded.

He was glad they'd chosen this time, at the beginning of the lavender bloom.

The truth, though, it didn't matter where he was as long as he was with Julia. They could have gone to Kathmandu or visited the White Temple in Thailand, gone hiking in Iceland, ridden horseback in Australia's outback, climbed Machu Picchu. Or just sat in his backyard.

Julia's hand was sweet and warm in his. Dinner had been sexy and evocative and fun. He'd enjoyed teasing her. He'd enjoyed feeding her. The walk along the river had been lovely, so normal, so casual, as if they'd been lovers for years. With the barriers breaking down between them, everything had a different feel, even a different scent, as if the grass and the flowers and the air around them gave off a more potent aroma. Excitement tingled along his nerve endings, his heart was in his throat, and his skin buzzed, making him feel as if he'd drunk too many glasses of wine when he'd had barely more than one.

How easily she could change his moods, talk him out of the doldrums when he started to think about everything he hadn't done for the kids, and about Elaine. It was Julia's special gift, making people feel better.

The truly amazing moment had come when she'd asked his advice. And taken to heart what he had to say. He felt as if she was turning the corner after Will's death, that she was thinking about the future again. He felt in his bones all the good she could do for people. As long as she had the invest-ments to keep going. He didn't know everything about her finances, but Will had always said there would be enough for her, that the trust from his grandfather would carry her through. But Julia was forty-five, only halfway through her life.

He had to hope that if she ever ran into problems, she would come to him.

But he appreciated her trust, the way she'd listened, how she turned his suggestion into something bigger, better, until she'd made the idea her own.

He wanted to watch her blossom and grow beyond Will's sickroom.

But that was later. Right now, all he wanted was Julia with him, all night, to wake beside her in the morning, and prove to himself this wasn't a dream.

They reached her door first, and he brought her hand to his lips, kissing her sweetly fragrant skin. "More than anything, I want you to invite me in. For the night. Will you do that, Jules?"

He didn't want to beg. He didn't want to push. He didn't want her to feel any pressure. He just simply wanted her. And the sweetness of her falling asleep in his arms.

She looked at him a long, tantalizing moment. Then she trailed her fingers from his temple to the corner of his mouth, going up on her tiptoes to press a kiss to his lips. "Ryder, will you stay with me?" She kissed the edge of his mouth. "And make love to me all night long?"

His heart soared right out of his body. He'd hoped, he'd prayed, and yes, he was pretty damn sure. But the moment she said she wanted him, it was as if her words set something inside him completely free.

She unlocked her door, wrapped her fingers around his, and pulled him inside.

They'd made love in his room this afternoon, a more masculine setting, less frills. But here in Julia's room, thick, soft carpets were scattered across the hardwood floor, the French doors covered by lacy curtains that brushed the floor and a large antique mirror above the ornate mantelpiece.

And then there was the bed.

A king like his, it was a huge fourposter covered by a mountain of pillows and a throw rug tossed across the bottom. The thick eiderdown exploded with bright colors.

All Ryder wanted was to make love to her in the middle of that color explosion.

❧ 18 ❧

Backing away from Ryder, a sultry smile on her lips, Julia crossed to the window, closed the French doors, and pulled the curtains against the night.

Then she returned to him.

She was all in, from that seductive smile to the tight beads of her breasts against the sundress she wore. God, he loved that she always wore those sexy sundresses. The formfitting bodice, the spaghetti straps baring the tanned skin of her shoulders. And they were so easy to get her out of.

"You have too many clothes on." She pulled his polo from his shorts, then shoved her hands under his shirt, her fingers warm and soft and sensual, sending a shiver of pleasure through him. Her scent was musky and sexy, the scent of desire and need.

"You're the one wearing too many clothes." He reached around her to slide down the zipper of her dress.

She tipped her head back, the invitation brimming in her eyes, on her lips. He took her mouth in a sweet, lingering kiss, exploring her, tasting her, exciting her.

She hummed her pleasure in her throat as he held her

tight against him, letting her feel exactly what she did to him, how hard, how desperate he was.

Pulling back, she skimmed her fingers beneath his shirt, pushing it up. "Clothes," she whispered. "Off."

He threw the polo, loving that she was directing their play.

Then she slipped aside the straps of her dress, letting the material slide down her body until it pooled at her feet.

He adored that she was losing her shyness.

Kicking the dress aside, she stood before him in blue cotton panties. Then she went for his belt and zipper.

He loved her eagerness.

Before she could push the cargo shorts over his hips, he reached into his pocket, pulling out the two condoms he'd stashed. As he tossed them on the bed, she dragged the shorts down.

Hunkered in front of him, her head tipped back, her eyes locked on his, she slowly, agonizingly traced her finger down his length. He was hard, he was ready, he could explode right now. But he held onto his control in a way he never could have all those years ago.

She rubbed her face against him, shooting another jolt of pleasure along his nerve endings. Then she opened her mouth and used her teeth through his boxer briefs.

The sight of her down there was riveting, the feel of her exquisite, the scent of her intoxicating.

"This is all mine," she said, talking to his body, not to him.

He loved that, too. Julia had never been playful when they were young. She'd been so serious about making love.

But he adored the way she played now. And he loved her sense of ownership.

She tugged the boxer briefs until he popped free, hard and ready. Years ago, he might have terrified her, because she wasn't overly experienced, because he was so crazed with hormones and desire.

But now, she slid his briefs down his legs, threw them aside, and sat back on her haunches to look at him. Just his body, not his face. There was something so erotic about her inspection that his muscles tensed and his skin tingled.

"Now that is quite a sight."

She glanced up at him, quickly, and back down. "I have to memorize it." She laughed. "If I were a millennial, I'd probably take a picture so I could look at it later."

He grinned. "A picture is worth a thousand words."

She wrapped her hand around him, squeezed skillfully. "And a bird in the hand is worth two in the bush."

Her humor amazed him. Will had been sick for so long that they'd all forgotten how to laugh. Yet Julia was laughing tonight.

"Now that you've got it in your hand, what are you going to do with it?"

She tipped her head to the side, studied him. "I once rescued a bird, and he liked to have his head stroked. Would you like that?" Her eyes twinkled as she looked up at him.

His heart and soul filled with her.

"You can definitely stroke my head." He couldn't stifle a laugh, didn't want to. Especially not when Julia joined him. But his laughter died as she rubbed a finger over his tip, finding the drop of moisture that pooled there.

"Oh yeah, that's crazy good." He closed his eyes to savor the sensation. Yet he didn't want to lose sight of her for too long. "You could even kiss it if you want."

Another droplet pearled on the tip, and she leaned in to whisk it away with her tongue. It felt too good even for words. Her long hair spilled down her back like a waterfall, her mouth glistened with his moisture, and her lips curved in a sweet, satisfied smile. She knew what she was doing to him.

Knew how badly he wanted to throw her back on the carpet right now and take her. His hand itched to tangle in her hair, push her down until she took all of him in her mouth, until he could bury himself in her heat.

"You can do whatever you want with me," he whispered to her.

"I know exactly what I want." She rose gracefully, grabbed the two condoms he'd thrown on the bed, and yanked the eiderdown to the end, scattering pillows all over. Then she pointed. "I want you right there."

Ryder obliged, crawling to the center of the mattress and flopping on his back, his arms and legs spread wide. He wanted those tantalizing blue cotton panties off her right now. But Julia kept them on.

Across the wide expanse of bed, she stalked him like a panther.

When she climbed on, she wrapped her fingers around him again, tight, perfect. "What if I want to do this?" She licked him like a popsicle.

It was enough to blow his circuits, but he held tight to his control. Barely.

"Like I said, anything you want." He didn't want to rush. They had all night. He wasn't twenty years old anymore when there was only the prize to attain, not the journey to revel in.

Then she took him all the way, deep, sweet. This wasn't the first time she'd taken him in her mouth, but he didn't think she'd truly enjoyed it back then. She'd done it for him, probably because he'd begged.

Yet now Julia seemed to relish the taste of him, the feel of him.

He didn't want to think about the fact that Will was probably the one who taught her.

Then he couldn't think about anything at all as Julia found

the perfect rhythm with her hand, her mouth, her tongue, even her teeth.

"Jesus, you have me in your power, completely."

Her hum against him created all new sensations.

She seemed to love the power. She'd been powerless against Will's disease for so long. Now Ryder wanted to give back to her all that she'd lost.

He arched, pushing himself deeper, and Julia took everything. He groaned, letting her know how amazing she was. He wasn't sure he could control himself for much longer, and as if she sensed how close he was, she reared up to straddle him.

Her hand still wrapped tight, she tossed a condom on his chest and ordered him, "Put it on."

She was elemental, powerful, sensual. She had complete control over him. She'd never been like this before. And he craved more.

"Yes, ma'am." Tearing the wrapper, he rolled on the condom, and gave himself to Julia.

She stretched over him, guided him, then slid down, until he was completely seated inside her. It was the agony and the ecstasy.

Throwing her head back, Julia moaned. "My God, that is so good". Then she leaned down, cupped his cheeks, and kissed him hard and deep. Until finally she pulled back, one hand on his chest holding her steady. "Get ready for a wild ride."

He didn't even laugh at the pun on his name. He couldn't, not now. She had him in thrall.

She rose, slowly, slowly, then slid back down with equally exquisite deliberation. "Oh my God." Her eyes squeezed tightly shut. "That is so good, just right."

He steeled himself not to grab her hips and pound into her.

He let her have him just the way she wanted, let her control the sex, let her take, let her use him. He was nothing more than an instrument to her right now. She had never been so immersed in the sensations, never let herself go.

But she used him so damn good, with a slow, steady, agonizing pace, her breath rising, keeping that rhythm until her legs trembled and her body clenched around him.

Then she demanded, "Now, touch me right now," her words barely more than a gasp.

He put his finger on her, pushing her button, making her crazy. She skyrocketed, crying out, then she shoved him, rolling, pulled him on top and wrapped her legs around him, one hand on the back of his thigh, the other on his arm.

"Do it hard," she ordered, forcing him to pound into her, to take her harder and faster.

Her climax rolled through her and straight into him, her body clenching, releasing, driving him wild exactly the way she said she would. She cried out once more, his name, then grabbed him by the ears and pulled him in for a deep kiss.

Ryder let himself go, right then, before she came down again.

They shattered into ecstasy together.

NOTHING HAD EVER FELT SO GOOD. SHE WAS BONELESS, sated, and something close to delirious.

After long moments, Julia was able to breathe again, able to think, able to remember every single moment of pleasure. She loved his weight on her, the full, heavy weight of a man.

Then Ryder slipped to the side. "I'll be back in a second," he said, sliding off the bed.

He padded into the bathroom, to dispose of the condom, she presumed. She didn't feel self-conscious about the condom or the noises she'd made or the abandon with which she'd taken him, telling him what to do, demanding her satisfaction.

She stretched languidly as he returned, and in his full naked glory, he opened the curtains and the balcony doors again, letting in night sounds and streams of moonlight. Finally, he gathered her close to lay in the circle of his arms.

She swirled her fingers in the soft hair dusting his chest. "Thank you. For letting that be all about me." Her voice was sleepy, satisfied.

He skimmed a finger up and down her arm, leaving tingles of fire in its wake.

"It should always be about you. If you leave it up to men, we'll just groan, take our own pleasure, and sometimes leave you unsatisfied."

She tipped her head to look at him, his eyes sparkling in the moonlight that fell across the bed. "I don't believe you'd ever do that."

He grinned. Then sobered. "I'm not completely sure I satisfied you every time we were together."

All those years ago. Julia wasn't sure either. She'd always been so nervous, so tense, afraid to let go, needing to make sure he was satisfied, that he'd want to come back again. Though he wasn't her first, she hadn't figured out how good it could feel. If she experienced even a wink of pleasure, she decided that was an orgasm and it was enough. Now, she couldn't remember if she'd had any real ones. Not that it mattered. She hadn't been with Ryder for the orgasms. She'd been with him because she thought they had a future. It might have been the nineties, but she still thought of marriage, home, and kids, even though the sexual revolution was long past.

"I think you satisfied me, Ryder."

He snorted a laugh. "You *think?* Is that supposed to make me feel better?"

She decided to tell him the truth. "I don't remember. I remember liking it when you held me in your arms afterward." Then she gave him another ounce of honesty. "I didn't like it when I woke up in your bed and you'd already gone without even saying goodbye." He was on the rowing team, he had practice, but he still could have kissed her goodbye.

He continued stroking her arm, as if it were a soothing gesture. "Will always said I was an asshole. I didn't want to admit that. But I was a complete asshole to you. You deserved better."

She'd had Will. A man who had loved her with everything in him the way Ryder hadn't been able to back then. "It is what it is," she said philosophically. "I wouldn't give up those years with Will. Not for anything. Not even when he got sick. Not even with the way it ended." Not even when she realized she would never have children. She didn't say it, but snuggled closer. "He needed me. And I needed to be there for him." She tipped her head back to look at Ryder. "But thank you for tonight. And for this afternoon." She drew her leg up, resting her thigh over him just below that precious jewel between his legs. And it was a jewel. She'd never known exactly how good sex could be. "Honestly, it's been so long, I almost forgot what sex was like. And even before—" She shrugged. "—it was never like what we just did."

"You've forgotten what it was like with Will, that's all, because he was sick for so long."

In the dark, after such perfect sex, she didn't want to lie. In fact, she wanted to talk. She'd been silent for so long, everything wearing her down on the inside because she could never say it aloud. It was one night, with this one man, and after everything he'd made her feel, she had to say it. "I don't think Will really enjoyed sex. Even long before he got sick."

"No way." His voice rose slightly.

Should she really be sharing secrets that should always remain hidden? Wasn't that disloyal? But Will was gone. She was alone. And she'd been silent for so long. "He liked that," she paused. "What I did to you. Before you put the condom on." Why was it so hard to say? So she said it. "I took you in my mouth. He needed that, too, before he could do the rest. But then, if we took too long with the actual sex, he'd lose it. I mean, he would try to make me feel good first, but... well..." But it had never felt the way Ryder made her feel tonight. Sex hadn't been a priority for her and Will. And later, it had been about making babies.

She waited for the guilt and disloyalty to smother her. But tonight she didn't feel any of that. In fact, she felt relieved.

Ryder's voice rumbled against her, still disbelieving. "But he told me sex was great when he was in remission."

She laughed, the sound hurting deep down inside. "It barely happened even then." Twice. And it hadn't been satisfying.

"I'm so sorry, Jules."

About five years ago, Will had been good for six glorious months. They thought he'd killed the cancer, licked it, won the fight, that they could start their lives again. More truth. "I wanted to try again for a child. But he was afraid. He didn't want to start a baby because the cancer might come back." She felt the tears stuffing her nose. "And in the end, it wasn't gone," she whispered. "He was right. Sex and babies would have complicated everything."

"But you wanted a baby to remember him by."

"I don't even know anymore. I honestly couldn't think straight. For so long I wanted to be a mother. Then we found out we couldn't have kids, that he was sick, and I stopped believing I'd ever be a mother. When he went into remission, I hoped. But hope doesn't last for long. And Will didn't want to risk it. Eventually I agreed with him, that it was a bad idea anyway." She stopped, trying to stem the emotions inside. When she could talk again, she told him, "It had been so long since he'd felt well for any length of time. Five years. And the remission was only six months. Besides, we'd never been able to make a baby before. Why would we suddenly be capable? What if the cancer treatments had killed all Will's sperm? And me? I was forty years old. What if my eggs were bad? What if I couldn't carry a baby full term? What if I had to start the whole in vitro thing?"

"I understand." He held her tight. "You were worn down."

She closed her eyes. "I was so exhausted. I used most of that time to rest. I thought about going back to work. But I couldn't face that either. I kept telling myself in a few months, when we knew he wouldn't relapse."

"Jules, you don't have to do this."

"But I do. Ryder, it's been in there for so long. I just wanted him to touch me. But he was afraid if—" Her voice broke. "He was afraid that if we started, something would happen, and there would be a baby. And he said he couldn't leave me to take on all that responsibility alone."

"Why didn't you ever tell me? Why didn't Will tell me? I could have talked to him."

She rested her hand on his chest, felt the steady beat of his heart. She'd been afraid to touch Will's heart for so long. Afraid it would stop beating. "We were scared. When you're that frightened, you can't talk about things. You can't even think about them or admit them out loud. I could never tell anyone that Will and I only had sex a couple of times in ten years. Twice at the very beginning of his remission. Then it was as if he got so scared he couldn't do it again."

And Julia had thought she would die.

RYDER'S HEART BROKE FOR HER. IT BROKE FOR WILL. HIS best friend had made it sound like that time was idyllic. Like he was having the best sex of his life. Like he couldn't get enough of it.

Ryder remembered thinking it was odd at the time that Will had even told him. They'd never really talked about their respective marriages, didn't confide their troubles. Ryder certainly hadn't. And it would have been weird, too, because he'd been with Jules, because there was all the history. But now it made a certain kind of sense.

It had all been a fairy tale Will had made up because of his fear about the cancer coming back.

It was so incredibly sad that Will hadn't been able to admit the truth. And it had taken five years for Julia to finally talk about it. Yet sex hadn't been a problem in just those six months of remission, she was saying it had been an issue their whole marriage. Ryder truly didn't get it. If he'd been married to Jules...

Tipping her head back to look at him, she said, "That's why tonight was so important, do you understand?"

Tears rumbled through her voice, but she didn't let loose with a single one. He wished, more than anything, that he'd been able to give this to her all along, to rebuild her confidence in herself, her sexual drive, her desire. And maybe there was still a bit of the youthful asshole remaining inside him because he felt a hint of gratification that he was the one who could do this for her.

"All I can say is that it's time to give it to you over and over." Then, because he knew she needed to hear it, he said, "While we're here." In his heart, he added the word *forever*.

Through the open window, a couple laughed on the driveway, giggling, obviously drunk, some sort of Scandinavian language, a lilt to it, snickering as they tried to get the key in the château's old-fashioned lock.

"I want us to be that couple down there," he whispered against her hair. "Laughing and giggling, even drunk, I don't care. I want us to feel that kind of happiness."

"I want us to feel the way we did ten minutes ago." She nuzzled his chest. "I want you to make me feel that way every day and every night. I want you to hold me in your arms while we sleep. I want you to make love to me in the middle of the night. Over and over. So I never forget what it's like."

He wouldn't let her forget. No matter what she thought, when they were home, he wasn't letting her go. He was going to make these few days together so good that she would never be free of him. That she wouldn't be able to walk away. She would beg him never to stop. Julia needed this. She needed to feel like a woman, like a sexual being, not forty-five years old and washed up. That wasn't Julia.

"I want you to be happy. I want you to enjoy every moment of life. I want you to find fulfillment and joy. I want you to live the rest of your life without regrets."

She was silent. And he knew she was thinking over every word, deciding if she could do it.

In these days together, he would make sure she believed that she deserved every single wish he'd made for her.

Then he rolled her beneath him, cupped her face in his hands, looking down at her beautiful face. "I'm going to make you feel that way over and over and over. That's my vow to you."

He started right then, with his mouth on her lips and his hands on her body, until she was begging for him to come inside her.

✸ 19 ✸

WILL

I never blamed Julia for our sex life. It wasn't her fault. It was mine. It was just that sex had never been an over-riding force in my life. When they tested me at the fertility center, they said I had a low sperm count. That was before the other tests that uncovered the cancer. So I chalked up my lack of libido to the sperm count issue.

I'm not sure Julia ever minded. We had sex more in the beginning, the first few months after we got together. And it was decent. I've got no complaints. Julia never complained either. I tried to concentrate on her needs. But somehow marriage changed things. It's like when you're sleeping in the same bed next to the same person every night you just don't feel the same urgency. Julia usually initiated it. Even then, though we hadn't decided on the right time to have a baby, she was always thinking that way. When Elaine had the kids, it was like Julia's libido went into overdrive. I know it was all about the babies.

But even then, I had a hard time keeping up with her. Had a hard time even getting it up. I had to make her blow me before I could get hard, like she was some sort of porn star fluffer. It was an embarrassing situation, and I never said a thing about it to Ryder. Mr. Virile. It was too humiliating.

If only Julia and I had been able to make a baby.

But there was the cancer. And Julia stopped initiating anything. I admit it was a relief that I didn't have to force myself to perform anymore. It's just the way for some men, a low libido. My doctor told me it's not that unusual, even before the cancer. It's not always like in the movies or the romance novels where a couple just can't get enough of each other.

Once, Julia suggested Viagra, and I told her that was just for old guys. I wasn't old.

But with the cancer, I no longer had to make excuses.

Until I went into remission. Though no one calls it that anymore. They just say your tests don't show any cancer for the moment. Hedging their bets. I did that enough when I was in practice.

I called it remission. Julia called me cancer free.

Cancer takes away all your control, all your power. You're at its mercy. You're sick and your hair falls out and there are times you want to just give yourself over to it and die rather than keep living through it all. Cancer saps you of everything.

And it saps your loved ones.

But the day that PET scan said I showed no signs of cancer, it was a miracle. Everything we'd been through, all the bad times, all the pain and the misery, all the degrading things Julia had to do for me, all that was over. We could start living again.

Julia could start living again.

The first thing she wanted to do was make a baby. It was unrealistic. All my little sperm, what few there had been, were dead dead dead by that time. I should have saved some sperm when we had the chance, but it was too late now.

But Julia believed everything was renewed, that we had a second chance.

We did it twice. And neither time really worked. It was as unsatisfactory for her as it was for me.

I didn't want to try again.

Yet there was something in me that needed to live every moment, live as hard and fast as I could. I had my control back, and I wanted my life back.

I never would have done it if I'd been in my right mind. But it was like I was on drugs, euphoric, terrified, full of joy, angry at what life had already taken from me. And there was this overpowering need to make up for it. This drive to do do do, everything I'd missed out on. I wasn't allowed to go back to work, not right away, and honestly I'm not sure I wanted to. Because I needed to *live*. Not watch more people dying.

So I did the unforgivable. I succumbed to that terrible driving need inside me. It was the worst mistake of my life. I regretted it every moment, sometimes right in the middle of doing it.

Then the cancer came back. And maybe it got me again as my punishment for what I'd done.

I hope that if there's a heaven, that everything is different up there, that you're allowed to say you're sorry and be forgiven.

Or maybe I'm just going to hell.

All I know for sure is that I will never forgive myself.

And if Julia knew, she would never forgive me either.

20

After that glorious night, after all the revelations, after baring her soul, Julia felt renewed. Energized. Maybe it was Provence, maybe it was the slower, relaxed pace. Maybe it was being with Ryder. Or maybe it was revealing all the guilty feelings that had been weighing her down, the confessions Ryder had listened to without judgment, letting her it get all off her chest.

She wished she could do the same for him. She'd heard his sigh when yet again his son didn't answer his call. But things had gone much better with Tonya. Julia hadn't been asleep when he slipped out of bed and stood by the window to make the calls, apologizing to his daughter because he was supposed to have called at nine.

But at nine, he'd been making love to Julia.

She didn't regret that. For now, it was her duty to help him enjoy every moment of their trip.

They checked out the next morning, skipped their usual pastry, and purchased fresh baguettes, along with meat, cheese, fruit, and a thermos of good French coffee for the day's drive to Arles. The town, Tonya had discovered for them, was like a mini Rome, with the ancient ruins of a Colosseum-style amphitheater, plus a necropolis, a forum, a theater, and the Roman baths.

They traveled by back roads, through the lavender and farmland, past big barns and freshly mowed fields, the hay packaged up like huge Easter eggs.

After an hour of driving, Ryder pulled off the road into a turnout with a single bench as if it were waiting for them. The fields had given way to marshland and a large pond with tall grasses.

They laid out their morning feast between them on the bench, complete with cloth napkins Ryder had found in a market stall.

"This is the life," he said. "Pick up your freshly made breakfast, take a drive out into the country, and treat yourself to a picnic."

"I could do this every day. Everything smells so fresh." Julia closed her eyes and breathed in deeply. "Hay and lavender and flowers in the air." She looked at him. "The sky almost seems to sparkle above us."

He poured coffee from the thermos, and they tore off hunks of soft bread, cut slices of cheese, and added meat to top it off. "I don't think anything's ever tasted so good," he said.

Julia nodded agreement, her mouth full.

An old motorhome rumbled by, kids hanging out the windows to wave at them. Then everything was still again. In the marsh beyond their bench, a heron stood stock still in the water.

Watching her instead of the scenery, Ryder snapped a photo, then showed it to her. "You look blissed out."

With her hair windblown, her smile soft, and her eyes bright, yes, she looked happy. "I look totally blissed out." She reached across their picnic to link her pinky with his.

"Because of the way you make me feel." She didn't care if it was admitting too much, especially since Will had been gone only three months. But it was how she felt, and there would be so much time for guilt when she returned home.

Ryder raised her hand to his lips. Kissed her knuckles, a long, lingering taste of her. She counted the remaining days in her head, all the glorious days with Ryder, all the sweet kisses, the tender touches. And the nights. She was going to enjoy every single one of them.

They arrived in Arles just after noon.

"Let's do something wild and crazy and totally not on our schedule," Ryder said. "Let's rent a scooter. There's some lavender fields up by an old monastery and a castle we can tour."

"That would be fabulous." They could see the Roman ruins tomorrow.

He caressed her shoulder. "Slather on some sunscreen so you don't get burned," he smiled. "On second thought, I'll slather it on for you."

"I'd like that." She'd love it. Except that they might never get to the scooter if he touched her.

They dropped off the bags at the pension she'd reserved for them. But Julia stopped before they got to the small reception desk, her hand on Ryder's arm. "Do you want to cancel the second room?"

He didn't hesitate. "Hell, yes." Smiling, he leaned down for a quick kiss that promised so much more.

It was sexy. It was exciting. It was a thrill. But she played it nonchalant. "Madam," she said sweetly, approaching the counter.

The lady, her hair pulled up in a neat chignon, smiled broadly, one front tooth slightly overlapping. *"Puis-je vous aider?"* She was about Julia's age, her hair blond with silvery highlights at the temples.

"Do you speak English?" It would be so much easier to explain without having to get out their French phrasebook.

"*Oui*. How may I help you?" she said in lilting English.

"I made a reservation for two rooms, but it turns out we'll only need one." Julia willed herself not to blush. She was a grown woman, she didn't need to blush just because she wanted to spend the night with a gorgeous man.

The woman looked at Ryder and that too sexy grin on his face. Then she smiled, a very knowing French smile. "But of course. I can make those arrangements easily."

Julia waited for a huge cancellation fee.

Still looking at Ryder with smiling eyes, the lady said, "At no charge, of course. I have a couple who would love to take the accommodation. They were hoping for a cancellation. It shall all work out perfectly." Her English was excellent. And so was her willingness to help.

"Thank you so much."

"In the meantime, please fill out our registration form. My name is Madame Brodeur and I will show you to your room."

Madame Brodeur led them to an opulent room Julia had never imagined they would find in a European pension.

"Please enjoy your stay," Madame Brodeur said in her elegant accent as she backed out of the room, closing the door, almost as if it were an invitation to use the bed right now.

Maybe she was just glad to have older lovers, instead of the young.

"Well, this is nice," Ryder said in total understatement.

A queen fourposter bed dominated one wall. The rugs strewn about the floor were a blue shag and matched the pristine eiderdown and the canopy over the bed. In front of the French doors, which opened onto a small balcony that was wide enough only to stand on, there was seating for two, low comfy chairs, a table between them. The walls were decorated with handmade needlepoints.

Julia wondered if Madame Brodeur was the needlepointer.

"You have to check out the bathroom." Ryder stood by the open door.

Not to say she was all about the bathrooms, but this one took her breath away. The clawfoot tub was enormous, more than enough room for two. The floor was tiled in blue and white octagons following the room's color scheme, and the white wall tile was finished off with a blue wainscoting halfway up. The white walls were topped by a blue crown molding. Two pedestal sinks stood next to each other with a small ornate dresser between them, an assortment of bath products in the basket on the tabletop. A mirror stretched across the wall flanked by two windows with opaque colored glass, the sun shining through them casting blue stripes across the tile floor.

She could say only one thing. "Oh my God."

Then she startled at a knock on the door.

Ryder answered, and Madame Brodeur stepped inside to hand over a filled champagne bucket and a box of chocolate delicacies. "I'm sorry I did not have these waiting for you." Her voice with that soft and lyrical accent fit perfectly with the Provence ambience.

They truly had stepped into a different world when they'd flown across the ocean.

"Thank you." Ryder took the champagne and chocolate.

The woman seemed to light up with Ryder's smile. She wore no wedding ring, and Julia imagined she enjoyed the role of facilitator, perhaps even inserting herself into the picture beside Ryder, a nice little dream of Provence.

She smiled at Julia, gave her a look that might actually been a wink. Yet Madame Brodeur seemed far too elegant for a wink.

Before she stepped out, Ryder asked, "Could you tell us where we might rent a scooter?"

"There are many choices. But I do have a card." She reached into one of the voluminous pockets of her skirt, which draped well below her knees. She handed Ryder a card, then delved once more into the pocket, retrieving another card. "We serve breakfast here, but these are very good choices for le dejeuner and le diner." Lunch and dinner.

"They all serve delicious foods, and the prices are reasonable."

"Thanks for the recommendations." Ryder pocketed both cards.

When the door closed, he said softly. "I'm sure she has some family businesses around town if the number of cards in her pocket means anything." He set the champagne in its bucket by the window. Then he corralled Julia, wrapping his arms around her and nuzzling her neck. "I've got half a mind to make love to you right now on that big bed."

She burrowed into him. "And what's on the other half of your mind?"

He laughed. "The other half thinks we should work up an appetite on a scooter. What do you think?"

"I want both." She pulled him down, kissed him quick. "But let's start with the scooter."

And he wanted everything from her.

"I have something for you before we go." He dug Will's mother-of-pearl box from beneath the clothes in his suitcase and held it out to her. He didn't know if this was the right time, but he wasn't sure he'd ever know when it was.

Julia stopped, and he thought her smile might die along with all her happiness of the last twenty-four hours.

Yet she surprised him, looking up at him with a glimmer of moisture in her eyes, taking the box from his hands.

"Thank you." Her voice was soft with emotion that matched her gaze.

"I put Dustin and Tonya's letter in there. I thought you'd want it as a keepsake. The letter as well as the box, I mean."

"Yes." She breathed in deeply. And she smiled. "I loved what they wrote. I'll always treasure their words." Then she turned to her purse and pulled out another envelope. "Let's put Will's letter in there, too."

He hadn't realized she'd been carrying it around with her everywhere. He didn't know what he'd thought, maybe that she'd put it in her suitcase.

When both letters were inside, she closed the lid gently, held the box to her chest a moment as if Will's essence was still with it. "Thank you. A keepsake is a perfect idea."

Then she put the box away, took his hand, and led him outside into the sunshine.

The day was glorious. Arles was a fairly large town, but quaint in the same vein as Aix-en-Provence. Maybe that's just how all French towns were. The streets were lined with shops she wanted to explore, the sidewalks teeming with locals and tourists alike. If it was this crowded now, she wondered what it was like later in the summer when tourist season was in full swing. Elderly women wearing long dresses, some of them with scarves over their heads, queued up at the fish shop. Old men drank coffee or beer outside small cafés. It was like a picture postcard.

Ryder rented a scooter for two, saddlebags on the back that he filled with drinks, fruit, and cheese, which was fast becoming their staple diet. Julia loved the food and the scooter and Provence and being with Ryder.

Climbing on the back, she wrapped her arms around his waist. "I should have worn Capri pants," she said through the helmet the rental shop provided. She didn't want to wear it, wanted to feel her hair flying free. But she wasn't a rule breaker either.

Ryder reached back to rub his hand up and down her leg. "Just checking your skirts, ma'am."

She swatted at him, laughing, then tucked her sundress down so it wouldn't blow up as they flew along.

"Besides, in that dress, you're perfectly color-coordinated with the scooter."

The little machine was a delightful turquoise blue, the background of her flowered sundress matching it. "I feel just like Audrey Hepburn in *Roman Holiday* when she's riding the Vespa with Gregory Peck."

And they were off, buzzing down the narrow streets, around walkers and bikers, and out into the countryside. It was like flying, like a dream, a fantasy. She held tight to him, feeling the ripple of his muscles as he guided the scooter.

"I should have gotten my own scooter," she yelled over the wind swishing by her helmet.

He didn't turn and she wasn't sure he'd heard her. And while she would have loved to be racing beside him—not that a scooter could truly race—at the same time she relished her arms around him and the thick hard feel of a man between her legs. It was sensual, and maybe that was far better than scootering on her own.

The sensations were glorious, the freedom, the scenery flashing by, and she found herself laughing even if Ryder couldn't hear her. Will would have loved this, too. They were living his dream, and she was glad he'd wanted so badly for her to make this trip. It was a time to heal, something she couldn't have done at home.

The sun on her arms and neck had healing properties. She felt as if Ryder's arms around her could heal her, too. Maybe that's what Will had intended. He wanted them both to heal in the warm sun and the fragrant air of Provence. He wanted them to be each other's stand-in.

As they flew along the country roads, she felt all the worries blow right off her shoulders, streaming out behind them, dissipating in their wake.

She squeezed Ryder harder, holding on tight to this new and exciting feeling.

❀

RYDER HAD PLANNED THIS SIDE TRIP FOR JULIA. IT WASN'T supposed to be about him. It was all about making her happy, helping her forget the trying months and years that had consumed her, even if her amnesia lasted only a few days. Yet the warm air of Provence and Julia's arms hugging him tight were everything he needed, too.

He pressed the scooter harder, pushing its limits, soaring along the road almost like a race car. He didn't want to stop at the fields of lavender in the monastery. He wanted to keep flying away with Julia. He didn't want to be around people. He didn't want to share her. But they did need to eat, and breakfast seemed like hours ago. Plus he'd promised her lavender and the monastery. All too soon, he guided the scooter down the long driveway and parked beside a picnic area with tables which were only half full.

They ate their lunch to the sounds of children laughing, people chatting, the scent of lavender all around them, the scent of Julia filling his senses.

There was something so amazing about being with her, streaming along the roadway, her body wrapped around his. Julia was all he needed.

When they were done with lunch, they toured the monastery, Julia's hand in his.

"Fascinating," she said, looking at him. He wanted to

think she was talking about him, not just the monastery's workings.

In the gift shop, Julia loaded up on lavender products, soap, lotion, candles. She sniffed a bottle of bath salts. "I like that." She held it out to him, but all he could smell was Julia's sweet scent. She eclipsed everything else for him.

As they headed out to the scooter again, Ryder touched her shoulder. "You're getting a little burned. You need more sunscreen." He stuffed her purchases into a saddlebag and retrieved the tube of sunblock he'd packed.

With the sun streaming down on them, he squeezed a dab on his hand, rubbed his palms together, and while she held her hair aside, he smoothed the lotion over her shoulders, down her back, along the line of her sundress. He felt her shiver at the intimate contact. He rubbed more sunscreen up and down her arms with a slow, sensual, lingering touch. It was almost foreplay. He stood so close, breathing her in, steeping himself in her scent, in the feel of her skin, until finally he noticed a couple staring at them. Ryder didn't care. He'd use any excuse to touch Julia.

"I should have made you wear a jacket to cover up." His pulse beat faster as if he were whispering dirty things to her, describing all the things he would do to her tonight.

Then he helped her with the helmet, and she climbed aboard behind him, tucking her skirt beneath her thighs.

Despite the helmets and the noise of the scooter and the rush of the air, he could hear Julia's laughter. This was so good for her. So good for him.

He found the castle twenty minutes down the country lane, its turrets rising above the trees long before they got there. He slowed for the turn into the long driveway lined by cypress trees, all trimmed to perfection.

Despite its proximity to the monastery and the lavender fields, the massive château wasn't crowded. He pulled into a parking spot, climbed off. Once Julia had removed her helmet, he locked both his and hers to the scooter. A hand on her shoulder, he leaned down to kiss the exposed skin of her neck. "No more sunburn," he said. "We need to be very, very careful with your fair skin. I should redo it every fifteen minutes."

She laughed at him. "You're just trying to cop a feel."

"Guilty as charged." He wanted to drag her into him, kiss her long and hard.

Instead she dragged him to the kiosk to sign up for a tour, the next one starting in fifteen minutes. They used the extra time to wander the magnificent grounds and view the castle from various angles.

A grand staircase flanked by lions led up to tall double doors, and turrets connected by a moat marked each corner. The lawn surrounding the château was meticulously manicured, so closely cropped it might have been done with clippers. Flowerbeds bloomed with color, and the shrubs had been shaped, some tall and boxy, others clipped into perfect pom-poms. Several people, couples and families, had spread out blankets to picnic on.

"You don't see that around America's historic homes. There's always keep-off-the-grass signs." Julia looked up at him. "I like this so much better."

They strolled hand in hand. "Maybe we should never leave." The idea was so appealing, to run away, to hide out here away from everything, no more work phone calls, no more calls from Elaine.

Julia glanced at her watch, reminding him it was time for their tour. Inside, they joined a group of fifteen and their guide started right on time.

"The paintings in this hall are all the old masters. There you see a van Dyck. And over there a Rembrandt." Their guide was perhaps in his eighties, his voice a little creaky, and his accent British, not French.

"Are the paintings original to the house?" a smartly dressed Italian woman wanted to know.

The old man shook his head. "Sadly no. Many precious items were stripped from the home during the revolution." He didn't need to say the French Revolution of the late 1700s. "Many antiquities were replaced during succeeding years, but we lost much of that again during World War Two. The Nazis were notorious for walking off with the artwork." He waved a hand down the length of the gallery. "These paintings were purchased during renovations done in the 1970s, to give the feel of what the house would have been like in its heyday."

The dining room on the main floor was dominated by a massive table. "King Louis dined here." He didn't say which Louis that might have been.

Standing on the edge of the grand ballroom, he described the parties. "Ladies dressed in elegant creations swirled around the floor, executing intricate dance steps, their part-ners dressed like peacocks. A small orchestra would have performed from the balcony above."

On cue, a waltz began playing over the loudspeakers and four couples wearing period costume and upswept hairstyles glided onto the dance floor to twirl about the room. The tour group loved it, clapping, smiling. Julia clung to Ryder's arm, smiling up at him, then back at the dancers.

She was happy, she was glowing, she was enjoying herself.

It was all he had hoped for.

21

"Wasn't that fabulous?" Julia held both his hands in hers.

"Yeah. Awesome." The château tour had been interesting, yet Ryder felt there were too many people, as if somehow they were stealing his time with Julia.

Except it wasn't *his* time. But for this little scooter jaunt today, they were completing a bucket list that belonged to Will, not them. Since he would never see all these sites, they had to do it for him.

Ryder didn't resent sharing her with Will. He just didn't want to share her with anyone else. It was a crazy notion, yet he could feel their time together slipping away.

Outside, when he made a move to unlock the helmets, Julia put her hand on his arm. "Let's get out the blanket and just lay on the grass for a while. Everyone else is doing it." She beamed a smile at him, as bright as the sun overhead. "I want to look at the clouds. What do you say?"

Yes. To anything she wanted. "I say it's a perfect idea."

They found a spot partially shaded by trees, the tip of

their blanket out in the sun so they could see the clouds overhead.

Settling on the blanket, Julia threaded her fingers through his. "What did I tell you? Isn't this perfect?"

He turned his head to peck a kiss on her temple. "Excellent idea." Bodies pressed together, hands clasped, it was more than perfect.

Clouds scudded across the sky, sometimes covering the sun, sometimes letting it beam down on them.

Julia pointed out shapes in the clouds. "That's definitely a frog getting ready to hop."

"Hmm. Maybe a rabbit."

She looked at him, feigning shock. "A bunny rabbit? There's no long ears. It's definitely a frog."

He harrumphed good-naturedly. "All right, I'll let you have that one. It's a frog."

The soft, fluffy clouds looked like mountains and Easter eggs and forest creatures. "And there's a tractor."

He laughed at her. "You've never even seen a tractor."

She scoffed. "Of course I've seen a tractor. We saw tractors out in the field just today. I know what a tractor looks like."

"Hmm," he mused. "If anything, it looks like a snail."

"No way. It's all blocky, not smooth and round like a snail shell. It's a tractor."

"You definitely win for originality."

She laughed softly next to him. God, he loved her laughter.

"Oh look." She pointed into the sky. "There's a pig."

He snorted. "Where's the snout? That looks more like an elephant, see it's long trunk?"

"But there's a curly tail on the end." She pointed with a flourish of her finger as if she were tracing the pig's tail.

"That could be the elephant's tail."

"And what you're saying is the trunk, well, that looks like a snout. An elephant's trunk would be way longer."

They bickered back and forth, his heart feeling full, feeling whole, after so many years of feeling heartless. "All right, I'll let you win that one. Because you're just too adamant. I know I'm not going to make you believe me."

She giggled, rolled over, rubbed her face against his shoulder. "I haven't looked for shapes in the clouds since I was a kid. With Felicity." She chuckled softly. "Well, not with Felicity. She was never the cloud-gazing type."

"I haven't done it since the kids were young." He reached over to run his hand through her hair. "But now I truly believe everyone should take five minutes every day just to look at the clouds in the sky."

"Or, if it's raining, to feel the rain on your face. We're always rushing, as if a little rain is going melt us."

"Like the wicked witch," he added.

"Exactly. Okay, so we're agreed, we're going to cloud gaze. Five minutes at least."

"Or all day long if we feel like it."

His phone rang, and he pulled it out, seeing Tyrone's name. There'd been work calls over the past few days, but for the most part Ty was taking care of everything, bothering Ryder as little as possible.

But today, Ryder found himself not wanting to answer at all.

At home, his phone had always taken precedence. It rang, he jumped. If he was needed at work, he ran to the office. But here in Provence, the office was an intrusion. Yet it was his livelihood, how he paid for everything Dustin and Tonya needed, how he would afford their college tuition.

"Sorry, I need to take this. Work." He was about to pull away when Julia squeezed his hand.

"Answer it from here. I don't mind. There's no reason we

can't lay on this beautiful grass looking at that lovely sky while you talk."

She was right. It was like taking the time to gaze at the clouds or feel the rain on your face. People were always rushing. And he didn't need to right now.

He answered without moving more than the muscles in his arm to put the phone to his ear. "Yo."

"Wow, you sound relaxed."

Tyrone didn't know the half of it. "I'll have you know I'm lying flat on the grass just staring up at the sky."

"No," Tyrone scoffed. "I had no clue you even knew there was a sky."

"There's definitely a sky. With clouds. And a big fat sun. And, wait for it, wait for it," he said with humor lacing his voice. "I'm actually smelling the lavender, too."

"Holy hell. I'm sending out the doctors. You've got a serious condition."

They laughed together.

"Sorry to bring you down out of the clouds, man. But we have an issue."

Ryder felt every muscle tense. He handled issues day in and day out. His life was a mess of issues. That was the CEO's job, handle problems, make decisions, settle squabbles, direct people. He remembered the days of old when he was a financial analyst looking at spreadsheets, putting together budgets, figuring out standard cost rates and return on investment. In ways, it had been a much simpler life.

"Okay, hit me with it."

"Neidermeyer called. He's, and I quote, 'extremely unhappy' with the prototype he just received. In fact, I would say he's flaming fire out his nostrils."

"At least it's not out of his ass," Ryder couldn't help adding.

Beside him, Julia laughed softly.

"Are you alone, man?" Tyrone asked. "Because we can talk later if you need."

"You're fine." He wasn't letting Julia go. "So what's his issue?" Neidermeyer was VP of R&D for a small concern they were working with. The business with his company was negligible, but still, you never crapped on a customer, large or small. He listened as Tyrone boiled down Neidermeyer's rant to the main points. And finally Ryder said, "All right, I'll give him a call."

"He just needs a little reassurance from the big boss."

"Tell me what our R&D is doing about it."

Tyrone laid out the facts succinctly.

Something strange came over him as he listened. For the first time in his working career, he simply didn't care. He wanted to tell Tyrone to handle it himself. He didn't want to call Neidermeyer. He didn't want to pacify people. He didn't want to lay down the law to his troops. He didn't want to look at budgets and tell his managers they needed to cut costs by this or that percentage. In fact, he thought maybe he didn't want to go back at all.

He wanted only Julia.

And his kids. But he wasn't sure how much longer they would need him.

He held Julia's hand trapped in his, breathed in her scent, sweet and sun-kissed. Turning his head slightly, he gazed upon her profile, her eyes closed, her smile beatific, and he wondered how long this feeling inside him had been growing. Not just about Julia but about work and life itself. Since Will's death? Even before they knew his death was imminent, when suddenly Ryder had to start thinking about the meaning of life?

When Ty was done, Ryder said, "I'll give him a call. Then I'll email you later and tell you how it goes."

"I'm sure it'll be fine."

"Yeah," Ryder agreed. He hung up, then held his phone above him, scrolling through his contacts for Neidermeyer's number.

"Sorry. I have to a call this guy." Again, he started to rise. Julia rolled over, propped herself on her elbow. "You can stay right here and call him. He's never going to know you're lying in the sun." She dropped her voice to a whisper. "With the woman you made love to last night."

Her words, her whisper, her scent, her pretty face, she lit up everything inside him. The last thing he wanted to do was call Neidermeyer. But he stayed right where he was, pushed the call button, then put the phone to his ear.

As soon as his call was answered, Julia began to play.

A DEVIL HAD COME TO SIT ON JULIA'S SHOULDER, AND AS Ryder said, "Hey, Colin, good to hear from you," Julia blew a warm breath against his other ear. Then bit his lobe.

He shivered. But he kept talking in the same natural tone. "Tyrone tells me we've got a problem."

Propped on her elbow, Julia leaned close to nuzzle his throat above his shirt, licking his skin, loving the salty taste.

Ryder shifted, but he didn't push her away. "No, Colin, I'm not minimizing the issues. But here's our plan to handle things."

He didn't miss a beat of the conversation as she kissed his neck, though she sensed a slight hitch of his breath. "Yes, definitely, we've got the guys working on that."

Julia let his words hum over her while she relished the deep timbre of his voice.

She glanced around to find that no one was paying attention to them. And really, she wasn't doing anything terribly naughty. She slipped one more button lose on his shirt and slid her hand inside. He was so warm, the feel of his skin so good. She nestled down beside him again and relished the length of his body against hers, savored the soft hairs beneath her fingertips, and glided over his skin, his heartbeat thrumming against her palm.

Then Julia got a little more daring. She teased his chest hairs until she found his nipple, rubbing the nub until it turned hard.

With a catch in his breath, he clamped his free arm around her, pulling her hand away and giving her little room to move. Julia smiled to herself. With her head on his shoulder, she watched the rise and fall of his chest, faster than before. His voice had taken on a harsher note. Looking down the length of his body, she saw exactly what she was doing to him. And she loved it. She loved the press of his arm around her, actually keeping her in place, her hand trapped against his chest, even if she couldn't stroke him.

He kept talking, calmly, smoothly, though taking a few deeper breaths.

Since she couldn't shift her hand, she moved her leg.

Having kicked off her sandals when they sat down, she now trailed her bare foot up his leg, her dress riding up, her thigh sliding higher along his. With one hand on hers and the other holding the phone to his ear, he didn't have an extra hand to stop her.

She teased him, tantalized him, never going too far. Keeping it light was almost more sexy than getting hot and heavy. If he'd really wanted her to stop, he could simply stand up. But he stayed, letting her play with him.

She felt young and sexy and carefree. And she wanted to do so much more.

"All right, Colin," Ryder said, winding things down. "Sounds good. We'll keep in touch. Any further issues, you can call Tyrone and he'll let me know. Talk to you later."

Then he tossed the phone on the blanket and rolled so fast she couldn't get away before she was trapped beneath him. He held her arms above her head. "You are one naughty woman." He stole a kiss, short but deep, and she felt him hard against her leg, showing her exactly what all her teasing had done.

"I wasn't doing anything," she denied, laughter in her voice, and something else, too, happiness, desire, a hint of power.

"You're very lucky we're in public, or I'd have to punish you."

"Such a big talker," she teased, daring him.

"Just wait till I get you back to the room," he threatened, leaning down to nuzzle her neck the way she'd done to him, his warm breath seducing her.

"I'm starving," she complained. "You have to feed me first."

"You're starving, all right, but not for food." He growled against her, the thrum of his voice reaching deep inside her.

He was so right. It wasn't food she wanted. She'd been starving for so long. And now she wanted to feast. On him.

In the next moment, Ryder rolled to his feet and held out his hand. With the sun silhouetting him, his gaze was dark. They'd been tussling on the ground like frisky teenagers, and the look he gave her smoldered, a look that stroked her starving soul.

She took his hand, letting him pull her up and hard against him, where he held her just long enough for her to feel how ready he was. Then he grabbed the blanket, crumpled it up, stowing it haphazardly under his arm.

"Home," he whispered under his breath. "Now." Then he marched her back to the parking lot and the scooter.

She felt powerful knowing she'd pushed all his buttons.

As he unlocked the helmets, she said, "I'm driving. You're riding behind me."

"No way."

She puffed up her chest against him, standing nose to nose, almost, because she wasn't tall enough. "You think I can't do it?" she challenged.

He went still, except his gaze, which roamed over her face. "I think you can do anything you want, Jules."

So she drove, a little shaky taking off—just like Audrey Hepburn in *Roman Holiday*—and felt a few moments of panic making the first turn onto the road. Then she got the hang of it, loving the feel of him surrounding her, his arms wrapped around her waist, his chest against her back, his body hard right at the base of her spine.

It was good. It felt crazy. She was tempted to pull to the side of the road and drag him off into a field or a forest. She wanted the sensations to go on and on, build and build. She wanted to take him to the breaking point, drag him back, then start all over again.

She'd never felt like this in her life, not even the first time around with Ryder.

Her emotions teetered on the edge of betrayal to Will. For all the years they'd been together, for all the things he'd done for her. Yet she had never felt this with Will.

But they were in Provence, and this was the trip Will had wanted her to take. In her wildest fantasies, this was what Will had wanted her to feel, alive, sensual and sexual, a woman in her prime. A woman who would do all the crazy things her body was begging her for.

She had tonight to experience it with Ryder.

She had all the nights left in Provence.

And she wasn't wasting a single precious moment.

❦ 22 ❦

With the rumble of the scooter and the feel of Julia between his legs, Ryder went a little mad.

Like a Viking with his war prize, he wanted to carry her upstairs to his lair, rip off her clothes, and ravage her with pleasure.

But as soon as they'd turned in the scooter, Julia grabbed his hand, and said, "Let's eat at the restaurant Madame recommended." She held his hand in both of hers, leaning back slightly, guiding him exactly where she wanted him to go.

"I'd rather go to our room and eat there." He gave her a lecherous eyebrow waggle.

She laughed at him. "Dirty old man. You just want to get your hands on me. You have to wait."

Christ, she made him even hotter. Julia Bellerman with a new attitude. He loved it.

"All right. We'll eat. But then you're mine." He punctuated with a growl.

She twitched her hips. It made him crazy. No wait, he

already *was* crazy. Out of control. Ready to do anything she wanted.

"We'll see," she teased. "It depends on how well you feed me."

She turned, twitched those sexy hips of hers again, and he had no choice but to follow. The streets were narrow and cobblestoned, and while there were no cars passing right now, mopeds and scooters and bicycles lined the sidewalk. Tourists were out doing all their touristy things, gazing in shop windows, eating macarons, buying lavender off an old woman's cart, and searching out restaurants for dinner.

There wasn't a single touristy thing on his mind right now. There was just Julia's newfound sexual confidence.

He was in for one hell of a ride.

They chose one of the restaurants on Madame Brodeur's card. It wasn't crowded and they could still get a table out front. Banks of flower pots surrounded the patio like a low wall, and lights hung from the awning, turning the patio into a fairyland in their glow.

Julia teased him throughout dinner, spearing a morsel of duck off her plate, holding out her fork. "Here, try this. It's so good." She licked her lips, firing him up as she fed him.

Then she'd say, "Please please please, let me have a bite of that." As if she were talking about something entirely different than what was on his plate. When he offered a forkful of his flaky salmon in pecan crust, she wrapped her fingers around his wrist, pulling him close, and ate it off his fork, her eyes all for him.

As she stole a flower of broccoli off his plate, under the table, she slipped off her sandal and caressed his leg with her foot.

He wondered how real this was, this new, smooth, sexy Julia, and how long she would stay with him. Or if she would vanish when they stepped off the plane back home.

He never wanted her to disappear. But he also recognized she was slightly manic, trying to live as much and as fast as she could. As if their time together was running out.

He didn't want to consider time right now. All he wanted was to enjoy the amazing tease she was putting on.

They shared a sorbet, feeding each other, never eating off their own spoon, only off each other's.

He didn't care if anyone was watching, judging. Because this was France, and they could do anything.

He slapped down cash as soon as the waiter left their bill. He'd had to ask for it, because in France they didn't rush their patrons out the door. Dinner was something to linger over.

But Ryder was done lingering.

He retrieved the key from Madame Brodeur, ready to race up the stairs when Julia decided to chat.

God, she made him crazy. And she made him laugh, because he was well aware she'd stopped on purpose.

Even that made him hotter. Her teasing made her sexier.

She leaned on the reception desk. "Thank you so much for that dinner recommendation. The food was absolutely delicious." She glanced over her shoulder at Ryder, a wicked, tempting smile on her lips.

"I am so happy we could give you such a good dining experience." Madame Brodeur beamed at them. "I took the liberty of adding more ice to your champagne bucket. When you didn't return before dinner, I felt you would need it."

"How very thoughtful of you," Julia said, her voice so sweet. And so teasing. Then she added, "We're simply exhausted after such a wonderful afternoon out. The scooter was so fun. And we were starving when we got back." She winked at Ryder. She was merciless. "So thank you for your recommendation. We didn't even have to make a decision."

He thought he'd have to drag her away, but finally, *finally*, she waved a hand and said, "Good night." Then she led him up the stairs.

In the room, he would have jumped her, but she said sweetly, "You open the champagne."

He did, and he poured, and he handed her a glass.

But when he tried to pull her into his arms, she held him off with a finger in the center of his chest. "Uh-uh." She shook her head. "You need to take a shower."

"What, do I stink?"

She laughed, shaking her head again. "No. But I want you to get yourself all soaped up." She lowered her voice to a seductive pitch that actually seemed to stroke his skin. "And while you're doing that, I want you to think about all the things I'm going to do to you."

His breath caught in his throat, and he wanted nothing more than to grab her up and toss her in the center of the bed where he would have his totally wicked way with her.

But even more, he loved her game. "All right. But I'm very fast."

She wagged her finger at him. "Be very, very slow. Take your time. Make it *really* good."

He stared at her. "Who are you?" he whispered, amazed and bewildered, dazzled and captivated.

"I don't know," she said just as softly. "But I like her."

"So do I." And he craved her.

He climbed under the hot spray and did everything she'd told him to, stroking himself as he thought of her.

It was too crazy good for words.

When he got out, he lit all the lavender candles Julia had bought, setting them around the bathtub. Then he poured in the lavender bath salts as he ran the water.

He left the bathroom with only a towel around his waist.

Julia's eyes went wide and dark and hot. "What are you doing?"

"I'm running your bath."

"But I'm not taking a bath."

"Oh yes, you are. And not because you stink."

She smiled, laughter in her voice as she said, "I most certainly do not."

Then he refilled her champagne. "I want you to get yourself all soaped up. And think about all the things I'm going to do to you." He pulled her close, kissed her hard. And turned the tables on her. "While you're doing that, I want to hear the water splash and I want to hear you moan. Because it will make me totally crazy."

He pushed her into the bathroom, champagne still in her hand, and closed the door.

The timing was perfect, giving him the chance to call Dustin and Tonya at the promised time.

Although it did feel a little hinky to be calling his kids when he had a hard-on. Especially with Julia in the tub just on the other side of the door.

"You okay, Dad?" Tonya asked. Yet again, Dustin hadn't answered his phone, and all Ryder could do was leave a message. Then he'd called Tonya.

"I'm fine." He pretended he couldn't hear Julia splashing in the bathtub. "Hey, sweetheart, seems like your brother isn't taking my calls."

Tonya made a noise, maybe a grumble. "He's just a big poop, Dad."

He was going to have to pry it out of her, though he already knew what she was going to say. "So why is he just a big poop?"

"Well... maybe... you know," she stammered out non-answers.

"Tonya."

Finally she said, "You know. Same old stuff. He doesn't like that you went away with Aunt Julia. Just the two of you. All alone. And his sucky attitude is getting worse."

Yes, he knew. Damn Elaine for putting that idea into Dustin's head. And for making sure it stayed there, too. But he wasn't about to turn his daughter into a go-between with his son. "Okay. I left him a message." He'd already left Dustin several messages.

They talked about her cheerleading tryouts. Cheerleading camp would start in the middle of July, long before school was in session, but they were already putting the team together now. He listened and thought he said all the appropriate things.

But he sure as hell wasn't doing a good job of ignoring Julia or the sounds she made.

"Okay, sweetie, I'll call you tomorrow. Have a good day. Love you." After she'd said the words back and hung up, he turned off his phone.

Behind the door, the water gurgled as it drained out of the tub.

Julia would be toweling off now, her skin pink and fragrant and glowing, not to mention hot.

He didn't wait another moment. He'd already waited more than he could bear, and now he was just this side of insane.

He opened the door without knocking. She'd wrapped a towel around her, completely naked under it. And he let his towel drop.

She stood stock still for five seconds. He counted them in his head. Then he was on her, lifting her high, until her towel fell away, too, and she wrapped her legs around his waist. He'd rolled on the condom the moment he'd heard the water circle the drain, and now he shifted her, letting her slide down onto him, holding her tight as delicious, delirious sensations flooded his senses.

She was hot, she was wet, and she was so ready for him.

Her arms wrapped around his neck, she pulled him in for a long, sweet kiss while he held still inside her.

When he didn't think he could stand another second, he turned, making his way through the doorway, counting himself lucky that they didn't fall. Then he collapsed with her on the bed.

"Oh my God, Ryder." She shut her eyes, tipped her head back, and writhed against him. He didn't let her go.

His last coherent thought was that he would *never* let her go.

IT WAS A NIGHT TO REMEMBER. JULIA HAD NEVER FELT more like a woman. She did sexy things, naughty things, even dirty things.

Ryder had loved every one of them. It was the craziness of wild desire. Letting go of every inhibition. She wasn't sure she would have been able to do it before. There was just something about this time, something about the freedom she felt in Provence, a freedom she would never have feel at home, the freedom of having no one to answer to, no one to check up on her. For so long, she'd had to account for every minute. Someone always needed to be with Will. Someone always needed to know where she was and what she was doing.

Now there was just her. And Ryder.

They slept late in the morning. He'd woken her up twice more in the night to make love. She'd never made love more than once in the night, not even on her honeymoon. Not even with Ryder.

Nothing had ever felt so delicious.

Because they hadn't come down for breakfast, Madame Brodeur left a tray outside their door. How kind of her. But she must have known exactly what they'd been doing all night.

Julia decided not to be embarrassed. This was France. This was Provence. The land of lovers. Where anything goes.

Ryder made her come again over croissants and coffee.

"You have a quite a knack for that," she told him as she lay gasping on the bed.

He laughed. "I'll get so much better with practice."

"Your practice is done for the day. We have sightseeing to do. All those Roman ruins."

"I don't need any sightseeing," he said like a grumpy old man.

"I do." How he made her want to laugh. Even though she was tempted to make love all day long, because that was something she'd never done either, they were in Provence, and lounging in bed for hours could wait until they got home.

She stopped short at the thought.

This was all they had. When they got home, it would be totally impossible. When they got home, no one would let them be together. He had children. He had a job. He had an ex-wife. And she had a life to start over without Will.

She scrambled off the bed, laughing, because she didn't want Ryder to know how her thoughts had suddenly spiraled down.

"I do believe Madame's croissants were the absolute best pastry ever," she told him. Or maybe it was just the amazing sex that made them taste so marvelous.

He made a grab for her. "I'll show you the best ever."

But she danced away, laughing. "Get dressed, you naughty man. We have so many places to see today."

She was going to live in the now, only for the moment.

She'd think about the rest when it was absolutely necessary.

❧ 23 ❧

"**D**o you want to rent bicycles?" Julia asked as they stepped outside their hotel an hour later. She was energized, feeling flighty and flirty and sated.

Ryder hauled her in with an arm around her shoulders. "Whatever you want, baby."

She loved the endearment. Will had never been one to use endearments, except for shortening her name to Jules.

But she remembered that back then Ryder had never called her Julia, always Jules or some other sweet endearment. He'd pull her close, right under his arm, and whisper in her ear, "Hey, Jules baby, let's go back to my room," or "Hey, baby, let's get something to eat before I devour you. I need my strength." Back then, all his words, especially the endearments, had warmed her and made her feel special.

The only thing she'd had to hang onto in all the years since was that Ryder had never called Elaine *baby*, at least not in front of Julia.

The same outfit that rented scooters also rented bicycles, and they tooled around the tourist sites in town. Julia wore her capri pants, afraid of the danger of catching her dress in the bike chain.

"Are you sure you're okay?" Ryder asked when she teetered dangerously almost right off the rental lot.

But Julia laughed. "I just need to get my bike legs back. It's been ages. But they say you never forget."

Avoiding the busier roads, they followed narrow streets which had mostly foot, bicycle, scooter, or moped traffic. They started their tour at Alyscamp, the roman necropolis, which had been a favorite subject of Van Gogh and Gauguin. It wasn't particularly crowded, as if weren't even on the tourist radar, probably because there was so many other things to see. Then they rode on to the Colosseum-style amphitheater, where they still held events like bullfighting and concerts. They wandered through the forum and the Roman theater.

Standing in the theater, she felt a bit teary-eyed for a moment, leaning close to Ryder to say, "Will would have loved this. It's almost like going to Rome."

He put his arm around her. "Maybe you need to actually go to Rome someday."

She nodded her head but knew it would probably never happen. She didn't want to travel alone.

They visited the Roman baths and had their usual picnic lunch down by the river. It had become a ritual, but this time, Ryder kept stealing kisses and Julia gave them up without a fight.

Their time together was idyllic, the sun delicious on her skin, the scenery gorgeous. Even the tourists didn't bother her. If you wanted the warm weather and the lavender fields and the blooming flowers, then you had to put up with a few crowds.

"You want to ride over to the Arles museum?" Ryder asked after he'd tossed their trash.

Julia had read online that many of the Roman artifacts were displayed in the museum, as well as replicas of what the amphitheater, the theater and the forum would have looked like.

"Of course."

In the museum, they strolled hand-in-hand, leaning close against each other as they read descriptive plaques or examined artifacts and marveled over the mosaics. Ryder was always right there, heating her up, turning even museum-gazing into a sensual delight.

He felt it, too. When they were only halfway through the exhibits, he pulled her aside, out of the stream of museum-goers, and asked, "Have you seen enough?" A hot glint glowed in his eye.

"Did you have something else in mind?" She pulled their clasped hands behind her back, tugging him closer.

"Oh yeah."

"Like what?" She tipped her head back and batted her eyelashes in a tease.

"It's better if I show you." The wicked half smile on his lips made her want to melt.

"Are you sure? Maybe you should tell me first. See if it's something I really want to do instead of examining all these magnificent artifacts."

His warm breath against her ear made her shiver. "I plan to taste every inch of you. Until you scream."

"I never scream," she whispered.

"You will. I promise."

He would make sure she did.

They took the shortest route back to the hotel, didn't even bother to drop the bikes off first since they'd rented them all day. Madame Brodeur gave them a happy yet knowing smile as she handed Ryder their room key.

He made good on his promise. Every inch. Until Julia had to pull the pillow over her face to muffle her cries.

It had never been like this the first time around. Who was different, her, him? Maybe both. She never could have let go like this when she was young. There'd been so many other things at stake. But here in Provence, in Arles, in this pension, this bed, there was only now, only pleasure, only Ryder.

They returned the bikes after what felt like hours in their magnificent bed, then strolled down by the river, followed by another bistro dinner.

The menu was all in French, and after the waiter left to let them peruse, Julia leaned forward. "I want to try something that I have no idea what it is. No translation. Just point to something and pick."

"I like the way you think. But what if you pick snails?"

"Then I'll eat snails." She laughed, then shuddered, figuring that at least she knew the word *escargot* and could avoid it.

"All right. I'm game." He laid out a menu between them. "You go first."

She chose something called *pissaladière* and Ryder ordered *croque monsieur*.

"Oh, of course, I should have known, it's a pizza," she said when her *pissaladière* arrived. Then she gave it a closer look. "I think those are anchovies." She scrunched up her nose. They *were* anchovies, spread out in a crisscross pattern with an olive in the center of each section. There was no pizza sauce, instead the crust was covered with sauteed onions and garlic, then the anchovies and olives.

"You don't like anchovies," Ryder said, as if she didn't know that.

She looked at his *croque monsieur* which was something like a grilled ham and cheese sandwich with more cheese melted on top.

"Do you want mine?" he asked.

She really did think about it for a second. Then she shook her head. "No. Thanks. I said I'd eat whatever I chose." And she did, taking a bite. "It's pretty salty," she said with her hand over her mouth.

"You don't have to eat it."

"I know." But she closed her eyes and kept chewing. When she drank it with the rosé the waiter had suggested, it wasn't too bad. "It's growing on me." She ate half, though it wasn't very large. Then held out a piece to Ryder. "You have to try."

He ate from her fingers, letting her feed him in the same way they always shared their food. "Yum." Ryder had always like anchovies. Then he cut off a piece of his sandwich and fed it to her.

"I like yours much better."

He fed her more of it, stealing pieces of her *pissaladière* off her plate, which was fine by her.

That evening, Ryder feasted on her. Then once more in the middle of the night. And again in the morning.

He couldn't get enough of her.

Julia never wanted it to end.

IT BECAME THE DELICIOUS ROUTINE ALL ALONG THEIR journey. They made love, they ate picnics in parks or at scenic spots they found along the road. They bickered over which was the best pastry or chocolate or coffee, they tried new dishes at every bistro they dined in, they rented bicycles or scooters. Once they rented two of them, racing each other down narrow country lanes.

Ryder called his kids every night at nine. No matter what he and Julia were doing. She never minded.

Dustin, however, never answered his phone. She knew it affected Ryder by the tenseness in his jaw, in his muscles, but he never said anything. He handled work calls when he had to. And if Elaine phoned, he answered because he was worried about Dustin.

Julia left the room or sat on a bench if they were strolling down a boulevard. She couldn't bear to hear the nasty things Elaine said.

From Arles, they stopped in Les Baux-de-Provence, famous for the ruins of an old castle and medieval village, then had lunch in Saint-Rémy-de-Provence. They stopped in the beautiful city of Avignon, where they stayed a full day to tour palaces and cathedrals and visit the broken Saint Bénézet Bridge. The following morning, they left Avignon to walk among even more Roman ruins, the Théâtre Antique in Orange, which was even more magnificent than the one in Arles. The ruins of ancient Roman houses of Vaison-la-Romaine in Quartier de Puymin were fascinating.

"I don't even need to go to Rome," she told Ryder. "Everything is right here." There weren't as many tourists, maybe because it was early in the season or because people didn't come to Provence to look at Roman ruins. They came for the sun and the food and the lavender.

From there, they visited a magnificent old abbey perched on a mountain in Gordes. They splurged on a stately château with a gorgeous view of the medieval village and the valley. Decorated with old paintings and antiques, it was living like a duke and duchess.

Then their last full day dawned. Tomorrow they would drive to Marseille, drop off the rental car, and catch a flight connecting in Paris that would take them back to San Francisco.

Neither of them mentioned this last day outright, but they got an early start on the two-hour drive to the seaside town of Cassis.

"We can't go to Provence and not spend at least one day on a beach where we can swim in the Mediterranean," Will had said. So Julia had booked a hotel overlooking the harbor.

After dropping off their luggage, the concierge directed them to the main beach in the town center, Plage de la Mer, and provided beach towels.

Julia wanted to enjoy the sun and the water, but somehow, knowing it was the last day, she felt... off. Unsettled. Even near tears.

But she peeled off her dress, having worn her swimsuit underneath, laid out her towel, and soaked up the sun, hiding behind her sunglasses so Ryder wouldn't see the anguish in her eyes.

Then he grabbed her hand, pulled her up. "Come on. We have to swim."

When she said, "I don't really feel like it right now," he hauled her up in his arms and trotted to the water's edge, wading in with her. Then he dropped her.

She came up squealing, laughing. "Oh my God, it's colder than I thought it'd be. Isn't the Mediterranean supposed to be warm?" Before he could answer, she tackled him down into the water as well.

They frolicked a while, then climbed out to warm themselves in the sun again.

"You need more suntan lotion." Ryder slathered it on without asking her. Up and down her legs, coming a bit too close to private parts.

"We're in public," she hissed, though it was no worse than anything else she'd seen on the beach.

Ryder just laughed and slipped his fingers down her back,

easing just inside her one-piece suit. "If I don't do it along the lines of your suit, you'll get burned right there."

She gave herself up to the sensual massage.

Then it was her turn to tantalize him, rubbing sunblock over his back and shoulders, making him groan with pleasure.

"Stop that," she whispered.

All he did was laugh.

She flopped down on her stomach again, letting the sun warm her, all the while unable to forget that this was the last day. The last day he would put lotion on her. The last day he would kiss her. The last day he would make love to her.

The last day for the rest of her life.

"Do you need to get anything else for the kids?" she asked before she started crying.

He didn't look at her, his head propped on his cupped hands, his sunglasses covering his eyes. "Yeah. I could do a little more shopping." He turned, lowered his glasses to look at her. "But not too much time. I have big plans for you." Then he winked, pushed his glasses back up, and pretended to sleep.

When they'd had enough sun and water and sand, they shopped, treated themselves to a last gourmet meal, then returned to their room where Ryder ran her a bath, using the last of the bath salts and candles she'd bought at the monastery.

It seemed like the last of everything.

She'd picked up more today in a little shop, needing the reminder when she got home, though she was afraid the scent wouldn't be quite so luxurious as the monastery's had been.

It couldn't possibly match, because Ryder wouldn't be there. Ryder had made it special.

The bath was large, a clawfoot with the taps on the wall at the tub's midpoint. She set her bath salts on a small shelf at one end and lit two candles. Small lavender accents in the center of each white tile on the wall matched the thick lavender bath towels.

Ryder entered the bathroom behind her. "Your champagne, madame." He carried a glass of his own, too.

They'd spent a fortune on champagne; Ryder never ordered the cheap stuff. They toasted, drank, then he put both glasses on the small table he'd set by the bathtub. Gone another moment, he returned with the champagne in its ice bucket.

"Let me help you undress." His eyes were hot and dark and just the way she liked them.

But she couldn't stop the refrain in her head. *I don't want to go home. I don't want to go home. I don't want to go home.* The exact opposite of Dorothy in Oz.

She let him pull the sundress over her head. Her shoulders were bronzed, the lines of spaghetti straps marking her skin after days of wearing sundresses, though she'd used an ocean of sunblock. She'd adored Ryder's hands on her as he'd rubbed it in.

They stood a long moment, Julia in just her panties and bra.

"May I take them off?" he asked, the banked fire in his eyes starting to burn.

"Yes." It was such a simple answer with such a complicated result.

First he hauled her against his chest, full body contact, reaching behind her to unclasp the bra. He backed off to slide it slowly down her arms, revealing her breasts inch by inch until he was breathing a little harder, a little faster.

Then he went down on his knees in front of her, just like the night she'd gone to her knees and taken him in her mouth.

By the time he'd slowly stripped her panties over her hips,

the material clung to her damp curls for a long moment. She was so ready.

And he knew it.

Sliding the panties down her thighs, her calves, lifting one foot after the other, he held the simple cotton panty to his nose as if it were expensive lingerie, breathing her in, looking at her as if he could gobble her up.

Then he rose and helped her naked into the tub. She settled down into the hot, silky, scented water, and he handed her the champagne.

Instead of leaving like he did every other night, Ryder stripped down. The beauty of him, glorious, solid, hard, left her heart quaking in her chest.

JULIA WAS BEAUTIFUL. HE WAS RAPTUROUS AT THE SIGHT of her.

It was their last night. Ryder wasn't going to waste a second, and she wasn't lounging in that tub without him. He stripped, standing naked a moment longer than he needed to because the look in her eyes made him harder and hotter, as if she'd been watching a strip tease. Then he slid in behind her, fitting her between his legs, pulling her back against his chest, her skin warm and wet and smooth. His mouth watered for her.

"Oh my God," she said in a breath, tipping her head back against his shoulder. "This is so good."

"Tonight is only going to get better, baby," he whispered against her hair.

Her breasts lay just below the surface of the water. Mesmerized by the sight, he couldn't help but touch them. A little tweak here, a light pinch there, and Julia was gasping.

He wanted to tease and tantalize, keep her high on sensuality for as long as he could.

"You need your champagne." Reaching down to the small table, he handed her a glass, then picked up his own. Clinking them together, they each took a long, sweet drink. He could stay like this with her all night, just refilling the tub with hot water.

"This is just too luxurious," she said.

He wanted to give this to her every night. The idea came to him that he'd send a bottle of champagne to her house, along with candles and bath salts. And think of her that way. Every single night.

She'd pulled her hair up in a bun, the tendrils that hung down flirting with his cheek. He played with the silky ends, couldn't resist her skin, trailing his fingers up and down her arms, sliding to her belly, tracing small circles, then making his way back up to her breasts.

Julia hummed her pleasure. When he cupped her in his hands, squeezing the tips between his thumb and forefinger, she let out a low moan that vibrated deep inside him.

The hard evidence of his desire stretched along her spine, and dipping down into the hot water, he slipped his hand between her legs, parting her with one finger and finding that pretty little button he loved so much.

She raised her knees, letting her legs fall apart and relaxed against his chest. And he slid deeper.

She was slippery and it was more than just the water. She wound her arm back around his neck and her breath hitched, then she moaned his name softly. "Ryder, please."

He would never have imagined the Julia he used to know allowing him to do this. It was so many years and so many lives ago. He wouldn't call her repressed back then, but sex hadn't been as easy between them. And maybe he'd pushed too hard as well.

"Do you like this?" He needed to hear her say it.

"Oh my God," was her only answer.

It was enough for him. "You feel so good in my arms. So hot. Tell me how badly you need this."

"I need it so bad, Ryder. Make me come, I want it bad." She arched, sending spikes of pleasure through his body as she rubbed against him.

He played with her, making her wild. There was so much pleasure in the feel of her. In this moment, he needed nothing beyond her satisfaction, nothing but the quiver of her body, the tension in her breath, her sweet cries of need.

He worked her gently. He didn't want her to go off too soon. He wanted this to last. Because it was the last night. Tomorrow they would take a flight from Marseille to Paris, then fly across the vast ocean to San Francisco. And that would be it.

As much as he needed more, tonight was all he might ever have.

He kept her hot and sweet, riding the fine line, cruising the edge, without letting her fall off.

"Don't let go yet," he urged. "Make it last. Hold on a little longer."

"Ryder, please, oh my God, Ryder." He let her beg, knowing he could make it so much better if she held out for the big bang.

"Enjoy it," he whispered. "Ride it for everything it's worth."

Her legs started to tremble, then her body shimmied and quaked. Finally her limbs tensed, and the moment had come, no way either of them could hold out.

Julia detonated like a firecracker in his arms. Crying out, clamping her legs together around his hand. She bucked and rolled, sloshing water over the lip of the bath. There was nothing else he could do but ride the wave with her, keeping her right on the crest, pushing her to go longer and harder.

She finally came down, collapsing against him, sighing out a long breath, then a soft, amazed laugh. He wrapped his arms around her, held her tight, absorbed her heat.

"This is just too crazy," she said softly. "I didn't know I could actually feel like this." She tipped her head back on his shoulder to look at him. "I'm forty-five. I thought women my age didn't even want sex anymore."

He laughed. "When I'm around you, all I want is sex. It's about the person you're with, not about the age."

"Maybe it's the newness of it."

"We're not new, Julia. We've been here before." He wanted her to admit it was about *them*.

But she fought him. "We aren't those two people anymore. We're completely different."

He couldn't stop the next words, though he hadn't planned to say them yet. "It doesn't have to end the same way it did last time, Julia."

She went very still against him, still and silent, until finally she asked, "What do you mean?" even though she had to know exactly what he meant.

"I mean that I made a mistake."

Her voice soft, wary, she asked, "Are you saying the last twenty-five years have been a mistake?"

He'd wanted to plan this properly, figure out the right words, the right time, the right way to say it. If he did everything right, he could convince her.

"No. I know you loved Will. And I love my kids. But leaving you was still a mistake."

"What about Elaine?"

Elaine was his biggest mistake. An even bigger mistake than leaving Julia. But he didn't want to talk about Elaine. "Let's talk about this later. This is our last night here."

She clambered away from him, heaving herself up, water streaming down her body. "It's getting cold." It wasn't.

He'd botched it completely, put pressure on her. He should have kept his mouth shut, even if it felt like the perfect opening, she wasn't ready to be pushed.

She grabbed the big fluffy lavender towel, stepped out of the bath onto the mat, wrapped it around herself, covering up all the beautiful, sweet skin. He stood, too, while she kept her back to him, and he reached for his glass, downing a gulp of champagne like he was drinking soda.

He'd been a screwup then. He was a screwup now. He never knew when to keep his mouth shut.

She brushed past him, back into the bedroom, leaving him naked and alone.

By the time he'd dried off and walked into the bedroom, she's pulled her nightgown over her head and covered up. Julia hadn't worn a nightgown since they began sharing a room.

And it spoke volumes.

He pulled on a pair of jogging pants, because he couldn't stand there naked.

Then he went to her, cupped her face in his hands. The only good sign was that she didn't immediately jerk away. "Jules, I don't want to fight." He kissed her cold, immobile lips.

Then slowly, as if she were separating her old self from the new full-of-life woman who wanted to enjoy, she softened against him. "I don't want to fight either." She leaned her head against his shoulder. "I don't want to talk about it tonight, but you're right, tomorrow is coming. Even as I tell myself going home doesn't matter, I know that it does. But I don't want to think about any of it now." She tipped her head back to meet his gaze. "Tonight I just want you to make love to me like it's the last time." They both knew she meant it *was* the last time.

They made love with a new ferocity. Each pushing the other higher, harder. He spread her legs and made love to her with his lips, his mouth, his tongue. She actually screamed out her pleasure.

She'd barely come down off her high before she rolled on top and took him in her mouth. She drove him to the edge, made him crazy, nearly pushed him over.

Until he grabbed her arms and pulled her up. "I need to be inside you when I come."

It was as if they were in a battle, their bodies slamming against each other, Julia exploding with one orgasm after another, until Ryder went over the cliff edge right along with her. Until they lay exhausted in each other's arms. Until neither of them could move.

It had never been like this when they were young. It was their age, their life experience, so many years of pain and happiness, anguish and joy. It was Will and Elaine and the kids. It was Will's death. It was their need to grieve for him. It was the way Elaine had blown his world apart. It was that nothing separated them now.

Yet everything separated them.

❄ 24 ❄

The previous night seemed like a dream to Julia.

And today they were flying back to Paris.

She wished they'd taken the train. It would have been longer, and she wanted that extra time. They'd packed, weighed, adjusted, making sure their bags weren't overweight after the gifts and souvenirs they'd bought. The drive to Marseille had taken a little over half an hour. Then there was the time spent dropping off the rental car, handing in the luggage, security, boarding. The flight to Paris was an hour and a half. The train would have been five hours. They could have relaxed, enjoyed, instead of what had seemed like such a rush. They still could have made it with plenty of time since their Paris flight wasn't until four in the afternoon. With the time change, they would be home around six in the evening.

She felt time tick-tick-ticking away. In one hour, they'd be landing in Paris. Then she counted the hours until they were home. *Home*. She'd never thought she wouldn't want to go back. *Home*. They'd have no time to talk, to analyze, to even think about what had happened between them in Provence.

Ryder would go back to work, back to his kids, back to his life.

And she would have to figure out what her life was.

As if she'd been planning the words for hours, she blurted them out. "Why did you leave me for Elaine all those years ago?"

He stared at her, his fingers tightening slightly around his coffee cup.

From the moment they'd scattered Will's ashes and Ryder had kissed her by the bridge, this had been coming. It was inevitable. The question had lain unanswered for twenty-five years. She had what he'd said was his reason, that he wasn't ready for a relationship. And she had her theories, about Elaine and how long they'd been sleeping together before he'd dumped Julia. And she had her need to believe Ryder. She had all Will's denials, too, that Ryder had never cheated.

But the fact remained, he'd married Elaine.

"I don't know, Julia." He set his coffee down, spread his hands on the tray table.

"That's not good enough," she said softly, not wanting to snap or yell or beg.

"I know it's not." Then he picked up the damn coffee again and sipped. As if his mouth had gone dry. As if he were nervous. "The truth is I had a bunch of reasons that seemed to make sense at the time." He lifted his shoulders, held out his hand as if he wanted her to take it. "But I was just afraid. I thought we'd gotten so serious so fast and that we had so many years ahead of us and I didn't want to get that serious. I wanted you. But..." He looked down at the tray table as if an answer were written there for him to simply read aloud. "I wanted you. But I didn't want to make a commitment, and I was afraid that's what you wanted. I sure as hell couldn't ask because it felt like just asking the question would somehow tie us down. I didn't want to end up like my parents, getting married before they even graduated. That's what people did back then. They got married, they started a family. I didn't know what the hell I wanted. Except that I wanted you without any strings. And I just didn't think I could have that."

But what about Elaine? She'd eventually tied him down. "I did want strings." There'd never been any question about that in her mind. "I wanted everything you were afraid of. I wanted a relationship. I wanted a commitment. And yes, down the road, I wanted marriage and children. You were right about it all."

She thought she'd see vindication in his eyes, but there was just a deep sadness. "Isn't that funny. Because I ended up with those things, and you didn't."

She felt such pain and such shame, closed her eyes against it.

"I didn't plan to marry her. And I never slept with her when I was with you. I'm not sure I even planned to ask her out after you and I broke up. She was just there." He looked down. "It was easy," he added softly. "I know how terrible that sounds. How young and stupid." Then finally he met her gaze again. "Then Will was there for you."

It was as if everything was suddenly fresh, the wounds new, the blood running bright red from her veins. "If you didn't mean to marry her, why did you?"

"Because I had to."

It was like a punch in the center of her chest, and she sat back heavily against the seat. "You had to? You mean she was *pregnant?*"

He closed his eyes briefly, then said, "Yes."

"But you were with her four years before that. You must have had some sort of plan."

His mouth lifted in a sad smile. "There was no plan." He shrugged and said again, "The relationship was just easy."

Easy sex, she thought. And realized that she had never been easy. She had wanted so much from him.

"I never said I was smart. In fact, I was an asshole. I was young and stupid and self-centered and selfish. I didn't know enough to see what a good thing I had with you. I didn't know enough about life, or anything else, for that matter."

She didn't disagree, even though she couldn't really blame him. They had wanted very different things. "But even back then you didn't have to marry her."

"It was the way I was raised. You take responsibility. We drove to Tahoe and did the quickie wedding thing."

"But wait." She gasped. "Wait, wait, wait. What happened?" She turned her head to look at him, her heart beating hard enough in her chest to actually feel it thumping against her ribs. "What about the big wedding? And you didn't have a baby until..." She trailed off, unable to wrap her mind around all these new facts.

He spread his hands. "She had a miscarriage a couple of weeks after we got married in Tahoe. I suppose we could have gotten a divorce then. But I had a good job, we were already married, and I guess I started thinking about the future. Like marriage and babies was going to happen anyway at some point. You were with Will, and..." He shrugged, as if he hadn't put all that much thought into it. And probably he hadn't all those years ago. "So we just stayed together. I thought it could work." He snorted out a sharp laugh. "Obviously *that* was wishful thinking. Since we hadn't told anyone about Tahoe, Elaine decided she wanted a big wedding. We pretended to everyone that Tahoe never happened. That the baby had never happened." A shadow crossed his face and it wasn't just a cloud outside the window.

"Why didn't you ever tell me?"

He snorted. That said it all. Why *would* he tell her?

"Did Will know?" She hated to think how much Will might have kept from her.

"I never told him. The two of you were together. I thought maybe you'd even get married eventually when he was done with medical school. After what I'd done to you, it seemed like my relationship with Elaine was my problem and no one else's. And Elaine didn't want anyone to know about the baby, at least not until she was showing." He shrugged. "It sounds bad saying it now, but she had a thing about me running to Will, or you, and telling our business." He shook his head. "Elaine always did like to control the narrative."

She'd always thought he and Will talked about guy stuff. She couldn't believe he'd gone through all that on his own. "And the divorce?" Now, because of Provence, because she'd started asking questions, she had to know everything.

He looked at his coffee, another sad half smile on his face. "She was having an affair."

It felt like another slap. Julia put her hand over her mouth.

"I don't know who she was sleeping with. I don't know how long it went on. I don't even know if it was the first time." He shrugged as if it didn't matter anymore.

"How did you know?" When Ryder grimaced, she quickly added, "Sorry, it's not my business."

He put his hand over hers, the first time he'd touched her since last night. "I'm an open book to you, Julia. Anything you want to know. I owe it to you." Then he told her. "I found another phone. The calls and texts were to only one number. The texts were all about sex, meet ups, hotel room numbers. Some of it was explicit." He avoided her eye when he said it. "But they never used names. I called the number, and no one answered."

"What did she say when you asked her about it?" She felt

like a voyeur peeping in the windows of his marriage. Maybe he hadn't even asked.

He shrugged, shook his head, gave a soft laugh. "She didn't deny it. We were too far gone by that time to even try to fix things. I just wanted out."

"I'm sorry." Julia didn't have any other words.

"Just so you know, I didn't tell Will about that either. You guys had your own stuff to worry about. He and I didn't really talk a lot about our lives. Or our marriages. Or our problems." He put his hands in the air. "So now you know the whole sordid story."

Julia felt as if she knew nothing. She'd always thought, at least until the divorce, that he'd led a charmed life. He'd gotten the woman he wanted, had two kids he adored. He'd made a lot of money, he was a CEO, for God's sake. She hadn't really questioned why they divorced. Will had mumbled something about growing apart. And consumed with Will's cancer, she never even asked for more information. She and Ryder had been friends, she'd leaned on him all during Will's illness, but she realized now that everything had been about her and Will, never about Ryder. Yes, she'd asked if he was doing okay, but she hadn't pushed when he said he was fine.

She hadn't been a good friend, while Ryder had been the best friend anyone could be.

Suddenly it didn't matter *why* he left her all those years ago. That was the past, their lives had diverged, and she had made a life with Will.

Now Will was gone.

As if he could read her thoughts on her face, Ryder said, "This doesn't have to end once we get home."

"What doesn't have to end?" She stalled, needing to think.

"Don't play games, Jules."

She closed her eyes, breathed in, smelling him, that subtle

aftershave, his male scent she'd come to crave. "I'm sorry, you're right. It's just that I don't know what to say. I mean—" She shrugged. "There's just way too much against us right now. Will's only been gone a couple of months."

"Three months," he said softly. Then he reached out, held her hand, tightened his fingers when she tried to pull away. "But we both know he's been gone for longer than that."

She put her hand to her chest as if he'd actually stabbed her. "I know," she whispered. "But I don't know how to let go."

"You already did, Julia. For this whole past week."

She couldn't look at him. "That was different."

"Why?"

"I don't know, Ryder." Her voice was harsh enough to hurt her throat. "It just is. It happened in Provence. It's not home."

"What happens in Provence stays in Provence?" A frigid note iced his voice.

"No." Except that it was exactly what she meant. "But home is where we have to live with it. And I don't want people thinking you and I were having sex before Will died."

"Making love," he said.

It stopped her cold. She could feel her heart beating against her ribs, her breath in her throat struggling to get in and out. "Is that what we were doing? Because I thought it was more like f—"

He put his hand over her mouth before she got the word out. "Don't say it, Jules."

She remembered the moment he'd done that on the train, the electricity between them. Now there was only an ache. "Don't call me Jules."

"I called you Jules before Will did."

"You called me baby." The pain in her chest surrounded

her heart, squeezed until she felt the tears at the backs of her eyes.

The silence was almost too long. Then he whispered, "Baby."

"Don't do this to me, Ryder," she said, each word succinct, sharp.

He did not let go of her hand. "And don't do this to *us*. We've found something amazing. Don't let it go."

"You were absolutely ready to let it go before." She knew that was cruel. Even as she said the words, she regretted them. But they were the truth. He'd failed in their relationship. He'd failed in his marriage.

She felt his withdrawal as he sat back in his seat, dropping her hand, his gaze turning bleak. "I've made a lot of mistakes, Jules. And I know I'll make many more. But the biggest mistake I *don't* want to make—" His voice came down hard on that one word. "—is to walk away from you a second time."

She was on the verge of apologizing, of taking back what she said. But it was honest. It was a fear she couldn't let go. And it wasn't the only thing that stood between them. "I don't want to be accused of cheating on Will."

"Neither do I. But most people will understand."

She jumped in because he had no clue what most people would think. "My sister won't. I'm not sure my parents will. And I'm pretty damn confident in saying that Will's parents won't."

"You're underestimating them. They know how bad things have been for you for ten years. They'll understand. They'll want you to find happiness."

They probably would. But not with Ryder. Not with Will's best friend. "What about my friends?"

"Do you really think your friends are going to believe you cheated on Will?"

She couldn't point to one person specifically, but that didn't mean she wasn't afraid of public scorn. Despite the cards and letters from friends, she had yet to reply. She'd told herself she needed to get to Provence, fulfill Will's last request, that she'd call everyone when she got home.

But now what would they all think if she came home from France and told them she was with Ryder?

Oh, she knew what *some* people would think.

She wasn't, however, going to win this argument. Ryder had an answer for everything. Except the most important thing. "What about Elaine? And your kids?"

"The kids will eventually understand."

"You're living in Neverland. Do you really think Elaine, after everything she's done to you, won't use this against you?"

It was a testament to his honesty that it took him so long to formulate a reply. "I believe Tonya will be fine. She asks about you every day when I call her." Then he shook his head, negating everything. "But Dustin, I'm not so sure. He won't take my calls. And Tonya says he's still upset because I'm here with you."

She put up her hands in a see-I-told-you-so gesture.

"I need to talk to him in person. I'll make him understand."

"Do you really want to lose your son over this?"

Gritting his teeth, he said, "If I lose my son, it will be because of Elaine. Not because of you and me."

She went after the only thing she truly could. "Elaine will make our lives a living hell. You know that."

It didn't faze him. "She's already made my life a living hell. I'm trying to turn that around."

"She's going to poison your kids against you. Is it really worth it? You could lose them forever." She was brutal. She was also honest.

"Elaine has wanted to take them away from me since the day I found that second cell phone and confronted her. She turned everything into my fault."

"But what about the affair?" She cocked her head, suddenly confused. "Don't they blame her for that?"

He blinked, swallowed hard. "My kids don't know."

"Really?" She stared at him, her mouth dropping open, the proverbial flies flitting in and out. She could almost taste them, acrid and bitter.

"I didn't want to put them in the middle of my fight with Elaine. I didn't want to use them that way. This was about Elaine and me, not about them. She's their mom. I didn't want them to be completely disillusioned the way I was."

She saw what his life was like. Taking his kids wrath for breaking up their household because he'd asked for the divorce. Of course they'd blame him if they didn't know the truth. She recognized the good and noble man he truly he was. He broke her heart all those years ago, but he'd never been the asshole he called himself. He'd never been a bad man.

Now he was so much more than the young man he'd been.

But could she put herself out there completely for him? She'd loved him once and lost everything. Then she'd loved Will and lost him, too. She couldn't put her heart on the line again. And the truth was that families could destroy a relationship. They could break you apart like tiny twigs under their feet. She'd been through too much; she didn't have the strength. She was weak, and she just couldn't do it. Not now.

"I'm so sorry for everything you've been through, Ryder. I'm sorry that your son won't talk to you. I'm sorry for the way Elaine treats you. But those are all the reasons nothing between us can work. We had our chance years ago and we lost it. It's not coming back."

"What about everything that's happened between us

here? Doesn't that count for anything?" He asked the question as if he were still fighting, but she heard the bleakness in his voice, sensed that he was on the edge of giving up.

"I'll remember it as the best week of my life. But if we don't stop it now, Ryder, it's going to turn into one big hot mess with our families and our friends. Then I won't even be able to remember this week without it being overshadowed by guilt. I know this from experience. I barely remember all the good times with Will before he got sick. Everything before his diagnosis is completely overshadowed by all the bad times. I don't want that to happen to my memories of Provence." Her memories of his touch, his kiss, his lovemaking.

He closed his eyes. Finally looking at her again with anguish darkening his gaze. "Please don't walk away from this, Jules."

She dropped her voice to a whisper, almost mouthing the words. "Please don't call me Jules."

RYDER'S MANTRA ON THE FLIGHT HOME WAS THIS: *I WON'T let this be over. It's not over. I won't let it be over.*

He called his kids at the airport just before they had to board their next flight in Paris. Dustin didn't answer.

Tonya had said only, "Have a nice flight, Dad." It was early back home, and her voice was sleepy, dreamy. "I'll see you soon."

He said, "I love you." But he was pretty sure she was already gone.

They were served dinner in first class, and this time they didn't share. Julia was right, his memories of the past week were already being overshadowed by the bleakness descending upon his soul.

He may very well have to pay the rest of his life for a mistake he'd made twenty-five years ago when he was a stupid, selfish, thoughtless kid. The only decent thing he'd gotten out of all the years since then were his kids. Now he wondered how close he was to losing Dustin.

Just the thought was like a vice twisting around his heart, squeezing until he thought he was having a heart attack. He had to say the words aloud, even if Julia didn't want to hear. "I can fix this thing with Dustin when I get home. I just have to talk to him."

Julia, always caring and compassionate, reached for his hand, holding on tight for a moment. "I know you will. He's a good kid. And kids understand a lot more than we think. You might never have told either of them what Elaine did, but you know your kids had to realize something was up with their mom."

"Maybe all Dustin ever saw was that I was consumed with work. That's what affected him the most." But he didn't want to lay all his problems on Julia's shoulders. He didn't want to try to bring her back to him by making her feel sorry for him. "I just have to talk to him," he said again. "He'll see that I love him. It'll all be fine. Now you should get some sleep."

"Maybe I shouldn't sleep. Then, by the time I get home, I'll almost be ready for bed, since it'll be past six at night."

She picked a movie, some sort of social commentary, which she quickly became engrossed in.

Ryder began to read. Even more, he began to plot.

No matter how much Julia said she didn't want a relationship with him, they'd found something special in Provence. If they could weather whatever storm that came, they would be so damn good for each other.

Maybe he should have told her he loved her. Because he did love her. Unquestionably. But he hadn't lusted after Will's wife for years. He'd appreciated the caring, loyal, stoic, selfless, loving woman that she was, but he'd separated himself from the feelings he'd had for her when they were young. And yet, she'd always been a specter, especially when things got bad with Elaine. Memories of Julia were hiding under their marriage bed, leaking out to give him a glimpse of what might have been. But Julia truly had nothing to do with his marriage. Not until his divorce and Will's health declined again. When they knew that his remission had been a blip on the radar before the ship sailed out of range. When Julia had needed his comfort on so many of Will's bad days.

Now he ached for everything they'd left behind in Provence. He'd already lost Will, and he couldn't lose her, too.

Which meant he needed to fix things with his kids. He needed to show Julia that her friends and family would be sympathetic.

He needed to find a way to prove to her they were meant to be together.

❧ 25 ❧

WILL

It's a horrible thing to live with fear day in and day out. It makes you do terrible things that hurt the ones you love. And I've done so many things I'm not proud of.

How different would our lives have been if I hadn't chosen the wrong path so many times?

I knew Elaine wasn't pregnant when they got married. I should have told Ryder.

You see, Elaine and I were friends. Not in any traditional sense, like bosom buddies or people who shared everything. We didn't even really like each other. But we had two things in common: Jules and Ryder. Everybody thought Elaine was a confident, self-assured, sexy bombshell. But underneath, she was as insecure as the rest of us, maybe even worse. And she was afraid Ryder would dump her to go back to Julia. Yeah, I was afraid, too. That was the bond Elaine and I shared.

In her fear, she liked to call me up for coffee. She wanted the latest on Jules. She wanted to make sure I knew what a precarious position we both were in. I always agreed to meet with her over coffee because I was scared down to my bones, too. Absolutely. Not just in the beginning, but forever, even after she and Ryder were married, even after Jules and I were.

Because Jules had never stopped loving Ryder. Even if she didn't admit it.

Of course Elaine didn't tell me about the baby until they'd already gotten hitched in Tahoe. At first she tried to get me to believe the lie that she was pregnant. Maybe she thought I could back her up with Ryder. But she didn't have a single symptom. No morning sickness, no fatigue, no food aversions, no headaches. And she certainly hadn't put on weight. She told Ryder that was because she felt so sick all the time. *Right.* When she tried to keep up that lie, I laughed at her. And I guaranteed that in just a few weeks she was going to have a mysterious miscarriage when Ryder wasn't around.

When she "lost" the baby just as I predicted and tried to tell me it was real and how awful she felt, I laughed at her again.

I didn't tell Ryder what I knew, or at least guessed. Even though I was his best friend and not Elaine's friend at all. I knew the fastest way to lose a friend was to tell him the truth about his wife. It's the age-old cliché about shooting the messenger.

In fact, we never talked much about his relationship with Elaine. Everything I knew all came from her. It was like that pretty much all our lives. We just didn't talk about Elaine or about Jules. Except one time, when I thought, hoped, prayed the cancer was gone. It was the only time I ever told him anything about Jules and me. I think I did it out of guilt. Remorse. Maybe even wishful thinking. As if I could change all the bad things I'd done by spinning a tale.

But the other reason I kept my mouth shut about Elaine and her lies was that Jules couldn't have Ryder if he was married to Elaine. Maybe that was the only reason, if I'm truly honest.

But here's the mitigating circumstance, at least for me. Ryder could have gotten out after the miscarriage, whether it was real or not. They could have gotten an annulment. But he stayed with Elaine, they planned that big wedding without even telling anyone they were already married or that Elaine had been *supposedly* pregnant. And I never told Jules, not about Elaine's fake pregnancy or that they'd gotten married in Tahoe. The only thing I could really do was stick by Ryder when he needed to talk. If he ever decided he wanted to talk. Which he didn't.

If it wasn't for Elaine, who *loved* to talk, I never would have known when things got rocky between them later on.

That was before she got pregnant with Dustin. She was afraid Ryder was going to leave her. She wanted me to feel afraid, too. She tried to convince me that if Ryder left her, then I'd lose Jules, too, that they'd get back together, that I didn't stand a chance. She said we had a joint project, that I needed to talk to Ryder, convince him not to leave her. When I told her we weren't the kind of besties who talked about relationship stuff, she was pissed.

Then next thing you know, Elaine is pregnant.

I thought it was another fake. But nope, this time it turned out to be the real thing. When I called her on it, she was the one who laughed. But I knew. She'd messed with her birth control to hold Ryder, and this time it had to be real. She figured she couldn't get away with a second miscarriage. But Elaine never flat out admitted the truth about anything. She'd just smile when I asked her a question or said I didn't believe her. And when she popped out the next baby lickety-split—Dustin and Tonya were not quite two years apart—she was solidifying her bond with Ryder. She never copped to using a second child once again as a way to hold onto him. She said she thought that breastfeeding stopped you from getting pregnant. But Elaine was too vain to breastfeed, especially not for more than a year. And she certainly didn't breastfeed Tonya.

If anyone knew about my strange relationship with Elaine, they would probably ask me why I never told Ryder any of this, why I didn't try to save him from her. The truth is that in the beginning I *did* tell him Elaine was bad news. Anyone could see that. But Ryder said it was just about good sex, that Elaine wasn't asking for anything else, that there was no attachment and they were only in it for fun. Later, when it was apparent she wanted to get her claws deep into him, it was too late for me to say anything. I was with Jules by then.

And I was afraid every step of the way after that.

But Ryder never stopped being my friend. I never stopped loving him for that.

What I know now is that the cancer was my punishment. My fear and lies and guilt coalesced into the disease. As if it were a malignancy formed straight out of the malignancy in my soul.

The worst was that once I got sick, I knew I was finally safe, that Jules would never leave me, that she was tied to me now.

Maybe that was my worst crime of all.

❧ 26 ❧

Ryder's campaign began the night after they returned from Provence.

Julia received a special delivery, the best champagne, a bouquet of lavender, lavender bath salts and candles, French chocolates. And mangoes.

She didn't need a card to know the package was from Ryder.

Lying in her bath that night, Julia was drowning in lavender and memories. She sipped the champagne and savored the chocolate and fruit. And remembered every detail of that first night when he'd seduced her with mangoes. She poured the bath salts and lit the candles and closed her eyes to relive the ways he'd touched her in the tub on their last night.

She steeped herself in the memories of every single moment she'd spent with him in Provence.

The following day, he emailed photos, her in the lavender field, on the scooter wearing her helmet, sitting on a bench gazing at a river, playing in the grass, staring up at the clouds.

All the memories rushed in like a flood. A flood of joy, a flood of loss.

Ryder knew what he was doing, forcing her to remember all the good parts and none of the bad.

Even putting Will's box, his letter along with Tonya and Dustin's inside, back on the mantel in the living room had served to remind her of everything she and Ryder had done in Provence. She'd waited for the guilt and yet it didn't come. At least not then.

She had coffee with her sister two days after her return, their same coffee shop, the same table, maybe even some of the same people sitting close by.

Felicity immediately jumped to the negative. "Mom and dad were really worried about you."

"I called them while I was over there. They didn't sound upset at all." Julia pushed the gift bag she'd put together across the table, trying to head off the storm. "A little something of Provence I thought you'd like."

Felicity took the bag, riffled through the tissue paper, though Julia wasn't sure it was long enough to even see the lavender sachets and candles. "Thanks. You shouldn't have." Then Felicity gave her a look, sharp and stern, as if she were not only the older sister, but the more reliable one. "I'm really worried about what people are saying, Julia."

"What are people saying, Felicity?" The only thing she could do was stare her sister down, force her to say what she *really* thought, that she wasn't worried about what people would think of Julia, but what people would think of Felicity by association.

"Just that it looks bad. Your husband's barely cold in the grave and you're off on a jaunt with his best friend."

Julia clenched her teeth, but when she spoke, she didn't raise her voice, didn't capture the attention of any other patrons in the sunny coffee shop. "First of all, Will doesn't have a grave. And it wasn't a *jaunt*," she said. "We went there to scatter his ashes. And everybody knows that was what Will wanted."

Felicity drummed her fingers on the table. "Everybody knows he wanted that. But nobody ever said Ryder had to go. It should have been his parents with you, his *family*."

Ryder had done more for Will than anyone. "Will designated Ryder." If she'd had Will's letter with her, she might have laid it in front of her sister, let her read Will's own words. But she didn't have to justify herself. "Will wanted me and Ryder to do it. Those were his express wishes."

Felicity's face was getting steamy, but she kept her voice well below the buzz of conversation around them. "I'm sure Will had no idea how people would look at this."

"What *people* specifically?" Julia insisted.

And Felicity hissed out, "Everybody. All our friends."

"All *your* friends? Or my friends?"

"They're the *same* friends." Felicity's eyes were steely.

"My friends aren't going to think that. All my *friends*," she enunciated the word sharply, "understand that everything I've done for the past ten years has been for Will."

"Oh, you're so sanctimonious, aren't you?" Felicity actually sneered.

Julia's coffee had gone cold, her mood had spiraled, and there was really no reason to stay. She answered anyway. "I'm not sanctimonious. I simply followed Will's instructions."

"But you slept with Ryder, didn't you?"

The question was a slap in the face. Julia hadn't imagined even Felicity would go that far. Instead of telling a lie, Julia went on the offensive. "What's wrong, Felicity? I don't understand why you're acting this way. Have I done something to make you angry? Is something going on at home that's putting you out of sorts?"

Felicity slapped her hand on the table, but when she saw

people glance their way, she leaned forward, her voice low. "That's just like you, to deflect this on to me. To put the blame on me."

"I'm not blaming you for anything, Felicity. I just don't understand why you even care about my trip to Provence." They had coffee once a month like it was an obligation, but they weren't close. Felicity had come to see Will only occasionally, and she hadn't brought her children at all, as if somehow his cancer were contagious. Just like Elaine, in fact.

"People are talking. If you can't understand how that affects the entire family—" Felicity raised an imperious and perfectly plucked eyebrow. "—then we don't have anything more to talk about."

Felicity made a move to stand up, but Julia reached out to touch her hand. "I must have done something to hurt you, Felicity, and I'm sorry for whatever it was. But this trip to Provence was something I *had* to do." She stressed the word, wanting her sister to understand that going to Provence hadn't been a choice but a duty. "And I'm sorry if you feel it reflects badly on you." She added the only thing left to say. "But I really don't see what it has to do with you at all. It's my business, not yours."

Standing fast, Felicity shot her chair back, catching it before it fell, drawing attention and the raised eyebrows of other people just the way she hated. "Until you understand how what you do affects other people, you and I don't have anything else to say. We need a time out." Then she turned on her Louboutin high heels and with flashes of red on her soles, marched out of the coffee shop.

She'd left her gift bag on the table.

For five seconds, Julia was the focal point of all the eyes at the tables around her, surreptitious glances, raised brows. But then the piped-in music took over, people turned back to their lattes and their conversations, chatter rising again to drown out the echo of Felicity's shoes.

Julia fished out her phone to call her mom. Her parents were really her only concern. Most of the couples Will and she used to know had drifted away when he got sick. Illness was hard to deal with, Julia understood that, especially when there were no more parties, no more trips to a show in San Francisco, no more outings. But Felicity acted as if they lived in a small town where everybody knew everyone else's business. This was Silicon Valley, for God's sake. She and Will had been tiny minnows in a vast ocean. Felicity's husband might be a prominent Silicon Valley plastic surgeon, but no one would even associate him with a sister-in-law he rarely saw.

Yet wasn't the issue of what other people would think one of the reasons she'd told Ryder they couldn't be together? And here she was castigating Felicity for worrying too much about what other people thought.

She wasn't reconsidering her decision. She *couldn't* reconsider. But she wasn't letting Felicity bully her either. Maybe it wasn't right to let anyone bully her into doing what they thought she should do. Or what they thought she *shouldn't* do.

Her mother answered on the third ring. "Hello, dear. How are you doing?" She was all solicitude.

Felicity had always been the one to tattle on her, not the other way around. And Julia wasn't about to tattle now. But she wanted to know that her parents were okay. "I'm fine. I just wanted to make sure you weren't hurt that I didn't ask you to go with me to Provence to scatter Will's ashes."

"Oh dear." Her mother sighed. "Don't give it another thought. The fact that you didn't ask actually made it easier. You know your dad doesn't want to travel abroad anymore. And you had to do what you had to do. I'm just glad that Will's best friend was there to keep you safe."

But what would her mother think of her relationship with

Ryder? The question wanted to leap off her tongue, but she squashed it before the words came out. This was her life. What she'd done in France with Ryder was her business. If—and that was a very big if—she ever decided to have more with Ryder, she wasn't going to ask her parents for permission. The only permission she needed was Will's.

She had a feeling he would give it without question.

The thought actually made her heart skip several beats. She didn't need anyone's permission but Will's? It gave her chills. It even gave her a thrill.

But it was impossible.

She had to push the point. "So it didn't worry you and Dad that Ryder went with me?"

"Whyever would it worry us?" Her mother puffed out a breath. "Felicity's been talking to you, hasn't she." It wasn't quite a question.

"She mentioned something."

"Well, I'm not one to tell tales, dear, you know that. But Felicity has her own issues. So don't you worry another minute about it."

She wondered what Felicity's issues were but didn't ask. It was enough to know her parents didn't feel the same way.

But that still didn't mean they'd approve of any relationship with Ryder.

She spent the next few minutes telling her mother all about her decision to become a hospice volunteer, how helpful hospice had been for her, and that she wanted to give back.

"That sounds like such a wonderful idea, dear. I do hope you have enough money to keep going if you don't have a job."

Her mother was aware of the trust that Will's grandfather had left him. And now the trust was hers. Julia wasn't worried. "I'm totally fine, Mom."

After a bit more chit-chat about the trip, they rang off.

Then Julia called her mother-in-law in case she needed to do damage control.

❀

RYDER HAD BEEN HOME TWO DAYS AND DUSTIN STILL wasn't taking his calls. The kids would be with him starting on the weekend. But the longer he waited, the further Dustin would pull away.

Leaving work right at five, he headed over to Elaine's, the house he had bought and paid for, the household he was still supporting until the kids were out of high school. He didn't allow himself one iota of bitterness, not even a moment of glee for the day both kids graduated and Elaine had to face that her gravy train was over. Okay, maybe a little glee.

He hadn't called Julia. But he'd set up a standing order of champagne, flowers, and chocolate to be sent to her every day. He was giving her time, but reminding her of all they'd shared.

He absolutely was not giving up.

Parking at the curb outside the house, he climbed the wide porch steps, ringing the bell beside the double doors. It was a two-story ranch style, even though a ranch style was usually only one level. Elaine had decided they needed more room so they'd added a second floor. At the time it had been much cheaper than moving to a larger home, and the neighborhood was good, though not the posh address Elaine coveted.

He half expected her to be watching out the front window and answering the door immediately, just so she could close it in his face.

But it was Tonya who opened up. Her long, dark hair, so much like her mother's, was pulled into a high ponytail. He liked to think that the light in her brown eyes was just like his, as was her smile. His daughter was such a wide-open person, and he adored that about her.

She threw herself into his arms. "Daddy." Excitement trilled through her voice.

Then she jumped back to gape at all the gift bags in his hands.

"You didn't think I'd forget, did you? I got you stuff that's all very French. And some things for Dustin, too."

Tonya's smile faded slightly, and she lowered her voice. "He's still mad you went away."

"I figured that. That's why I've come by to see him. And you, of course." He punctuated his words with a smile.

"Way cool." She practically dragged him over the threshold into the wide front hall flanked by the formal dining room on the left and the living room on the right. For the second story, they'd added a staircase, making a narrower hallway back to the kitchen and family room. They'd converted one of the downstairs bedrooms to an office for him and kept the master suite down there as well. The kids' rooms were now upstairs.

Elaine padded out of the kitchen.

Barefoot, she wore skinny jeans and a blowsy top. Her hair hung loose and her makeup was fresh, as if she were expecting a lover. He could smell meat cooking. Elaine was a decent mother in many ways, homecooked meals, carpool duty.

She jutted her shapely hip, propped her hand there. "What are you doing here?" she said with the usual snide tone she saved just for him.

"Daddy brought us presents from Provence," Tonya said brightly, as if she were trying to head off a fight before it began.

"Well, I can just bet there isn't a bag for me."

"Then you'd be wrong." He shifted all but one of the bags to his other hand. "Provence is famous for its lavender. I brought you some."

Actually, Julia had bought it, saying he couldn't walk into the house with presents only for the kids.

It would be a mistake, however, to even mention Julia's name.

Elaine snatched it out of his hand, looked inside, sniffed as if he'd handed her a bag of dog crap. "Lavender sachets," she drawled. "How special."

Ignoring Elaine's display, he gave several bags to Tonya who tried to bank her excitement. She pulled out a couple of scarves. "I love them, Dad. Scarves are totally in." She draped a scarf around her neck, knotted it expertly. "When school starts again, everyone will be so jealous that mine came all the way from France."

He'd also bought an assortment of lavender products, plus a pretty sweater Julia had helped him pick out. "Straight from the Paris fashion houses," he said, although he had no idea.

She squealed with delight. Elaine pursed her lips with boredom. Though there might have been a glimmer of envy in her eyes. It was a very nice sweater.

"I've got some things for Dustin, too."

"He doesn't want to talk to you," Elaine snapped.

But Tonya was already rushing up the stairs, calling as she went, "I'll get him."

"He's not going to want them," Elaine said with that same cutting drawl. "He doesn't want anything from you. He doesn't get why you had to go to France with that woman."

"He knows it was what Will wanted. In fact, Will even told both the kids that he wanted his ashes scattered there."

"Right. As if Will would try to explain anything to a couple of kids."

He didn't remind her that Will had doted on their children, that he'd even asked for their help in planning a trip to Provence for the anniversary. Dustin didn't have a problem then. The problem had come when Elaine discovered that Ryder was going, too.

Tonya bounded down the stairs like a typical teenager, sliding to a stop at the bottom.

Dustin was behind her, descending at a much slower, maybe even hesitant, pace.

Tonya grabbed the bags still remaining in Ryder's hand and shoved them at Dustin. "Dad brought us a bunch of cool stuff from France.

"Thanks," Dustin mumbled without even looking in the bags.

He didn't want to have this conversation in front of Elaine. "Why don't we go for a walk?" He included Tonya in the invitation.

"Dinner is almost ready." Arms crossed, Elaine drummed her fingers on her biceps.

"Can't Dad stay and eat with us?" Tonya asked, her face brimming with hope.

"No," Elaine snapped immediately. "There's not enough."

"All right, why don't Dustin and I talk in the living room for a minute until dinner is ready." He looked at his daughter, sending her silent plea. "I can come back after you've had dinner, and we'll all go for a walk."

Elaine sniffed like an annoyed diva. "I really don't think Dustin has anything to say to you until it's *your* weekend."

Ryder watched as Dustin shuffled his feet, looked as his mother, then at Ryder.

He recognized the malicious glint in Elaine's eyes as she said, "I'm not sure he wants to spend the next week with you either. Right, Dustin?" She tapped her fingers impatiently on her crossed arms.

She'd obviously been working on Dustin. Ryder tried to

counteract the venom. "I can't force you, son. But I missed you. And we haven't been able to talk a lot on the phone."

"Right." Elaine's annoying drawl was grinding down his very last nerve.

"Dustin's going to come." Tonya said. "I told him we're going to the Santa Cruz Beach Boardwalk. And he wants to go."

A drive to Santa Cruz was news to Ryder, but he could see his daughter's brilliant mind working the problem. She wanted everything to go back to normal. At least as normal as it had been after the divorce.

"Oh, so now you're bribing the kids." Elaine turned her glare on her son. "Fine, Dustin. You go. I think it will actually be good for you. Maybe your father can try to explain his incomprehensible actions." She looked at Ryder, her smile silky and cruel. "If there can possibly *be* an explanation."

He knew just how much crap she would fill the kids' heads with before Friday night. He'd have a week to undo the damage. If he could.

"So shall I come back after dinner for a walk?" he asked Tonya, with a glance at Dustin.

"No," Elaine said. "You have them next week. You need to be satisfied with that."

He waited a beat. Neither of the kids said anything. He accepted defeat, at least for the moment, and hugged Tonya. "I'll see you on the weekend."

Then he took a big leap and hugged his son. For just a moment he felt Dustin's arms start to go up. But in the next, the boy went rigid and stepped away.

Ryder didn't let a single emotion flicker on his face. "I'll call you guys tomorrow, like usual, see how you're doing."

Then he left.

He could only imagine the vitriol Elaine would continue to spread over dinner.

But he had next week to work on it. After two weeks in Provence, it would be difficult to squeeze in any more time off, but Ryder didn't care. He'd take a couple of extra days with the kids, maybe Monday, make it a long weekend.

Once he'd fixed things with them, he'd figure out how to fix everything with Julia.

❧ 27 ❧

The following afternoon, Julia made the drive to her in-laws up in Marin.

Verna had prepared coffee and scones.

"It's kind of you to come see us, dear," Verna said.

Julia waved a hand over the spread in the living room. "You're so sweet preparing all this."

"It was just a little bit of baking," Verna demurred, pouring the coffee out of the service that had been in her family for generations. Her gray hair was perfectly coiffed, her nails polished a pale pink, her lithe figure accented by a muted blue pantsuit.

The Bellermans lived in the same five-thousand-square-foot house in which they'd raised their three sons. The formal dining room sat twenty-four. Despite being in their seventies, the Bellermans still did a lot of entertaining, and Verna always used the best china. After the boys moved out, they'd converted the bedrooms into guest rooms, a home office, and a workout room. The off-white sofa Julia sat on was comfortable and pristine. She'd never been good with white, sometimes spilling out of sheer nervousness. Now she perched on the edge, figuring any spills could more easily be cleaned off the hardwood floor.

"Harold will be here in a moment. He's just freshening up after his workout."

"Wonderful. I brought pictures for you of the bridge and the stream where we scattered Will's ashes." She'd created an album of the best photos to show Will's parents.

Verna smiled softly, sadly. "We were out to visit Will the other day, and believe it or not, there were flowers growing everywhere, almost right up to the cliff edge. It was glorious."

"I'm sure it's absolutely beautiful, Verna." Julia ate a bite of her scone, putting her fingers to her lips as she chewed. "Goodness, Verna, these are delicious." Then she pushed the small bag she'd brought from Provence across the coffee table. "I brought you something that might go very well with these scones." Verna was a wonderful baker.

"Oh dear." Verna put a hand to her cheek. "You didn't have to."

"It's just a little something. To commemorate the trip."

"These look yummy." Verna pulled a jar of lavender honey and one of fig jam out of the bag.

Harold entered then, and Julia rose for a hug.

"You looked well rested and even a little suntanned." He sat on the sofa beside her and buttered a scone while Verna poured his coffee. His hair was a steel gray, and he didn't wear an ounce of flab on his well-worked-out frame.

"The weather was gorgeous," Julia told them both. "I'd expected much more rain, but we barely had our umbrellas out. We were outdoors so much of the time."

"Be sure to try the fig jam or the lavender honey," Verna told Harold, undoing the lids. "Julia brought them all the way from Provence."

"I see Ryder even fattened you up a bit," Harold remarked, Will's same twinkle in his eye.

"Harold dear, women do not like to be called fat."

He dipped a small spoon into the fig jam and slathered it on his scone. "You know I didn't mean it that way, sweetheart. But we both know that Julia lost weight over the years. So a little gain is healthy."

Verna changed the subject expertly. "I believe I'll try the lavender honey." She smiled at Julia. "It sounds so exotic and delicious."

Julia had tasted it in France. But somehow it was even better on Verna's scones.

When the treats were demolished, Verna wiped her fingers. "I'd just adore seeing the pictures now."

Julia opened the album. "I've got everything in order by day."

"So organized, dear."

Julia scrolled to the page with Will's bridge and started there. "We scattered Will's ashes right here at the base of the bridge. It was where he wanted to be."

"Oh, it's lovely. I couldn't have asked for a better resting place." Verna put her hand on the photo as if she could actually touch Will.

"The hydrangea bushes were in full bloom. It was an idyllic scene."

The photos reminded her of that first kiss with Ryder, and guilt nibbled at her stomach.

"Here's what I want to do, dear." Verna opened her iPad, turning it so Julia could see the array of photos.

"Oh, you're right, Verna, the flowers are gorgeous."

"I knew you'd think so. I'd like to frame some of the photos, the very best. Something from here." Verna tapped the photos of the Pacific Ocean view where they'd scattered Will's ashes along the cliff top. "And something from Provence. You pick out your best ones and send them to me.

I'll put them in one of those collage frames, one for you and one for us. I'm sure Will would love that."

Verna ran her finger over a particularly good photo of the bridge and the hydrangeas, her eyes going moist for a moment. The Bellermans had never been demonstrative people. At Will's memorial, Verna had dabbed surreptitiously at her eyes with a hankie, her only sign of grief. They had all become resigned to Will's death long before it happened.

"This one, absolutely." Verna tapped the picture. "I almost wish now that I'd gone with you."

"You know that's not what Will wanted," Harold said, his tone slightly imperious.

"Yes, you're right," Verna agreed. "It was supposed to be your anniversary trip, wasn't it, dear? He didn't want old fogies hanging around with you."

"You're not old fogies," Julia assured them. "Here, let's look at the rest of the photos." She showed them all the places that had been on Will's list.

She thought of the photos Ryder had emailed her, the ones he took of her in the lavender field and lying on the grass staring at the clouds. She hadn't added them to the album, unable to share them with anyone. They were her own personal memories.

"Here's the monastery with the lavender fields. That's where I got the honey."

When the last page of the album had been turned, Verna put her hand on Julia's arm. "This is a lovely tribute. Tell me, dear, were you able to enjoy yourself? Under the circumstances, I mean?"

The guilt wasn't just nibbling now, it was devouring her insides. "I promised Will that I wouldn't be maudlin. And honestly, the only day that was a bit difficult was at the bridge. It was that final goodbye. But the rest of the time,

Ryder and I were determined to enjoy everything just the way Will wanted."

They'd enjoyed each other. Thoroughly. What would Verna and Harold think? They'd be horrified.

"Dear, I'm going to say something very strange. You might even think it's inappropriate. But there might never be a better time."

Julia began to feel nauseous. As if they knew. Good God, she was suddenly *sure* they knew.

"And Harold agrees with me that we need to say this to you."

Harold nodded, but he left the talking to his wife.

"Will said he didn't want us to go on this trip." Verna paused. "He wanted it to be what he called an odyssey, for you." She patted Julia's knee. "And for Ryder."

Julia didn't know what to say. She didn't even know what that meant.

"Ryder's had such a bad time these past few years." Verna made a face, pursing her lips. "The divorce, the battles over the kids. But even so, he was wonderful with Will. A lot of people would have just walked away, but he was always there. And we're so grateful for that. He's family."

Julia finally managed words. "Will wrote a letter to Ryder. He told him all that."

"I'm so glad. But there's another thing." Verna sipped her coffee as if she needed a moment, then finally set her china cup on its saucer. "It was Will's greatest wish that the two people he cares so much about, the two people who were there for him in every way, that you both find happiness again."

Her queasiness was growing. Verna couldn't mean they should find happiness *together*. That was too much. "I'm as happy as I can be for now. We fulfilled Will's request, took this trip for him. And I know," Julia added, "Ryder will eventually find happiness, too."

Harold patted her knee. "That's not exactly what Will meant."

Verna took over again. "Dear, what we're trying to say is that Will wanted you to be together again. You and Ryder. That was why he wanted you to make this trip together. So you could finally air your differences from so long ago. Come to an understanding."

What was that feeling suddenly clogging her throat? Fear? Disbelief? Guilt? Joy? "You can't mean..." She couldn't finish. She even had trouble breathing.

"Will felt he'd been instrumental in keeping you apart all those years ago."

"That's not true." She wasn't even trying to defend Will. It simply wasn't the truth. "Will was the one who helped me put myself back together after—" She stopped. "You know Ryder and I were dating before, that we broke up. And Will was there for me when I needed him. He never came between us."

"Honestly, dear, Will didn't give us details."

Harold added, "We didn't need them. But he obviously felt some sort of responsibility," he continued to explain. "He was very clear that when he was gone, he wanted you to be there for each other."

Julia shook her head, her mind suddenly fuzzy, as if she'd drunk too much of the good champagne Ryder was still sending to her house. "I will be there for Ryder. And he'll be there for me. But I don't think we can do what you're asking."

"Well, if the feelings aren't there..." Verna shrugged, though looking at Julia with a keen gaze.

And Julia felt a new horror. "You know, there was nothing going on between Ryder and I before Will died. Ryder helped us a lot, but there was nothing like, well—" She stumbled over her words. "There was nothing."

Verna held up a hand, palm out. "Of course that's not what we meant at all, dear. Will never thought that." Then she put her hand to her chest. "*We* never thought that. It's only what Will hoped for you after he was gone. He didn't want you to go through the rest of your life alone. Not you. And not Ryder."

"I don't know what to say," she told them, her heart fluttering, almost giddy. And yet there was something so wrong about it. It couldn't be right to feel this hopeful. Will was gone. He'd had so many bad years. And now to hear that he'd actually urged his parents to give her permission to be with Ryder?

It was crazy. What would people say?

Should she even care what people said?

Maybe the only question was whether she wanted to be with Ryder.

But what about Elaine? What about his kids? What if they hated him for being with her?

There were so many questions and thoughts, it felt like her head might actually explode.

Suddenly she couldn't stay there anymore. "I better go. Thanks so much. It was so good seeing you." She was rushing, words flowing out of her. "I'll send you more pictures. Having them framed would be great. I'd love it, too. But I really need to go now."

"Oh dear, we've upset you." Verna stood, came around the coffee table, held out her hands. "You don't need to go. It was the wrong time, too soon. We should have waited."

Julia felt trapped. Verna on one side, Harold on the other, the only way out was to jump over the table.

She'd already done exactly what they'd said Will wanted. She'd slept with Ryder. They'd made love over and over and over in Provence, made beautiful, wonderful, amazing love. She'd felt everything she'd never felt with Will. It couldn't be right, no matter how much permission Will and his parents gave her. Felicity was right. Everybody would think they'd been sleeping together before Will died. Everyone would believe that while Will lay in his hospice-provided bed, she and Ryder were screwing in the guestroom.

She couldn't live with that.

Verna was speaking, her voice seeming to come from very far away. "It's okay, Julia. We're sorry. Please don't worry." They must have seen the panic in her face.

Finally, Verna stepped aside, letting her out.

Julia couldn't remember the words any of them said. She didn't even give them a goodbye hug. She just ran. Ran back to the place where Will had died. Maybe she needed to sell the house, get away from the reminders, start fresh.

She arrived home before five to find another delivery of champagne and chocolate and flowers from Ryder.

The sight made her heart want to claw its way out of her chest as if it weren't actually a part of her.

Her mind had whirled around the insane conversation the entire drive home from Marin. The craziness of Will actually telling his parents that she and Ryder should be together after twenty-five years.

Is that what Will *really* thought? That for twenty-five years he'd been second choice? What about their last ten years? Had he been thinking she and Ryder were waiting for him to die so they could be together? Had he lain in their bed wondering if, out in the living room, she and Ryder were...?

She wanted to crush the flowers, throw out the champagne, and grind the chocolate up in the garbage disposal.

All Ryder wanted to do was remind her about everything they'd done in Provence.

Obviously what happened in Provence *didn't* stay in Provence.

She grabbed the champagne, twisted off the little wire cage, and popped the goddamn cork. It smashed into the ceiling, barely missing a light fixture. Champagne sprayed in an arc across the floor. She went a little crazy and guzzled the foaming wine right out of the bottle. It was good. God, it was so good, it made her lightheaded, alien, as if she weren't in her own skin.

There were so many images in her head, Ryder at the bridge, Ryder leaning down to kiss her, Ryder in the tub with her, Ryder drinking champagne with her, Ryder feeding her bites of his beef or his salmon or his caramel flan, Ryder with windblown hair on the scooter. Ryder making love to her for hours.

So many images of Ryder. So many feelings, so much sensation.

And Will actually thought she should have it all? For keeps?

Without even filling a glass, she carried the champagne outside, threw herself into a deck chair, and put the bottle to her lips, drank deeply as the clouds scudded across the sky.

The clouds. She remembered the day they'd lain on the château's lawn and watched the clouds, picked out the shapes. They were supposed to do it every day. They were supposed to watch the sunset. Every day. To remind themselves of all the beauty in the world. To stop life's merry-go-round for a few minutes. To live in the moment. But they hadn't. She'd forgotten.

But she watched the clouds now.

There was a blooming rose above her. And wasn't that a chocolate truffle over there? And that cloud there looked like one of the perfect pastries they'd feasted on in Provence. She could taste the chocolate and the cheeses and the fresh baguettes. She could smell the lavender of Provence once again.

It was as if the champagne and the clouds released a barrier deep inside, and she remembered Will's letter as if his words were written inside her head, inside her heart. That she deserved to be happy. That she was a good person. Even if he hadn't put it specifically in the letter, after what his parents said, it was clear. He meant that she deserved to find happiness *with* Ryder. That she deserved to feel the way Ryder made her feel.

Ryder made her feel so wonderfully, perfectly, amazingly good. He made her feel beautiful. He made her appreciate her body again. He made her see herself as more than just a husk, as more than an older woman past her prime. He gave her the ability to stand in front of the mirror and like, no, *love* what she saw. A woman totally in her prime.

Could she listen to Will's parents, take their words to heart, the words they said came from Will?

Could she overcome her worries about what other people would think?

Could she deal with Ryder's family?

But none of those questions was the most important. Maybe all her doubts about what everyone else thought or what everyone else would do really came down to one thing: fear. Was she willing to risk her heart again with Ryder? Could she move past her fear of getting hurt again, of losing again?

"Is it really so impossible to find happiness?" she whispered aloud.

She didn't dump out the champagne or crush the flowers or grind up the chocolate. She sat for a while just picking cloud shapes out of the sky.

Then she returned to the kitchen, set the champagne on a tray, arranged the flowers in a vase, laid out the chocolates on a plate, and retrieved the good crystal from the china cabinet. She carried the tray to the master bedroom and placed it on the bathroom counter.

She ran the bath, poured in the lavender salts and lit the candles Ryder had bought for her in Provence, and climbed into the gloriously hot water, letting it soothe and relax every muscle.

And finally she texted Ryder.

❦ 28 ❦

Ryder stared at the text on his phone.

The front door is unlocked.

His insides tangled around each other, constricting his lungs until it was hard to breathe, squeezing his heart until his brain turned numb without enough blood to feed it.

Of course it was all in his head.

But she had texted him. She had typed something other than *Thank you* or *We shouldn't do that.*

He was still at the office, staying late to finish up so he could take a long weekend with the kids. Tyrone would cover for him. He'd thanked him profusely. Even after the Provence trip, he had plenty of vacation time built up. He didn't normally take vacations. CEOs were supposed to be at the beck and call of the stockholders and the Board of Directors.

It was time to make a change. The past few years, he'd spent so much of his free time with Will, taking the kids along with him, something he didn't feel guilty about. Dustin and Tonya had adored Will. They adored Julia. Now he would show them they would adore her as more than just their Aunt Julia.

Maybe she could go to the Santa Cruz Beach Boardwalk with them this weekend. It was Friday, the start of his week with the kids. He wasn't scheduled to pick them up for another couple of hours. Elaine liked to make things difficult, insisting they have dinner with her since she wouldn't see them for another week.

So when he finally left the office, there was time to kill.

Julia's door was unlocked just as she said it would be. He walked in the way he always had, then followed the scent of lavender down the long hallway. Past the den, the home office, the guestroom, into the master bedroom by the mirrored closet and built-in drawers that had once held Will's clothes, around the bed Julia had slept in with Will, past the old-fashioned vanity filled with perfume bottles and pots of creams and the makeup Julia rarely used. She was beautiful without it.

The bathroom door was ajar, the lavender-scented air steamy. He pushed it open, heard a splash in the water. A plate of chocolate lay on the wide lip of the bath, and on the tub's corner sat a glass of champagne.

On a tray on the countertop, she'd arranged his flowers, the bottle of champagne, and had poured another glass.

She waved a hand. "That's for you."

He entered, picked up the champagne, turned.

She was unashamedly naked in the steamy water, letting him look his fill. The fact that she didn't move and didn't cover up said everything.

"Have a seat," she directed, pointing at the closed toilet lid. Ryder sat. It felt like one of the most intimate things he'd ever done with a woman.

Leaning forward, her beautiful breasts rising above the water, she picked up her champagne flute.

She took his breath away, made him lose his voice. The tub was huge. He could have climbed in with her. But he wanted to watch.

Leaning over the edge, she clinked her glass with his. "I see you got my text." Then she settled back in the water.

He didn't know what to say. He didn't want to beg and scare her off. He wanted to dive on her and simply take.

Instead he said something completely innocuous. "You and Will never remodeled."

Julia sipped her champagne and smiled as if she understood that he was speechless for anything that mattered. "I love this old forties style. The tubs are absolutely enormous." She stretched out. "Look at this, I can barely get my feet on the other end." He looked until a halo seemed to form around her. "I bet you could stretch out, too," she said, the invitation in her words, in her eyes, in her smile.

But he didn't move to accept her offer. He took in her sleek lines and sweet curves, saying inane words instead of telling her how beautiful and perfect she was. "You and Will kept it in good shape, I guess it didn't need redoing."

"The house had only two owners before we bought it, and they both cared for it lovingly." She moved in the water like a mermaid, pulling her legs up, her knees barely above the water, then stretching straight out again. "In the kitchen, the previous owners added pull-out shelves in all the lower cabinets and put in that big pantry. So I didn't even need to remodel with the new style everyone has with those pullout drawers. And what we've got is solid, let me tell you."

He loved her voice. He loved her face. He loved her body. He loved her soul.

After another sip of champagne, she leaned forward once again to set it in the corner of the tub. "The water's starting to cool." She rose gracefully, water sluicing down her smooth, perfect skin, and held out her hand. "Could you pass me that towel?"

Then she turned and pulled the old-fashioned block out of the drain, her bottom sweet and inviting, still high and shapely.

He wanted his hands all over her.

Instead he handed her the towel.

She wrapped it around herself, then stepped out of the tub onto the mat, so close to him he could smell the lavender on her skin. She smiled down at him, turned, tugging the towel up around her shoulders, drying off. Unhurried, she grabbed her robe off a hook on the door, pulled it on, covering her gorgeous body. Then she handed him the towel. "Could you hang that for me, please?"

It was as if they had always been together. As if this were a normal evening ritual.

She held out her hand, and Ryder took it, letting her lead him back into the bedroom. "Let's lie down on the bed and talk for a bit."

He was mesmerized by her voice, by her words, by her. And he lay on the other side of the bed, propping himself on his elbow, his head on his hand, while she rolled to her side facing him, shoving pillows beneath her head.

He didn't want to think about the fact that this was the bed she'd shared with Will.

He concentrated on her. She was nothing like the woman on the plane, denying everything they'd shared, saying it could never happen again, that it was all over.

"What happened?" he asked.

She reached out, trailed a finger down his arm. Even through the material of his dress shirt, her touch was hot, made him burn.

She knew exactly what he was asking. "I want to see Verna and Harold."

The thought stopped his heart. Will's parents were the last people who would approve.

Yet Julia was different after visiting them.

"What did they say?" he asked softly.

"I didn't tell them about us. About what we did in Provence. I didn't have it in me to say that."

He nodded, let her go on.

"They had lovely pictures of the flowers growing on the cliff over the ocean where they scattered Will's ashes. Verna's going to put them in a collage photo frame along with pictures from the bridge in Provence. They want me to pick out some of the nicest ones. I thought maybe we could look through the ones you took, too, and see if there's something even better than what I've got."

He felt as if he were going crazy, talking about photos of Will's final resting places or whatever the hell you called it when you divided someone's ashes and scattered them on two different continents.

What about the two of them? What about Will? What about the future?

Waiting was killing him, but Julia had to get there in her roundabout, mesmerizing way.

"They talked about Will." She waited a beat, forcing his heart to rise into his throat. "And they talked about you, Ryder. How much Will loved you. How much you did for Will. And how grateful they are for that. How grateful Will was." She put her hand on his for a moment. "I'm grateful, too."

He blinked, couldn't speak.

He wanted to scream, *Just tell me*.

Instead she lay down next to him in her fluffy robe, her feet bare, damp tendrils of hair stuck to her throat. More beautiful than any woman he'd ever seen.

"And they talked about a few things Will told them. They

said he wanted me to be happy after he was gone. Will wanted you to be happy, too." She reached out once again, curled her fingers through his. "Will wanted us to be happy together." She squeezed. "And I want us to be happy together, Ryder."

He felt an inexplicable rage take him over. "So suddenly it's okay because *Will* gave us his permission? Because his parents are also approving our relationship?"

In spite of the tension hardening his face and all his muscles, she smiled and said very gently, "No. I don't need Will's permission. Or his parents'. Something else made me want to change."

"What?" The word rasped in his throat, harsh and hard. Though he couldn't articulate what made him so angry. Was it because someone else had to make it okay for her to be with him? That she couldn't choose him on her own?

"I thought about what you said. About regrets. I don't want any more regrets."

He held his breath.

"And I'm also afraid," she whispered, and the words broke his heart. "But I don't want to let fear rule my life anymore."

"What are you afraid of?" He kept his voice as low and soft as hers.

"I'm afraid of getting hurt again."

His anger seemed to drain away as quickly as it had come over him. "I'm not going to hurt you this time. I swear it." But he felt the heavy ache of what he'd done to her before.

She laid two fingers against his lips. "I know. And I have to trust that everything is different now."

He wanted to haul her into his arms, hold her tight. But that moment wasn't here yet. "Trust me." He knew how much he was asking. He knew how he'd wronged her. "I'm so sorry for what I did."

She shook her head. "I know that, too.

"Can you forgive me?"

"I could never have made love with you in Provence if I didn't."

Yes. They'd made love. It wasn't just sex.

"That's what made me realize, too, that if I walked away from you, yes, it would be because I was afraid that people would say hurtful things, that my friends would wonder what you and I had been doing behind Will's back." She put a hand to her chest. "*I* was the one letting other people come between us. But even more, I've let fear come between us. I've been afraid of getting hurt. First you left me, then Will left me. And it's scary to think about having your heart crushed again."

He ached for what he'd done. But she'd also lost Will in the worst way possible, ten long years of losing him. She had a right to her fears. "I know. I understand how hard it is."

"But I'm tired of being afraid. So tired." Her sigh was long and weary. "I don't need Will's permission. He's gone now. I just need my own permission. And yours. That's all we need, just you and me to say this is what we want." She stroked her fingers lightly across his cheek.

He thought about his kids. He wondered if he needed their permission. Maybe all he needed was to tell them how happy being with Julia made him. Could that possibly be enough? It *should* be enough.

"Dustin's angry," he said softly. "But I think it's all coming from Elaine, the things she says."

"I don't like to see him upset." She shook her head. "But I believe he'll get over it."

He couldn't help bringing up her own words. "You said families can ruin everything."

She touched his cheek once more. "Only if we let them. It will only ruin us if we start to fight about them. That's something else I realized, too. Felicity was so angry that I went

257

away with you. But really it's all about what she thinks people will say about *her*. When she understands that nobody's going to say anything about her, she'll get over it. Maybe that's true for Dustin. We just have to understand what he needs. We can figure that out, can't we? Together?"

He closed his eyes, breathing in deeply. "I'm not sure how easy that will be. And Elaine won't be easy at all. She'll work on him. She'll work on Tonya." He looked at her again, his heart filling up his gaze. "But I'm not giving you up because of it. I'll make it right with Dustin no matter what she does." He made it sound so doable, but it wouldn't be just a few snappy words and explanations and heart-to-heart talks. It would take everything in him to break through.

But he would. Because he wasn't giving up Julia again.

He said the only thing that really mattered. "I love you, Julia. I always have."

She rolled into his arms, saying the words he'd waited to hear for twenty-five years. "I love you, too." Hugging him tight, she whispered, "I never stopped loving you, Ryder." She pulled back to look at him. "I thought it was a betrayal of Will to even think that. But I believe now that he understands." She put her hands on his face. "I loved Will with all my heart." Then she lowered her voice. "But I'm not sure I was *in* love with him. Not the way I felt about you. But I was never a bad wife."

He didn't want to feel that little burst of triumph. It was unworthy, and he squashed it. "You were the best, Julia. No one could ever have taken care of him as well as you did."

She smiled softly. "I did my best. And I think that's why I can love you now. That's all in the past. And we hold the future."

Ryder held her tight. And reveled in his future with her.

❦ 29 ❧

They lay there together without making love, without even kissing, just holding hands, fingers entwined. Their words were like vows, as if they'd made the ultimate commitment to each other.

Julia had never felt more content. When she was younger, there was always a job to be done or a project to finish or the burning desire to have a child or buying a house or just daily living. Something always stood in the way of complete contentment. She didn't blame Will for that. People were responsible for their own happiness.

Then there'd been Will's illness. When contentment stopped being part of their lexicon.

But now, with Ryder, she could allow herself contentment, even happiness. She'd revealed everything, all her guilts, all her fears, all her desires. This moment was close to the bliss of making love, almost a physical feeling, relaxing her bones, her muscles, her mind.

"You're so beautiful," she said.

"You're beautiful."

"Your hand is so big and warm and safe."

"Your hand is so delicate and smooth and sweet."

"It's sort of like being on drugs, this feeling."

He smiled, that Ryder smile that reached deep down inside her, touched her, surrounded her.

She could lay like this forever.

She would have, too, if there hadn't been a subtle flicker of something on the periphery of her vision. It drew her to the closets and built-in bureau lining the short entry hall to the bedroom.

And there she saw Elaine reflected in the mirrored doors.

She lay for just a moment, trying to comprehend, wondering if it were a vision, a warning, a nightmare. It didn't make sense. *Couldn't* make sense.

Then her frozen limbs finally moved, and Julia scrambled off the bed, clutching her robe around her. Not from guilt, but from absolute terror.

Because it *was* Elaine.

Ryder rolled over on the bed to see what made her jump. Then he rose to his feet, slowly, menacingly. "What the hell you doing here, Elaine?"

"I followed you. And I waited long enough for you to assume a compromising position." Elaine smiled maliciously. "You were gracious enough to leave the door unlocked."

"So you just walked right into someone else's house?" He spread his hands in disgust.

"You did." Her smile was so smug, so knowing, so cruel. "It was like an invitation. If you didn't want me in here, you should have locked the door." She sounded calm, reasonable. But as she strolled into the room, running her fingers along the mirrored door, then a drawer, Julia could see the fire in her eyes.

Elaine was beautiful. She had always been beautiful, and she was beautiful now. She was one of those women who aged gracefully, never looking her actual number of years. Her figure was voluptuous but not fat, her skin wrinkle-free, her lips full, her hair thick and lustrous.

"You need to leave," she told Elaine, without the quaver in her voice that she felt in her belly.

"I'll leave when I'm ready." Elaine's tone was snide, her lips curled in the slightest of snarls.

"You can leave *now*," Ryder said.

"And what are you going to do, darling, pick me up and throw me out?" Her smile was rabid. "That's not going to play very well when I take you to court for manhandling me. The judge will be sure to give me the children."

"Don't threaten me, Elaine." But he didn't advance on her, didn't pick her up or throw her out. "Take me to court. I'll tell the judge you're stalking me."

She put a hand to her chest. "Me? Stalking?" she said innocently. "Why, I just happened to be driving by when I saw your car sitting in *her*—" She pointed with a crimson-tipped nail. "—driveway."

Elaine would lie to the judge. It would be the typical *he said, she said*.

"And I'd have to point out that you don't have a single reason to be driving by." Ryder was just as capable of a nasty, derisive tone as Elaine was.

"I knocked, of course." She cast a flaming glare in Julia's direction. "No one answered. I was worried. I had to come in to make sure you were both okay. But you two were so engrossed in each other, you failed to hear my knock." Then she turned fully to Julia. "So how long have you been fucking my husband?"

The words slapped Julia back two steps. "I haven't—"

"Don't bother to lie. I can see it written all over you." Elaine flourished her hand, from the damp tendrils of Julia's hair to her robe to her bare feet to the imprint of their bodies on the bed.

Ryder stepped between them "Shut up, Elaine. I already answered your questions. And you already know there was nothing going on between Julia and I while Will was alive. You want to make something of it, go ahead. But it's not going to get you the kids. And you're not grinding more money out of me either."

Julia was sure it was all about the money. And Elaine's envy. But that didn't stop the roiling in her belly; it only made it worse.

"I have pictures of your car in her driveway over and over and over." Elaine's smile was reptilian.

He raised one brow. "So you have been stalking me."

She trilled out a nasty little laugh. "I just happen to be driving by on my way to do other things, like pick up your kids or take them to a game or go shopping for them."

In two strides, Ryder towered above her. "I haven't been here over and over and over," he imitated her. "And even if I had been, we're divorced. No matter what evidence you think you have, it doesn't matter. We've been divorced for four years. Your lawyer isn't going to take this to court. And even if he does, any judge would throw it out."

"Oh, they're not going to throw it out," she said, rearing up to go toe to toe with him.

Julia was afraid they might actually come to blows.

Elaine slammed him with her words. "Will told me every dirty detail of what he knew you two were doing."

The words shoved Julia back against the wall. "Will never told you anything." But even to herself, her voice sounded weak.

Elaine drove a dagger through her heart. "Will told me *everything*." Droplets of spit flew off her lips.

Ryder sneered at his ex-wife. "That's total bullshit."

"Is it?" Elaine's smile was pure evil. "Who do you think all the texts were from on that phone you found?"

It was like the moments after an earthquake, when everything settles, and there's utter and complete silence as you wait for an even bigger shockwave.

And it came. "We were seeing each other for months while he was in remission." Elaine smiled.

Julia wanted to throw up all over the bed she'd slept in with Will.

Ryder had found that phone. With sexting. And hotel room numbers. Clandestine meetings.

The words simply burst out of Julia. "That couldn't have been Will. It wouldn't have been Will. Never."

Elaine left a stunned Ryder and marched on Julia. "Poor Julia." She widened her eyes, cocked her head, and made a sad round O of her mouth, her voice soft and sorrowful and innocent. "Don't you remember all those times he went MIA, telling you he had to get out of the house or go crazy?"

It was exactly what Will used to say. *I have to get out of here, Julia, or I'll go crazy.* It couldn't be true, none of it could be true.

"You're lying, Elaine." Ryder had found his voice, and it was as strong as ever. But two minutes too late.

Elaine had the upper hand. "He would have left you," she said, and Julia felt a drop of spittle land on her cheek. "But then he got sick again. And he needed you to nurse him. I certainly wasn't going to do it."

No, no, no. But she thought about all the times Will had left the house in those months when he felt normal again, healthy, human. She thought about the two times they'd tried to make love, and it hadn't worked. She thought about the hours he was gone when she believed he was trying to figure out what to do with the rest of his life. He was so distracted, turned off to her, not just sexually, but in every way.

Those months should have been a renewal of their love,

their marriage, their relationship. But that never happened. Instead Will's cancer came back.

And all those times he was gone, he'd been with Elaine.

"I don't believe you." She made her voice as strong as Ryder's even as she felt weaker than Will in the last few weeks of his life.

"Think about it." Elaine's voice was a knife edge that sliced Julia's insides. "You'll see how it fits perfectly."

Ryder grabbed her shoulder, pulled her away, but Elaine shrugged him off. "Don't you dare touch me. I will report you."

"You've done your dirty work." His voice held the low growl of warning. "Now just get out."

But Elaine wasn't done with Julia. "Just think, while you and Ryder were being so honorable, loving from afar, never saying it aloud, but wishing, wishing, wishing." She giggled, a hard, harsh sound. "Will was with me."

Ryder laughed cruelly. "I thought you said we were screwing all the time. That Will knew and told you all about it. Changing your story now?"

She waved him off as if he were a gnat. "That was later. During this honorable time when you knew you had to stay apart—" She was like a romance narrator, overdoing it. "—all the while Will and I were meeting every day and fucking our brains out."

Julia didn't have any words to fight her. She didn't even deny it. She wasn't sure she could.

Ryder did it for her. "You've always been a liar, Elaine."

But Elaine turned every vicious cell she possessed on Julia. "He told me everything, about how he couldn't make love to you after he got well again."

Each word hammered into Julia's soul.

"Just shut the fuck up, Elaine, and get out." Ryder's words

were useless. The only way to stop Elaine was to put his hands on her.

Ryder would never do that.

Instead he held out his hand to Julia. "If she's not leaving, we will."

But Julia couldn't take his hand. She had to hear the rest. And Elaine knew it.

Her expression was superior, victorious, lighting up her face. "He told me how you moped around the house, like you didn't have anything to do anymore now that you couldn't play the martyr by taking care of him. You were driving him crazy."

"Julia," Ryder said, his voice low and harsh and broken. "Come on."

"You were so pathetic. 'I don't know what to do with the rest of my life, Will.'" She imitated Julia so well. "He was sick of it. He just wanted you to get on with it. Get out. Do something, anything, just so he didn't have to be responsible for you anymore."

She hadn't been moping. She'd been recovering from the previous five years. But she had said those words, so many times. And if Elaine knew...

Julia couldn't even think it.

Then Elaine said the thing that crushed the rest of her world. "And I didn't even have to blow him first the way you did, Julia. He was ready the moment he saw me. And he wanted it bad. He never had trouble finishing with me. Not like he did with you."

Elaine never saw the punch coming.

Not until Ryder's fist smacked into his palm only inches from her face.

She shrieked and jumped back, holding her cheek as if he'd actually hit her. "What the?"

"The next time it will be your face. Get out. And take all your lies with you."

For just a moment, Elaine stood there, as if she were stunned.

Then her face melted into the cast of the evil queen in *Sleeping Beauty*, her mouth curved in a beautiful crimson smile as if her lips were slashed with blood. She looked at Julia, sighed contentedly "I'll leave now. My job here is done." Then she dramatically wiped her hands clean, turned on her heel, and marched out of the house.

She didn't even slam the front door.

In the deep, deep quiet, Julia heard her car start, roll out of the drive, and fade into the distance.

She hiked up her robe, ran down the hall, flying to the door and throwing the lock. Tugging the handle to make sure it wouldn't open. Then she raced to the back door, checked it, too, found it locked, thank God. She thought about checking all the windows and all the French doors, but she hadn't been out to the backyard in ages. Everything would be locked up tight.

Elaine couldn't get in.

But she'd already done the damage.

THERE WAS A HYSTERICAL EDGE TO JULIA'S RACE FROM ONE end of the house to the other, locking, checking.

The only good thing was that she'd locked Elaine out. And locked him in.

But he'd lost Julia again anyway.

He grabbed her by the shoulders, made her look at him. "She was lying, Julia. About everything. That's what she does."

"She knew things." Julia shook her head. "She *knows* those things." Her voice was deep, panicked.

"She was just making guesses. Educated guesses. It's probably not far off to say things might have been difficult during that time for both of you."

"She used my exact words. That's what I said to Will, that I didn't know what to do with my life."

He shrugged, but he felt a queasiness in his gut. During that remission, Will had talked about the amazing sex he was having. But it hadn't been with Julia. She'd said that much. He was sick even thinking about it.

But Julia was his now and he couldn't let Elaine—or even Will—take her away. "So Will might have said something to her at one time or another. An offhand comment. She was lying about the rest. Will would never do that to you."

But he didn't have answers that would satisfy either of them. He knew only one thing to be true. "She wants to ruin us in any way she can."

"And she will, Ryder. You know that. I know that."

He wanted to shake her. "We can't let her lies change things for us."

"I thought it could work." She shook her head. "But I don't think it can."

They'd been so close, so very close

Then Elaine had ruined it all again.

She didn't say anything, stared hard at his chest, and he knew deep in his gut, his heart, his soul that he was going to lose.

"It changes everything," she said softly.

"All right, say it's true, even though I know she's lying, what if it's true?" He held her tight, afraid she might walk away from him. But Julia just stood in the circle of his arms, not moving, not touching him. "What difference does it make to us now? To our relationship? I love you. You love me.

267

Whatever happened, that's all in the past. It doesn't have anything to do with now."

She lifted her face, looked at him, her eyes hollow and lifeless. "I don't care what people think of us. What they say about us. Their judgments can't hurt us."

"Then what's the problem?" Besides the ache in her heart that Will might have betrayed her.

"The problem is that Elaine will never let it go. She will make up lies and mix them with the truth and we'll never know what's real and what's not. She will never let me have you. She will take your kids. She will wreck every good thing."

The queasiness in his stomach turned to true nausea. Because Julia was right. "I'll make her go away. She just wants more money out of me. She's worrying about when the kids graduate from high school and her cash flow dries up. She's using the kids as hostages. But I can fix that." He quaked with the desperation to convince her.

Julia rose up on her toes, wound her arms around him, held him tight. Then she whispered in his ear, "It doesn't matter how much you pay her. Because she will poison Tonya and Dustin against you." She pulled away, standing in front of him. "If she's capable of sleeping with Will, then she's more than capable of alienating your kids. She's already started with Dustin."

Truth. Elaine wanted money. But she wanted to punish him, too. "*If* she slept with Will," he said with harsh emphasis. "Don't you wonder why she waited until after Will was gone before she told you? Because she knew Will would have denied it. We can't let her lies destroy us, Julia. Please." He wanted to beg.

"It doesn't matter." She put her hand to her chest. "It hurts here, deep inside, because if Will did it, he had reasons."

He wanted to shake her. "He couldn't possibly have had any reason."

She shook her head, slowly, sadly, staring at his chest. "He always knew he was the second choice. He always knew you were first, Ryder."

He stepped away then, leaned down, hands on his knees, breathing hard, not wanting her to see the guilt swimming in his eyes. "We were so close, Julia." He held up his thumb and forefinger a quarter inch apart. She'd almost been his again. Then he stood up straight. "I can't deny that I wanted you. But I never, not once, let Will know that. I would never hurt him that way." He could only *pray* he'd never hurt Will that way. But had he?

"But I hurt him that way. Because he always knew." She blinked, then she actually smiled. "But I can forgive myself for that. Because I stood by him all those years. I took care of him. I never left him. I believed in him. So I can forgive myself. And Will forgave me, too, in the end. Even if he did what she said, I know he forgave me in the end."

Ryder cupped her face in his palms. "There was nothing to forgive. You never did anything wrong."

She stepped back, forcing him to drop his hands. "That doesn't change anything now. It doesn't change what Elaine is going to do. You need to think of yourself and the kids first. Make it right with them. Maybe later, someday, there's a chance for us. But I'm not going to be the reason you lose your kids."

"I won't lose them," he said.

"You need to leave, Ryder. It's what we both have to do." She turned her back on him and walked down the hall to the bedroom. The room she'd shared with Will.

She closed the door.

He heard the lock click.

And he knew he'd lost her.

MAYBE HE SHOULD HAVE STAYED. BEATEN THE DOOR DOWN. Tried to talk to her. To convince her.

None of it would have worked.

Goddamn Elaine. She was spiteful, vicious, cruel. She was evil. And she would have fucked Will just to hurt Ryder. Because she knew he didn't love her anymore.

Ryder drove aimlessly at first. He could have gone to pick up the kids, since obviously Elaine wasn't fixing dinner for them.

His lying, scheming ex-wife. She had to ruin everything around her. She had to spew her vitriol, her lies. How could she besmirch Will's memory that way? Will would never ever do that. Not to Julia. Not with Elaine.

He pulled to the curb on a tree-lined residential street he couldn't identify and pounded the steering wheel until his fist ached.

She was lying. She'd always told lies. Because Will would never...

Not to Julia. Never.

But what about the sex? All that great sex he was having because he was suddenly miraculously cancer free?

It hadn't been with Julia. Maybe Will made all that up, maybe he'd wanted Ryder to think he was doing great. Maybe he was trying to hide his terror that the cancer would come back.

Bile rose in his throat. A kid rode by on his bike, gave him the stink eye as if he were some dirty old man hanging out on a street corner. He started driving again, turning right, right again, then left, aimless wandering, voices in his head. Julia telling him that she had to take Will in her mouth to get him going. Elaine putting it so much more succinctly.

How could Elaine have known about that?

Unless Will told her.

But why would he tell her?

Unless...

It was unthinkable, unbearable, unbelievable.

But Julia believed it.

"How could you do that, Will?" he whispered aloud, and slammed on his brakes before he blew through a stop sign. At the next turn, he pulled into a parking lot, found a spot, shut off the engine.

He didn't look at his watch, didn't wonder if he was late.

What the hell? Could Will really have done that to Julia? He was cancer-free. At least he thought he was. He should have been working on his marriage, paying attention to Julia after the years she'd sacrificed for him.

"You lied to me." He had to say the words aloud, as if Will could hear. "You screwed over your wife. How could you do that, buddy? How could you treat Julia like that?" He leaned forward, looked out the windshield up at the sky, the sun going down, the stars starting to come out. If Will was up there, he could hear. "What the fuck, Will? Just what the fuck?"

He could have pounded the steering wheel again, but instead he collapsed against it.

Will had betrayed Julia. He'd betrayed them all. "Did you, Will, did you really?"

And as if Will was inside his head, as if he were whispering his guilt, Ryder finally knew that it was true.

Elaine's lover had been Will. All those text messages he saw on that phone were from Will. The sex stuff. The stuff that made him sick. Will had done that.

His gut raged. "How could you hurt Julia that way?"

But he knew how. Elaine. She'd manipulated Will. She'd taken a cancer survivor and used him to crush Julia. Will hadn't been in his right mind. He was crazy with relief and scared as hell the cancer would come back and Elaine had used him. Because Will had always believed he was the second choice.

Maybe he was getting back at Ryder himself.

His head and his heart felt like they were squeezed in a vice.

He couldn't think about it another moment.

What he needed right now were his kids.

❧ 30 ❧

WILL

It was the worst thing I've ever done.

I never ever want Julia to know.

I didn't just betray my wife, I betrayed my best friend. I betrayed his kids. I don't have any excuses. I'm not even sure I have any reasons. I could say it just happened. Because it did. I'd always been Elaine's sounding board, and she'd always been mine.

I thought I had a new lease on life. I thought I was free. And yet, inside, the fear lurked that the monster would come back. It could be hiding out there, waiting for me just around the corner.

Julia wanted to make love, even make a baby. It was so much pressure. And I couldn't, I just couldn't.

I should never have called Elaine, should never have asked her to meet me at that damned coffee shop. But even more, I shouldn't have told her what happened in our bedroom.

But I did tell her. She knew everything.

God help me, I wanted to feel like a man. I needed it. I had been sexless for so long. All my life. Sometimes I wondered if I'd ever been a man. I'd never been good in the bedroom. I never wanted it the way some men did. Yet, for the first time in my life, I found I needed it. Badly.

I hated myself. But it didn't stop me.

It was crazy. We got those phones, and I sent her dirty texts. I didn't even know who this person was sending those texts. And yet, God forgive me, it made me feel manly. Virile. When we were together, we went at it like animals. It was the most thrilling, debilitating, terrifying time of my life.

I've never felt so alive.

I told myself Elaine would get tired of it, that things would return to normal, and I could get back to my real life with Julia. I went back for my three-month check and things were great. And I couldn't stop with Elaine.

She wasn't ready to let me stop.

It was a game to her. Something she was doing to Ryder. And even worse, a way to get back at Julia. When she talked about us leaving them and being together, she only wanted to hurt them. It was never about me.

During our pillow talk, she told me things. She finally admitted she'd never been pregnant when she got Ryder to marry her. And she'd gotten pregnant with Dustin when it seemed like Ryder was thinking about divorce. I'd always suspected, of course, been ninety-nine percent sure, in fact, but Elaine confirmed it.

They were crazy times, I must have been out of my mind. And maybe Elaine was, too.

Then I had my six-month check.

And it all fell apart.

The thing that terrified me and kept me awake at night, kept me returning to those sleezy motels with Elaine, it finally happened. The markers were bad, just like I'd feared.

The cancer got me again.

In the deepest, darkest recesses of my mind, I believed it was because of the things I'd done with Elaine.

CHAPTER 30

Then I committed the next great sin of my marriage. I told Elaine the cancer was back before I ever told Julia.

The next thing I know, Ryder found her phone. Our secret phone.

She called me, cruel and vengeful. She was done with me, the jig was up about our affair, and now it was time to make Ryder and Julia suffer.

I think she would have told Ryder, except that I had her secrets to hold over her now. I knew all the lies she'd told to keep Ryder.

I told her I wouldn't keep her secrets. If she revealed mine, I'd spill all of hers. It scared the crap out of her. She didn't know what Ryder would do. I told her she'd get nothing in any divorce settlement because I would testify on Ryder's behalf. I would tell him everything I knew. She'd tricked him the first time, and she tricked him again when he was planning to leave her, letting herself get pregnant for real that time.

Yet I'm not really sure Elaine would have told our secret anyway. At least not during the divorce. In that first moment of anger, she'd wanted to inflict maximum damage. When she came to her senses, she realized she'd never get the kids and she might not get a dime out of Ryder. Really, what judge would award anything to a woman who'd slept with her husband's dying best friend?

So she never told. And I never told. Julia was safe from the worst thing I'd ever done.

But I wonder what Elaine will do once I'm gone.

I don't trust her.

But I have no way of stopping her.

Julia lay on the bed, curled in a fetal ball long after
Ryder left.

Turning him out had broken something inside her.
But she had to be strong for the both of them. She
absolutely could not allow Elaine to destroy his relationship
with his kids. And that's what Elaine would do in order to
make sure Julia never had Ryder.

She knew it just as she knew that Elaine hadn't lied about
Will, about the affair. Will have been different during that
time, manic even. Elaine could only have known those things
if Will had told her. And Will would only have told her if he
was having an affair with her. Julia didn't believe he'd said all
those cruel, mean things, but he'd told Elaine enough so she
could put her own nasty spin on everything. After, when the
cancer returned, he'd said it was his own fault, payback for all
the mistakes he'd made. Julia had thought he'd meant the
mistakes made over a lifetime, the wrong turns, the times
he'd been insensitive or careless or selfish. Things everyone
looked back on and regretted, things you wondered how you
could possibly have done.

Now she knew *this* was what he'd meant. What he'd done with Elaine.

She lay there waiting for the heaviness of betrayal to crush her.

Yet it didn't come.

She could almost understand why Will had done it. The affair didn't have anything to do with her or their marriage or their lovemaking. Will had needed something different, something wild, something to make him feel completely alive. After years of believing his death was imminent, he'd been given a reprieve, and he'd needed to feel crazily, passionately full of life. Elaine had done that for him. She'd probably even played on his need, used him to get back at Ryder, and even more so at Julia.

For Will, maybe any woman would have done so long as it wasn't Julia. Because Julia was part of the illness, part of the fear. With Julia, he'd always felt second best, not because of anything she'd said or done, but because of his own insecurities. Will had needed desperately to run away from all that. Maybe deep down he even knew the cancer would be back.

And it did come again, the way they'd both feared yet had never wanted to admit to each other. The cycle began once more, the misery, the pain, the frantic desire to grab onto any new treatment that came along. Before he became extinct.

If he found something that made him feel alive for a little while, so be it. She wished that it had been anyone but Elaine, but what he'd done didn't actually hurt her, as crazy as that seemed. She'd never stopped loving Will. And yet, as awful as it sounded, she'd never been *in* love with him. God help her, she should feel guilty for even having that thought, but she couldn't summon any guilt. She'd made her confession to Ryder, and what she'd told him was true. She'd been a good wife to Will. She'd stood by him until the last moment. She'd given her very best. Now she was beyond feeling the hurt a normal person would. She couldn't even feel the betrayal.

She could only feel the ache of losing Ryder.

And she could hate Elaine. Oh yeah, she could do that. She was well aware of what Elaine would do.

No matter how much Julia cared for Ryder, no matter how much she might love him, precisely *because* of how much she loved him, she could never put him through Elaine's wringer.

RYDER WANT TO SHOUT AND RAGE. HE WANTED TO SMASH things. He wanted to drive right through the front door of the house and run Elaine down.

He'd never known how violent he truly was.

He parked the car at the curb, shoved the gear into Park, and left the keys on the front seat so he wouldn't be tempted.

He could blame Will for the affair. He could hate his memory. But deep down in his guts, in his heart, and in his soul, he knew the only one responsible was Elaine.

She was a vengeful bitch. And Julia was right, his ex-wife would ruin his kids. She'd already poisoned Dustin.

He needed to talk to both Tonya and Dustin, think of a way to fix this. That was his job, solving problems all day long, week after week, year after year. And this was the most important problem of his life. He had to do something before Elaine turned his kids into bitter carbon copies of herself.

He rang the bell.

Elaine opened the door, hand on her hip, a malicious smile on her lips. "Well, I didn't think you'd have the nerve to show your face here."

It was almost comical that she'd just admitted to having an affair with his best friend, yet she could still play the affronted heroine as if the last hour had never happened.

She was barefoot, wearing leggings and a crop top that accentuated her curves. Any other woman, he would have called luscious. But Elaine looked like the bitter shrew she was.

He stared at her, actively hating her in a way he'd never done before. "What you did was disgusting. What I do, what Julia does, it's not your business."

Her lip curled. "What I'm doing is protecting my children from your debauchery."

"Aren't you afraid I'll tell them about you and Will?"

She smiled, triumph in her eyes. "No. Not at all."

The fight was coming, the anger rising, the red haze of it already coloring his vision. He had to stop, couldn't do this now, not with his children in the house, possibly overhearing everything.

"Are the kids packed and ready to go?" They had clothes and DVDs and sundries at his house, but there were always books and laptops and whatever thing of the moment they absolutely couldn't live without.

"They aren't going with you. I told them everything about you and that woman. And neither of them wants to be around you." A condescending, self-satisfied smirk disfigured her face.

He did not get violent. Pulling his phone out of his pocket, he called his daughter. "Hey sweetie," he said when she answered. "You guys ready? I'm on the porch." He didn't say their mother wouldn't let him in. He wouldn't play Elaine's game, badmouthing her to the kids.

It wouldn't endear him to his children.

"Sure, Dad, I'll be right down." She didn't sound angry, not even upset.

"What about Dustin?" he asked his daughter.

Elaine looked bored, crossing her arms, studying her fingernails, rolling her eyes.

"He's taking his time," Tonya said. "But he's coming."

He heard her before he saw her, then she was racing down the stairs, her backpack over her shoulder, Dustin behind her, slower, slouching, sullen.

Tonya sidled past her mother to get out the door, then backed up and kissed her cheek.

Elaine turned to Dustin. "Remember what I said," she told him, and he nodded grimly.

Ryder didn't say he would have them back next Friday. He didn't say anything to his ex-wife at all. There was nothing to say. He could argue, he could fight, he could read her the riot act. But she would never change. She would only get worse. His job was to get through to Dustin before it was too late.

As Dustin would have walked out the door, Elaine took his arm. "What about a hug, honey?"

Dustin hugged her, but it was loose, quick, emotionless, then she let him go.

Ryder was sure as soon as she closed the door, she would be on the phone to one of her sex buddies.

Damn, he was sounding petty. It was beneath him. Just as running her down with his car was beneath him.

He needed to concentrate on the kids, figure out exactly what lies Elaine had told and do damage control.

"I promised you guys the Boardwalk," he said, as he almost sat on his keys, remembering them before he accidentally set off the car alarm. "You want to head out there tomorrow?"

"The traffic will be a freaking mess," Dustin said, sitting next to him in sustained sullenness.

Ryder rolled away from the curb. "Well, I'm taking Monday off. We'd be going opposite the commute, and the traffic won't be too bad then."

Tonya grabbed the front seat. "You're taking a day off?"

He smiled at her in the rearview mirror. "Yeah."

"But you just took two whole weeks. How can you do another day?" She stared at him as if he'd just hatched out of a pod.

"I've got vacation time saved up, and I'd like to use it with you guys." Next to him, Dustin was staring out the window, curled in on himself, arms folded, shoulders hunched.

Tonya clapped her hands. "Dad, you are awesome."

"You can't make up for years of not being around," Dustin said, his voice hard and unyielding.

"Maybe I can't make up for stuff I did in the past. But I can do better in the future."

"Right," Dustin drawled. "And that's why you're screwing Aunt Julia. So you don't have to spend so much time with *us*."

"Hey," Ryder said sharply. "Do not talk like that. I don't like that kind of language about Julia or anyone else." His son sounded just like his ex-wife. Just the way Ryder had feared.

Dustin hunched, ignored Ryder.

While Tonya said in a childish voice, "Is it a true, Daddy?"

He had never screwed Julia. What they'd done was making love. "Look, why don't we go for Starbucks or ice cream or something? Then we can sit down and talk." It wasn't bribe. If they went home, Dustin would stomp up to his room and slam the door. Then again, Ryder might not even be able to get him out of the car.

"I've got a better idea." Tonya said.

Ryder glanced at his daughter's face in the mirror, giving her a slight nod.

"Why don't we go see Aunt Julia?" Her voice wasn't tentative. It was sure.

But Ryder snapped before he thought better of it. "No way. We don't need Julia in the middle of this."

As he turned back to the road, he felt Tonya's eyes boring into him. "This has everything to do with Aunt Julia. She should be able to say her piece, too. Right now we're only hearing your side." She paused before adding, "And Mother's side."

"Your mother doesn't have a side in this."

Was his daughter trying to manipulate him? He was the father, she was the child, and letting her best him would set a bad precedent.

Then again, she made perfect sense. Because Julia had the biggest stake in this.

Tonya said exactly what he was thinking. "It's the best thing to do, Dad. You know it."

When he stepped back from his own sense of what fatherhood should be, he knew Tonya was right. In fact, she was brilliant. He thought of Elaine's warning as Dustin walked out the door. *Remember what I said.*

His ex-wife was playing games. Maybe Ryder was, too, by trying to keep Julia away from them. The only two not playing the game were Tonya and Julia.

"Dustin?" He glanced at his son beside him. "What do you think?"

Dustin harrumphed like an old man, his crossed arms lifting and flopping back down on his stomach. "Whatever."

"That means he thinks it's a good idea," Tonya interpreted.

His gut roiled at the thought of subjecting Julia to Dustin's hostility. He realized, though, that he could talk and explain and cajole all he wanted, but on his own, he wasn't going to fix this.

And his daughter was willing to help.

"All right, let me pull over and call Julia." He didn't want to put her on the spot by having her on the car's Bluetooth. "She might not want company this late," he warned. After what had happened with Elaine tonight, he wasn't sure she'd want any of them in her house ever again.

"That's all right, Dad. I'll call her. If I do it, then she's going to know exactly what to expect."

He shot another glance his daughter's way, really looked at her for at least as long as it was safe. She was an amazing young woman. He loved her, but he'd never quite appreciated her strength and maturity as much as he did in this moment. And he nodded his agreement.

Tonya scrolled through her phone a moment, then put it to her ear. His heart was beating far faster than the tick of the seconds going by.

Finally, his daughter said, "Hi, Aunt Julia." A pause. "Yeah, I know." Julia's voice was just a hum in the car, like radio music played low, the words unrecognizable but the tone sweet. "Here's the thing, I'm with Dad and Dustin." She paused again as Julia said something. "I know it's getting late and all, but we'd like to come see you. You know, to talk. Because Mother said a few things that I think we all should talk about." She was silent a long moment while Julia's lyrical tones played through the car. "Yeah, Dad agrees to this." He felt her shoot him a look. "He didn't want to bring you into the middle of it, but I convinced him you're already in the middle. And we all need to talk." She leaned forward in her seat, looking at Dustin, saying, "Especially Dustin. So can we come by now?"

He felt the hum of Julia's voice deep inside. He wondered if he could give her up even for his kids. It was selfish, he knew, but if he couldn't turn them around, he would be forced to walk away from Julia.

Losing her again would kill him.

His daughter said, "Okay. Thanks a lot. We'll be right there. We're already in the car."

He should have felt guilty letting his daughter do the work for him, as if he'd made her some sort of go-between.

But instead he was immensely grateful for her love and support.

Somehow, despite all the anger and the recriminations and the lies, he and Elaine had managed to raise two amazing human beings.

❧ 32 ❧

When they pulled up, Julia was standing on the front porch, the door open behind her as she waited on the doorstep for them.

Tonya yanked on her door handle and dashed out of the car, throwing herself into Julia's comforting embrace. He heard Julia say, "I've already got the kettle boiling, sweetheart."

Ryder climbed out, feeling Julia's gaze on him over his daughter's shoulder, light and sweet and warm.

In the backseat, Dustin didn't move. Ryder leaned down. "Are you coming in?"

He couldn't drag Dustin out of the car. So he went to Julia, the love of his life, and his daughter, two of the most important people in the world to him. Dustin made three, whether or not he got out of the car.

"I've got coffee brewing for you," Julia said. "And orange juice or whatever Dustin feels like." She turned to Tonya. "Hungry? I can make grilled cheese sandwiches or something."

"We already ate," she answered politely.

Julia put her arm around Tonya's shoulders, leading her inside. "I'm sure Dustin will be along when he's ready."

"If he doesn't come in on his own, I'm dragging him." Tonya's face was set in determined lines.

Julia laughed. God help him, how much he loved that laugh. "That might actually make things worse," she said.

They left the front door open for Dustin. Ryder found himself praying that his son would come round, at least enough to come inside and hear them out.

In the kitchen, the kettle was boiling and the coffee pot finished its last few chugs. Julia had already out set out creamer, sugar, milk, and honey. She knew his family well.

She poured coffee, tea, and a glass of orange juice for Dustin, all the while chattering about what Tonya was doing for the summer.

He wanted to touch Julia, take her in his arms, kiss her. He wanted to beg her to change her mind, to let him into her life. Yet somehow he couldn't even talk to her, and all he gave her when she handed him the coffee was a mumbled, "Thank you."

They were all seated when the front door slammed, Dustin making a statement. He stomped across the hardwood floor of the formal dining room and into the breakfast nook, throwing himself into the vacant chair, sullen, glum, but saying, "Sorry, I didn't mean to slam it," to Julia.

She smiled, even as her blue eyes turned pale. She pushed the glass at him. "I hope juice is okay. I don't have any sodas."

Dustin mumbled something that might have been a thank-you.

Ryder opened his mouth to start the conversation, but his daughter jumped in first. "I'm sure you've already figured out that we're here because of my mother." He picked up on a lilt of denigration he'd never heard before. "She made allegations about you, Aunt Julia. And my dad."

Julia didn't ask what kind of allegations. "I'm sure that most of what your mother says isn't true."

Ryder jumped in, incapable of letting Julia take the brunt of this. "*None* of what your mother says about Julia is true."

"Right," Dustin muttered next to him. Ryder wanted to scold him for his attitude.

But Julia made the unprecedented, and perhaps unwise, move of putting her hand on his arm. Her touch was warm, and Ryder couldn't shake her off. But he noticed that both Tonya's and Dustin's eyes fell to that simple gesture.

"Your mother has accused us of some bad things," she said. "I won't repeat them. I just want to say that your father and I honored your Uncle Will above everything else." She pushed the bottle of honey to Tonya, watching as his daughter squeezed it into her mug.

Dustin took a great gulp of his juice. It almost seemed like a truce.

"But," Julia looked at him, her gaze roaming his face like a physical touch. "With your father's permission, I'll tell you what *is* true."

He debated whether the truth should come from him. But he wondered if Tonya had brought them here because she needed to hear it from Julia. Maybe Dustin did, too. They both needed Julia's side of it, to show her innocence in all this. So he nodded, wondering what she'd say, if she'd deny everything, their feelings for each other, the beauty of their lovemaking.

"It happens that while we were in Provence, your father and I fell in love."

His heart surged. He even had trouble catching his breath.

And he thought the grinding sound that filled the kitchen might actually be Dustin's teeth.

Tonya looked at Ryder. "Is that how you see it, Dad? That you and Aunt Julia fell in love while you were in Provence?"

He didn't know what she was asking. A white lie to soothe their feelings, validation of Elaine's accusations? "Yes, we fell in love. This isn't something that just happened because of the situation or because we were in Provence. It's real."

Julia squeezed his arm, and he went on. "I'm not exactly sure what your mother told you." He was, but it didn't bear repeating. "I only know what she said to us." He paused and looked at Julia, meeting her eye, seeing the emotion banked there. "And if she said those same ugly things to you and your brother, then you need to know that none of it is true."

He looked at his daughter, then Julia, and finally Dustin. He prayed for understanding. "What I feel for Julia isn't going away. You can approve or disapprove. But I can't change the way I feel."

Dustin slapped his glass down on the tabletop, orange juice sloshing over the edge. Julia shoved napkins into the pool to sop up the mess.

"How do you think that makes Mom feel?" Dustin lashed out.

Ryder wanted to say that he didn't give a damn what Elaine felt, but he knew that was a bad idea.

Tonya jumped in. "Oh, for God sake, they're divorced. They've been divorced four years. Mother shouldn't care what Dad does anymore. And you know she has—" She cut herself off, looking sideways at Ryder, as if she knew the tricky territory she was stepping into. Tonya didn't want to tattle on her mother. "Maybe this will finally give Mother a chance to move on, too."

"Don't you get it?" Dustin glared at his sister. "If it weren't for Aunt Julia, they might have gotten back together."

Beside Ryder, Julia closed her eyes briefly.

"I was never going to get back together with your mother." He kept the sharpness out of his voice. This was his son, not Elaine. "Even without Julia, my life with your mother ended. And nothing is going to resurrect it. Not now. Not in the future."

Yet Dustin continued spewing all of Elaine's lies. "But what about Uncle Will? He was your best friend. How can you do this to him?"

"I will always love your Uncle Will. He was like my brother. And I'll miss him every day. But he's gone, Dustin, and I can't bring him back," he said, shaking his head as he spoke. "And you know what, I don't think he's looking down from heaven and getting angry over what he sees down here." He wasn't going to talk about Elaine, about the affair. They didn't need to know.

"Actually, Uncle Will wanted you to be together." Tonya laid her palms flat on the table as if she were laying out the truth before them all.

"What's that supposed to mean?" Dustin scowled, so like his mother, but he was just a young man. He didn't have to end up bitter and cruel the way Elaine had.

"I used to sit with Uncle Will a lot before he died. Don't you remember?" she challenged her brother.

"I remember," Dustin snapped at her. "I sat with him, too. We used to play chess all the time. And he never said anything to me."

"Yeah, well, there were times when it was just me and Uncle Will. He used to talk to me. And he told me that his greatest hope was that Aunt Julia and Dad would finally find happiness together."

Ryder felt his heart split wide open, felt himself falling into the void.

Julia didn't say a word.

"That's bullshit." Dustin's mouth was a thin, white line.

Ryder said softly, "Watch your language, please."

"It's true," Tonya said.

"So why didn't he tell me?" Dustin argued, bunching his fists on the table.

"Because he trusted me not to go ballistic," Tonya said simply. She seemed so grown up. "He told me I wasn't to say anything, not to anybody. That they—" She jutted her chin at Julia and Ryder. "—had to come to it when they were ready. So they wouldn't feel guilty or all torn up about it." Then she gentled her voice and crawled her fingers across the tabletop to within an inch of Dustin's hand. "But this is like an emergency situation. And I don't think he'd mind if I told the truth."

Dustin's fingers twitched, as if he were actually thinking about taking his sister's hand. Or jerking away. "But what about Mom?" His voice had suddenly turned small, like a little boy.

"Mother will be fine," Tonya insisted. "Maybe this will help her get over this weird obsession she has with Dad so she can officially move on. I mean, it's not like she actually likes him, right?"

How wise his little girl was. At first he'd felt he was letting his daughter fight his battle. But now he saw that Tonya was the only one who actually understood Elaine. She didn't make excuses for her. She *got* her. Maybe in a way none of them could, Tonya realized what her mother needed. A clean break. Elaine had slammed him and Julia over her affair with Will, she'd done her damage, she'd gotten out her anger and her jealousy. Maybe she could finally let it go.

"I feel bad for her," Dustin whispered.

Ryder wanted to hug his son, hold him close, soothe away all his hurts like he did when Dustin was a boy. "You and Tonya will always be there for her.

"And we'll always be here for you, Dustin," Julia said.

Finally, Dustin raised his head, a sheen of unshed tears clouding his eyes. "It's going to be really hard. She'll be so mad."

"At first," Julia agreed. "But you love her, and Tonya loves her. And she'll be okay. You'll all be okay."

Ryder had his doubts. Elaine would keep working on Dustin every chance she got. But he saw that his son's anger was out of loyalty. "I love you, he said. "I will always love you two. No matter how angry you might get with me, I'll always be here for you. You can always talk to me." He rested his hand on the table, palm up. And waited for Dustin, his heart struggling to climb back out of the hole it had dropped into.

Until finally, thank God, finally, Dustin put his hand in his.

They were all holding hands, completing a circle.

Tonya, Dustin, him. And Julia.

"I MISS UNCLE WILL," DUSTIN SAID, HIS EYES OVERLY bright with tears he was too afraid to shed.

"I miss him, too." Even as her heart was breaking, Julia felt it stitching itself back together again.

"We all miss him," Ryder said, squeezing her hand especially tight.

"He was the best." Tonya closed her eyes, as if she were saying a prayer for Will.

"The letter you wrote for him was the most beautiful thing I've ever read." Julia felt her eyes go a little misty as she looked at Tonya and Dustin. "I can't thank you enough for that. I know Will was smiling as he looked down from heaven while your father read it aloud. Thank you."

"It's how we felt about him, you know," Tonya said. And Dustin nodded.

"I'm keeping it in a very special box in the living room so that I'll always remember what you said." She didn't tell them it was in Will's urn, the box that had once contained his ashes and was still so special to her. She remembered the months it had been in the living room where she couldn't bear to go in and see it. Everything felt so different now.

They sat there a long moment, hands clasped, a circle of people who had loved Will.

Julia felt as if he were in the room with them, hovering over them, giving them his love and his blessing.

She didn't know why Will had told his parents and Tonya that he wanted her to be with Ryder. She didn't know why he'd never said anything to her. Maybe it was her history with both of them. Maybe it was a topic they just couldn't handle. Would she even have listened when Will was alive? No, she would have tried to shut him up.

But when he'd written that he wanted Ryder to be his stand-in, he'd meant it in every way.

She gazed at the beautiful man beside her, her hand so warm and secure in his, and she knew Ryder would never be anyone's stand-in.

When she gave herself to Ryder again, it would be with her whole body, her whole heart, her whole soul.

That's what Will had given her by telling his parents and Tonya, but never Ryder or her. He'd put the choice in their hands. Yet he wanted the ones he loved to know it was what he hoped for.

She wasn't going to let Elaine ruin it. Ryder's children weren't going to turn against him. Julia saw that clearly now in a way she couldn't when she lay alone on her bed curled into a ball. Alone. Sometimes you needed someone else to make you see the truth. She recognized it the moment Tonya called her. There was hope, so much hope. It gave her the courage to admit her feelings to them. To Ryder. She was done changing her mind, saying yes, then no, rethinking, vacillating. Now the answer would always be yes.

"I've got this great idea. Tell me what you think," Tonya said. She was an indomitable spirit. Despite the fact that she was thirty years younger, Julia knew she had a lot to learn from this young woman. She was truly amazing, an old soul with understanding and caring far beyond her years.

"What?" Julia asked, her smile not only on the outside but filling her up on the inside.

"I think we should all go to the Santa Cruz Beach Board-walk first thing tomorrow. I don't want to wait until Monday." She glanced at Dustin. "If we go early, we can make it over there before the traffic gets bad." She looked at her father. "What do you say, oh ancient one?"

Ryder let out a whoop of laughter. Julia hadn't heard him laugh like that in years. And it was so good.

"Who are you calling ancient?" he asked.

Tonya beamed at him. "Three times my age. That totally makes you ancient."

"You need to mind your manners, young lady," Ryder teased. He looked at Julia. "What about you? Are you up for a jaunt to the Boardwalk tomorrow?"

She waited for Dustin to object. He didn't. "What do you say, Dustin? You want a ride on the Giant Dipper?"

She could almost hear Ryder holding his breath.

Finally, Dustin said, "Well, I guess so," like a typical teenager who didn't want to appear too excited about anything.

They finished their tea and coffee and juice and talked about all the rides they wanted to go on tomorrow. "The

Giant Dipper," Julia said, then she lightly punched Ryder's shoulder. "Remember that time we went over there on Valentine's Day and it was raining so there was no one there and the guy just kept asking us if we wanted to go around another time?"

He laughed. "We must have gone around ten times. We were soaked."

Tonya made a face. "You guys are weird." But Julia didn't miss the sparkle in her eye.

Even Dustin seemed to smile, a teeny-tiny one, but a smile just the same.

Everything would be okay. Ryder wouldn't lose his kids. She wouldn't let him. And maybe, if Elaine no longer thought she could get to Ryder through Dustin and Tonya, she'd leave them alone.

Julia would never forgive Elaine for what she'd done to Will. But she could forgive Will and live with it.

Half an hour later, she walked them all to the front door, and as the kids scrambled into the car, Ryder wrapped her in his arms. "You changed your mind. I thought after what happened earlier, you'd never let me back in." After the wrath of Elaine.

She tipped her head back to look at him. "I never changed my mind about how much I love you. I just couldn't bear it if you were to lose your kids because of it."

"I'm not going to lose them," he promised.

"I know that now. They love you. As rough as things can get, I don't believe they'll ever turn against you, no matter what Elaine does. You've raised wonderful kids."

His eyes gleamed with acknowledgement. "I love you," he whispered. "Thank you for talking to them."

"I love you. And you know I love them. It'll be okay."

He looked down at her, the porch light shining in his eyes. "I know it will. We have the rest of our lives together." Then he kissed her, a real kiss, all his love and desire filling her with his scent and his taste.

When he let go, she saw Tonya's smile. And Dustin looking at them without a glower.

After all the years of hiding her feelings even from herself, she would never have to hide again.

❈ 33 ❈

WILL

I have a plan. Maybe it will make up for what I did with Elaine. If anything could ever make up for that.

You see, if I tell Julia that I want her to be with Ryder, she'll totally freak.

She'd never understand all the things I did, all the decisions I made that kept her away from Ryder even when I knew she'd never stopped loving him. If I hadn't stepped in after they broke up, if I hadn't turned her into *my* girlfriend, no longer Ryder's, they might have gotten back together. If I'd told Ryder about Elaine's lies, he might never have married her. He could have gone back to Julia. But I made sure he stayed with Elaine. I kept all her secrets.

In a sense, I stole Julia's happiness. Her life would have been so much better with Ryder. She would have been a mother. She wouldn't have spent the last ten years of her life caring for a dying man who eventually cheated on her with the worst person ever.

So I've done the only thing I can. I've planned their future together.

I've got my angels working. Ryder's perfect daughter

knows exactly what I want. And I told my parents. They want Julia to be happy as much as I do. They know what it's been like for her.

And I'm sending the two of them alone to Provence. What better way to bring people together than giving them a dying wish they have to fulfill? Two weeks in the beautiful French countryside should be long enough for them to work it out.

They should have been together all along.

My last gift to the two people I love most in the world will be bringing them happiness for the rest of their lives.

Maybe that will be enough to get me through the Pearly Gates if they exist.

EPILOGUE

They were married four months later in a quiet ceremony with only their family in attendance. They weren't trying to hide their nuptials, but they also didn't want a huge fanfare.

Her parents had flown out from Florida, and Felicity attended with her children. Ryder's parents were there, and Will's parents came, too, but not his brothers, who'd both said it was too far to fly. Julia didn't question that.

She and Ryder had visited Verna and Harold to tell them about their marriage plans, and Julia had apologized for practically running away the last time she'd seen them. They'd both been ecstatic to know that Will's last wish had come true. Any lingering guilt Julia might have felt melted away.

The most important attendees, of course, were his children. Dustin had even dressed up in a monkey suit, as he called it.

He was coming around, the last dregs of his anger draining away as he finally accepted that his parents were never getting back together.

They didn't invite Elaine.

Dustin never said that Elaine was continuing her campaign of poison. If she was, he didn't let it get to him. Julia and Ryder had taken the kids on some day trips over the last few months, and twice up to the Legion of Honor in San Francisco. Julia was pleased that Dustin hadn't slouched around bored and in a bad mood. Those difficult times seemed to be over for him and for them.

They hadn't written any special vows, and the ceremony was simple and brief. Julia wore a cream sheath with lace sleeves, and she felt elegant without being showy. Ryder was gorgeous in a black tux.

They were married under a flower-covered arbor on the green grass of a nearby country club. After the minister said, "I now pronounce you man and wife," Ryder cupped Julia's face in his big strong hands and kissed her. It was lingering and gentle and sweet, the way their life together would be.

He murmured, "I'm twenty-five years late doing this, but I love you."

Julia whispered, "I've always loved you," without feeling it was a betrayal of Will. She'd never held anything back from Will. She'd given him everything she could.

Hand in hand, they turned to their family for hugs and well wishes.

When Felicity put her arms around Julia, her voice was soft. "I'm sorry I was a bitch. You two are perfect together. I should have been more supportive."

Felicity's dire predictions had not come true. Julia had been reconnecting with friends in the past weeks and months. They'd all been understanding, happy for her. No one had judged her, or her lack of communication while Will was ill. They'd even understood that the wedding would be only family.

She held her sister tight. "It's okay. I know you were going through a rough patch."

Felicity had caught her husband cheating, and she'd suffered in silence far too long. The divorce was in progress, the acrimony in full swing. How sad it was that she and Felicity hadn't been there to help each other through the difficult times. They'd stepped up their coffee dates to twice a month, and over time maybe they could find the closeness they'd never really had. Julia could only hope, and she could only try.

Dustin's hug was tight. It felt good. It felt real.

Tonya threw her arms around Julia. "I'm really, really happy for you guys. Uncle Will is smiling down, I know."

"I think so, too," Julia said.

Tonya sucked in a deep breath, as if she thought she needed courage. "I'm trying to decide if I should call you Julia or not."

She stroked a hand over Tonya's cheek, careful not to smudge the girl's makeup. "Julia would be great. You don't need to call me *Aunt* Julia anymore."

"I was thinking more like, would it be okay if I called you Mom?"

Julia's heart burst, and she hugged the girl tight, afraid she'd ruin her own makeup with her tears. "I would love that," she whispered.

With Ryder beside her and his children's acceptance, there had never been a more perfect day.

THE CHAMPAGNE WAS FIZZING, THE CHOCOLATE MELTED ON his tongue, and his wife lay next to him on the bed, nestled in his arms.

They'd flown to France for their honeymoon. Ryder wanted to make love to her in Provence, reliving every moment of their last trip without all the guilt.

"I told you everything would work out," he said, kissing the top of her head.

She tipped back to look at him, a sparkle in her eyes. "Is that how married life is going to be, with you saying 'I told you so' all the time?"

He pecked a kiss on her lips. "Totally. I'm going to tell you how I'll make you scream when you come, and when you actually scream, I'll just smile and say 'I told you so.'"

She laughed. God, how he loved her laugh. "Are you going to make me scream right now?"

"Absolutely. Over and over." For the rest of their lives.

She was deliciously naked. He was achingly ready for her.

But there were so many pleasures he had to shower her with before he buried himself inside her.

He'd planned a week in Arles. They'd missed a lot of the sights in that ancient town, and it was only an hour from Avignon, another city they hadn't fully explored. Despite being mid-October, the temperature was in the high sixties during the day, though they would probably need their umbrellas at some point during the week. Sadly, it wasn't sundress weather, and Ryder did so enjoy Julia's sundresses.

He'd flown them first class, but everything was different, new, wonderful in so many ways. But also the same. They'd shared their meals, watched a movie, then fallen asleep together on the plane, feeling refreshed when they landed. Unlike before, they flew from Paris to Marseille and rented a car. On the way to Arles, they stopped in Aix-en-Provence, eating at their favorite restaurant there. They made a side trip to Saint Jean de l'Ange for the merlot chocolate, both of them agreeing it was the best ever, though that might have been influenced by the evening they first made love.

That night, Ryder had booked them into the same pension, and Madame Brodeur remembered them immediately.

When she saw the Mr. and Mrs. on the register, her hands flew to her mouth. "*Félicitations!*" She put them in the bridal suite at no extra charge. "This will be perfect for you," she said in her musical accent.

Ryder had ordered champagne, saying, "I'd appreciate it if you could add a few slices of mango to the tray, if it's still in season."

She waved her hand. "Of course. And this one will be on the house. I feel as if I saw a fledgling romance your last time here. We are so happy you've chosen to come back to us."

"Thank you, Madame Brodeur, that's very kind of you."

That night in June had been their first time staying in the same room. A new beginning.

The bridal suite was on the top floor, and they'd left the balcony doors open to let in the sound of the nightlife down below on the street. He didn't care if anyone heard Julia's cries of pleasure. This was France, after all, the country of lovers.

"Oh my God." Julia sighed her satisfaction as he circled her breast with a slice of mango. He'd dropped mango chunks into the champagne glasses, too, letting them soak up the sweet wine.

But right now, all he wanted was sweet Julia, with a topping of fruit. "I really need to eat this mango."

He trailed the fruit from her breasts down her belly, following with his lips, cleaning up every drop of juice on his way, licking, sucking, relishing. Then slowly, slowly, his tongue caressing her, he crawled down her body.

She was panting by the time he reached the prize between her legs. He drizzled cool mango juice down her center, and she gasped, grabbing locks of his hair in her fingers. "Ryder," she moaned.

Then he took her with his mouth, shooting her to the heights of bliss the way he had night after night since their return from Provence four months ago. He planned to make her scream like this every night for the rest of their lives.

She exploded in a blast of starlight, and before she came down, he filled her body with his heart, his soul, his everything.

The next time she came, they came together.

Then he carried her into the bathroom. He'd already lit the candles, filling the room with the scent of lavender. He returned with the champagne, the mango pieces still sizzling in the sparkling wine. Twisting the taps, he filled the tub with hot water while he held Julia close, his hands all over her, keeping her body stoked.

"You're incorrigible." Her eyes were closed, her voice dreamy.

"I just want to make sure you're completely satisfied."

"You're certainly doing a five-star job," she said as he helped her into the tub, climbed in with her, and they sank down into the water together, the scented bath salts rising in the steam around them.

He leaned back with her. "While we're here, shall we continue our hunt for the best pastries and coffee?"

She laughed softly, a sweetly seductive sound. "I've already decided the best pastries were the croissants Madame Brodeur brought us that first morning."

"You mean the first morning in bed when I made you—"

She elbowed him lightly. "Yes, that very morning."

"Hmm." He growled against her neck. "I'll have her send up some in the morning."

"Oh, I'm hoping you do."

And he would make her feel so good. For the rest of her life.

"The best pastries, the best chocolate," he said, "now we just need the best coffee and we've accomplished everything we said we would on our last trip."

She tipped her head back. "Don't forget about cloud-watching and sunset-gazing."

"Of course." They might not have managed it every day back home, but many nights they'd enjoyed sitting outside in the evenings, unwinding, talking over the day.

When the tub was full almost to overflowing, he turned off the taps, pulling her back against him. "I've been thinking about our first anniversary."

She laughed. "It's only been two days."

"No time to waste. I'm already planning our anniversary trip to Rome." He wanted to give her everything she'd thought she couldn't have.

She reached back to stroke his chin. "I'll go wherever you want."

"It's where you want to go." He would go anywhere, as long as he was with her. "You know, I never used to like baths. But I love them with you."

"Life's simple pleasures." She sighed with utter contentment.

"Maybe we should get a hot tub."

She hummed thoughtfully a moment. "With a bath, the water starts to cool. But in a hot tub, you just get overheated until you have to climb out. Unless we had a pool where we could do a cold plunge." She tipped her head back to look at him. "Do you remember when we did that at the resort in Palm Desert?"

He remembered. It had been years ago, before the kids were born, on one of their couples' vacations. "I remember. It was January and the pool heater was broken."

"And when we got overheated in the hot tub, we jumped in the pool." She shivered dramatically. "It must've been fifty-five degrees in there."

He laughed. "It was certainly a shock to my gonads."

"Yes, but when we climbed back into the hot tub, it made my whole body tingle."

He stroked her arms, her skin turning pink from the heat. "I can see buying a house with a hot tub and pool in our future."

"Actually, we could add that to my house. There's plenty of room in the yard." Her voice was nonchalant, but he thought she might be holding her breath, waiting for his reaction.

"How big is the lot?" he asked with the same feigned nonchalance.

"Half an acre, I think."

He considered it. The house was built in a big T, with the bedrooms down the long wing at the back, the living room, dining room, and kitchen at the front along the top of the T.

"We could put the pool in the area by the living room with the jacuzzi at the far end by the master bedroom," Julia said. "With a door into our bathroom. Then we could just step in and out and wouldn't have to go all the way around."

"It sounds like you've been thinking about this a lot."

She laughed, the feel of it vibrating through him. "I've been thinking about our living arrangements. Your house or my house. Or buying something else. And you've got the kids coming over every other week. They'd love a pool."

He'd been thinking about it, too. Before they'd gotten married, he spent the week with the kids at his house, Julia coming over to visit but never spending the night.

When it was Elaine's week with the kids, he stayed the entire time at Julia's.

He supposed he should have felt uncomfortable sleeping in his best friend's room with his best friend's wife. But somehow, knowing that Will actually approved, understanding that he'd engineered the trip to Provence to bring them together, Ryder had exorcised all the ghosts of the past.

Julia tipped her head to look back at him. "Would that be

okay, if we lived in my house? We could rearrange, maybe make the living room into a family room, so the kids can each have their own bedroom."

"You really have been making plans."

"I love that house. I always have. The kids always seemed to like it, too." She fluttered her eyelashes at him. "They can actually walk to the mall. It's only a block." She was silent a moment. "I just never got the feeling that your house was somewhere you loved."

He nodded, his cheek brushing her hair. "It's just a place to live, close to the kids' school so they could walk. But now that Dustin has a car, he can drive them both." Dustin had been saving for a car, and he'd bought something used over the summer. Ryder had pitched in for the amount he was short.

"So if you agree, we can talk to them about it when we get home."

He wrapped his arms around her, hugged her close in the warm, scented water, dropped a kiss on the top of her head. "Yeah. Let's talk to them about it. And you and I can talk about the hot tub and pool."

"I was thinking about getting a dog, too. Or a cat. The kids would like having a pet, don't you think?"

He thought about the future, the boundless opportunities. "A dog, maybe. We could take it on long hikes in the woods." He was no longer willing to let work rule his life. He would take the time to enjoy every moment with Julia, and with his kids.

He felt her smile. "I'd like that." Then she leaned forward to retrieve their champagne glasses from the small table. "To our new life."

"To our fabulous, wonderful, amazing, new life." They clinked glasses.

He broached the subject that had been on his mind for

weeks now. "Have you thought about having children? With me, I mean?" he added as if she needed the explanation. "I know you always wanted to be a mother."

She was still a very long time, sipping her champagne. Then she turned in the water, sweeping her hand down his arm. "Tonya said the most amazing thing at the wedding. She asked if I would let her call me *Mom*."

His heart contracted. For so long—he couldn't even remember when it started or why—Tonya had called Elaine *Mother*. As if calling her *Mom* wasn't right or real. And yet, his daughter had offered that honor to Julia.

"I almost cried." She put a hand to her chest. "And I realized I can truly be a mother to her. We've always been able to talk. She listens to my advice." She laughed softly. "And I listen to hers. When I think ahead to when she has children, I know I can hold them in my arms and feel like they're *my* grandchildren. And I think Dustin might let me act like a mom, too."

"I feel a little weepy myself," he said. Even if he meant it as a joke, he felt the tiny prick of tears at the back of his eyes.

"My life is full, Ryder. It's full with you, full with my hospice work, full with our future plans. And it's full with the thought of grandchildren. You know, I actually feel like I've had a hand in raising Tonya and Dustin. I love them as if they're mine."

He hugged her tight, her body scented, her skin hot. "I love you. I loved you all those years ago, even if I messed up so badly. And I love the beautiful, wonderful, woman you are now."

"I will always love you," she whispered.

He saw that even after twenty-five years, even after all the mistakes, all the grief and pain and loss, that life could be perfect.

They had found each other again. And they would always be together.

Ryder whispered, "Thank you, my good buddy Will."

Julia added her voice. "Thank you, my sweet Will. I know that wherever you are, you're happy and smiling down on us."

The *Once Again* series, where love always gets a second chance.

Look for **Wishing in Rome**, the next *Once Again* novel.

ABOUT THE AUTHOR

NY Times and USA Today bestselling author Jennifer Skully is a lover of contemporary romance, bringing you poignant tales peopled with hilarious characters that will make you laugh and make you cry. Look for Jennifer's series written with Bella Andre, starting with *Breathless in Love*, The Maverick Billionaires Book 1. Writing as Jasmine Haynes, Jennifer authors classy, sensual romance tales about real issues such as growing older, facing divorce, starting over. Her books have passion and heart and humor and happy endings, even if they aren't always traditional. She also writes gritty, paranormal mysteries in the Max Starr series. Having penned stories since the moment she learned to write, Jennifer now lives in the Redwoods of Northern California with her husband and their adorable nuisance of a cat who totally runs the household.

Learn more about Jennifer/Jasmine and join her newsletter for free books, exclusive contests and excerpts, plus updates on sales and new releases at **http://bit.ly/SkullyNews**

Pretty In Pink Slip

Stand-alone
Baby, I'll Find You | Twisted by Love
Be My Other Valentine

Books by *Jasmine Haynes*

Naughty After Hours
Revenge | Submitting to the Boss
The Boss's Daughter
The Only One for Her | Pleasing Mr. Sutton
Any Way She Wants It
More than a Night
A Very Naughty Christmas
Show Me How to Leave You
Show Me How to Love You
Show Me How to Tempt You

The Max Starr Series
Dead to the Max | Evil to the Max
Desperate to the Max
Power to the Max | Vengeance to the Max

Courtesans Tales
The Girlfriend Experience | Payback | Triple Play
Three's a Crowd | The Stand In | Surrender to Me
The Only Way Out | The Wrong Kind of Man
No Second Chances

The Jackson Brothers

Made in the USA
Monee, IL
07 November 2023

45973502R00187